EIGHT MINUTES

EIGHT MINUTES

Lori Reisenbichler

LAKE UNION
PUBLISHING

Text copyright © 2015 Lori Reisenbichler

Published by Lake Union Publishing, Seattle
www.apub.com

Amazon, the Amazon logo, and Lake Union Publishing are trademarks of Amazon.com, Inc., or its affiliates.

ISBN-13: 9781477821824
ISBN-10: 1477821821

Cover design by Kimberly Glyder

Library of Congress Control Number: 2014949399

Printed in the United States of America

This novel is dedicated to my son Hugo, who introduced me to John Robberson, and to my husband, Tom, who knows which parts are the truest.

CHAPTER ONE

EIGHT MINUTES

Not once did I think something happened to Eric. That's how denial works, evidently. I think I had to believe he didn't get my messages. I simply could not entertain the alternative.

So I was alone. Fine. Between the physical pain and the mounting regret at not calling my girlfriends earlier, I became a funnel of righteous indignation that twisted tighter with every contraction. Later, I would have a full range of emotions, but at the time, I was uncontrollably pissed off as I delivered my son at 11:09 p.m., surrounded by my female doctor and two nurses.

Even with all the classes, I wasn't prepared. I'd read the book but didn't know what to expect. It hurt more than I'd imagined. It went faster than I'd anticipated. I cried and slobbered and grunted and, most importantly, did not feel beautiful or noble or life giving, as I'd hoped. The pain filled my head with meanness. *Fuck this*, I thought, *I should've done it like my mom, where they hand you a highball and roll you into surgery with your makeup on.*

But while I missed my mom, I wasn't like her in many ways, and this was one of them. Eric knew that. But where was he?

Not with me. Not with our son, who was barely a minute old. I gulped the baby up with my eyes, tasting every tiny finger and every perfect toe, searching for Eric in the fresh, tender Toby. I'm not exactly religious, but I can spot an angel. I could see his soul glowing right through his skin.

I was convinced Eric would be there when I woke up, apologizing and regretful, but at Toby's first feeding, all I got was his voice mail for the fiftieth time.

An unfamiliar physician strode into my room. Dr. Curt Thornton III, with the demeanor of a man tired of his role in this kind of conversation, said Eric was in intensive care on the third floor. Later I recognized what he had told me—and what he had withheld.

He told me the head-on accident had occurred in the afternoon, but he didn't mention that it was a result of Eric changing lanes on a hill in an attempt to pass a tractor-trailer. He didn't discuss how long it took the paramedics to cut my husband out of our new Prius.

I held my breath.

Dr. Thornton said it could've been a lot worse. He reported the hairline fracture in Eric's hip socket, pressing his right fist against his cupped left palm as he explained the part with the fracture. The cupped palm, not the fist. Dr. Thornton then told me about the second fracture, in Eric's femur, and explained that he'd lost consciousness at the accident site. However, the doctor did not describe how this hindered the paramedics' discovery of the internal bleeding caused by a slow, seeping leak in the artery in his hip.

He made sure I understood that the ER physician had acted quickly and ordered a CAT scan, which is how they found the pooled blood in Eric's pelvis. He did not mention that prior to that discovery, my husband entered the doughnut-shaped CAT scan talking, but when the tech pulled him out minutes later, saying, "Good job, buddy," Eric didn't answer because he had no pulse.

Dr. Thornton didn't describe what I would later imagine when I read Eric's medical records. The crack in the tech's voice as he called a code blue. The frenzy in the frigid room as the cart rolled in. The crinkle of the bag on Eric's face; the shouts for fluids, for blood, for a pulse as the CPR failed, as the paddles failed, after eight full minutes with four people working. The heroic resolve of the muscular attending physician with a weightlifting hobby who, when asked, wouldn't call it, didn't stop, didn't wait on the chest spreader, but instead, against protocol, reached for a knife and sliced my husband open right under his ribcage and went in, squeezing the life into Eric with his hands, beating him back to fatherhood with his fists.

Eight minutes is too long. Most don't revive. If they do, they're never the same. I'm glad I didn't know that as I lay in the maternity ward.

Dr. Thornton continued, describing the emergency surgery, explaining how he not only repaired the artery, he took care of the ruptured spleen. He had not mentioned the spleen until then. He assured me again that Eric was going to recover and be my husband and Toby's dad.

I demanded to see Eric. They wouldn't let me take the baby. I slumped into a wheelchair at the nurse's insistence and sobbed a low moan all the way to the ICU.

His nurses warned that he'd be unresponsive at worst, loopy from the painkillers at best. As soon as they left the room, I gingerly pushed the tubes aside, put my hands on his shoulders, and shook him. Hard. I had to see his eyes open.

I shook him again, babbling the whole time: I loved him, I wanted him, I needed him. He started to blink. Choking back tears, swallowing panic, I pressed my face to his and whispered, "Our baby is here. You have to see him. You have to."

I wasn't sure if he winced or winked at me, but he garbled, "'kay."

I nodded, reached for his hand, and thought I heard him say something that sounded like "sugar." I didn't know what that meant, so I settled for kissing his eyelids as they were closing. I withdrew to my wheelchair, dizzy as if the whole world had wobbled off its axis. I'm not sure how long I sat there in a stupor before this unsolicited realization hardened in my core: the unimaginable could happen.

CHAPTER TWO

JOHN WHO?

Waterson?"

"Wah-buh-son," Toby says. He has just turned three, so his r's and l's sound like w's.

"Robertson?"

"Wah-buh-son."

"Robberson?"

This time he nods his head with each syllable and enunciates "Wah. Buh. Son," which I take as a yes and the last time I'll be able to get a decent answer before it all becomes a game.

"John Robberson?"

He nods in the backseat, the tips of his curls wet with sweat. He has my dark hair and his daddy's light eyes.

Shifting out of mom voice, I turn to Eric. "Who is John Robberson?"

"I have no idea," he says, without taking his eyes off the road, "but he's been talking about him since we got back from the Boneyard."

They've spent the day at the Boneyard, which is part of the Air Force base near Pa's house in Tucson. Due to a favorable lack of humidity, about four thousand military airplanes are parked there, anticipating the recall order that might someday return them to active duty. In reality, tourists are the only ones paying them any attention.

Eric pulls into a parking space at the grocery store and hurries around to open my door. I nestle in the crook of his arm, ever grateful I married a tall guy. I've been on my share of flat-heels dates. He's six-four, all legs. We worried that he might lose some height after the accident, but he doesn't even limp anymore.

When I release the harness, Toby springs out of his car seat and jumps between us, commenting on the gaudy shamrocks—which he thinks are symbols for his mid-March birthday—in the store windows. He insists we swing him as we walk. One, two, three, wheee!

I worry we're going to pull his arms out of their sockets. One look at his baby-toothed grin, mouth wide open the entire time his feet are in the air, and I tell myself he's fine. He's so easy; the kid even laughs in his dreams. The first time it happened, I jolted awake and made my way down the hallway to stand over his crib. Tiny Toby, deeply asleep, laughing out loud with his eyes closed. I returned to bed, satisfied I'd done my job well that day.

We push the cart up and down the aisles. I fight the temptation to overpurchase fresh fruit and vegetables. What I don't serve tonight will rot in the crisper drawer of Pa's refrigerator until the next time I come. I suspect he eats a lot of junk food now. We pass the cereal aisle where I once scolded him for buying Cap'n Crunch instead of Grape-Nuts.

"I'm a grown-ass man, baby girl, and if I want Cap'n Crunch, I'll buy Cap'n Crunch!"

Well, if he's a grown man, why does he eat like a little kid? I didn't say it, but I did stop commenting on his food choices after that.

Toby says, as we pass the coffee aisle, "John Wahbuhson wikes coffee."

"Let's get some for Pa, then." Eric puts a can of decaf in the cart.

I don't think anything about it until Toby does it again, saying that John Wahbuhson says you should wink when you talk to girls. Toby sits in the grocery cart, blinking at me, and for the third time today, I'm talking about John Robberson.

I do what I always do when I'm trying to get something clear in my head: I recap. I learned this in a management-training seminar, and it's a job skill that has lasted far longer than my severance package. I lean against Eric's arm. "So . . . to get it straight in my mind: while you guys were at the Boneyard, Toby met someone named John Robberson, but you didn't? Was Pa watching him at the time?"

Eric turns the corner with the cart. "Yeah, you know. We were man-watching him."

This is an old argument for us, dating back to Toby's first steps. I think we should be able to see him—physical eye contact as often as humanly possible, preferably every waking minute. Eric thinks a general sense of Toby's proximity constitutes supervision. All he needs to know is which room contains his son. This is what he calls "man-watching," and it is a distant cousin to babysitting.

He accuses me of overreacting, but I'm not. It's an early-detection response that gets activated during labor and delivery. I believe a mother's intuition works like sonar: each kid emits a sound only his mom can hear.

I remember joking about it at a playgroup with my relatively new mom-friends. "And I'm pretty sure a penis scrambles the signal," I'd said, a tad too loudly, and was rewarded instantly with a sugar rush of laughter that left me hungry later.

They talk like this a lot, adding to a running commentary of mild complaints about their husbands. I used to be able to play along, but now I grow tired of women whose primary source of comedic material is the ineffectual doofuses they married. I'd like to see how they react when that doofus is lying in a hospital bed after technically being dead for eight minutes. It's hard to be cynical and grateful at the same time.

I'd been too embarrassed to tell Eric about my stupid joke. Ever since I added "mom" to my résumé, I have caught myself saying things like that more often than I'd like to admit. In the few solitary moments I can grasp, these tiny breaches of my own standards compel me to stare in the mirror, to lean in close, to bore past the brown and yellow flecks in my pupils, searching for the Shelly behind the mom.

I know she's in there.

This is only one of the things nobody tells you. I've got a whole list of questions I can't ask in a Mommy and Me playgroup. Mostly, I wonder if I'll ever recognize myself again, or if my gut instinct is now permanently tuned to the vigilance channel. I hate that my first assumption is the worst-case scenario. I can tell something has shifted. Slipped. It feels like I've left a part of myself behind, the carefree part. Do you ever get that back?

To be fair, not everything about motherhood is disorienting. Some changes have left me feeling more like myself than ever. Once Eric went back to work and I could finally stay home with Toby, I realized I could dress the way I wanted, instead of the way I had to, so now my closet is full of prints and natural fibers. I don't have dry cleaning anymore. Or makeup. I threw away any shoes that hurt my feet, pierced my nose with a baby diamond, and quit fighting my curly hair. And when I'm with Toby, I feel like someone finally colored in the background on my page.

Here in the grocery store, I know better than to mention the man-watching again, so I ask Eric to walk me through their day. He says they took the Boneyard bus tour and Toby sat by the window, bored. No big deal. Then they went to the flight museum next door.

"I let him run around. Maybe one of the museum guides talked to him."

I'm trying not to make a big deal out of the word "maybe."

As we pass the bakery section, Toby tells me another of John Robberson's preferences: oatmeal cream pies. I figure I'll play along.

"I don't think Pa needs an oatmeal cream pie. It might give him a big ole bellyache. Does John Robberson get a bellyache from them?"

Toby gets a puzzled look on his face. "No bellyache." He touches Eric's abdomen when he says it. Only Toby says "bewwy ate."

I whisper to Eric, "Are you sure you didn't see this guy?"

"No, ma'am." He shakes his head. "I did not," he adds, "neglect my duty while a malevolent pervert enticed our son to wink at girls, drink coffee, and partake of the ever-alluring oatmeal cream pie."

"Okay, okay."

I should let it go. If it makes Toby happy to keep jabbering away about John Robberson, what's the harm? I've almost convinced myself—until I realize Toby's never seen an oatmeal cream pie.

We usually shop at an organic grocery. There's nothing close to an oatmeal cream pie available there. So how could he pick it out on the shelf, much less know the right name for it? Even at his preschool, Toby gets snacks like peanut butter and apples, not processed, pre-packaged goo smashed between two cookies with almost no relationship to actual oatmeal.

I'll check with Pa later. About John Robberson, maybe the oatmeal cream pies—but not the man-watching. He'll be on Eric's side about that.

Toby says, "John Wahbuhson says I'se supposed to go see Kay. But I don't want to."

"Who is—"

Eric swerves toward the checkout. "Let's take Pa his groceries."

CHAPTER THREE

AN ALTERNATE TRUTH

oday, the window over my kitchen sink allows me a peek at the ethereal blooms on our desert willow tree. My tea-kettle makes a sputtering sound, and I pluck it off the burner a split second before it whistles. I sprinkle a little extra nutmeg into my chai and slice a handful of fresh cherries to add to Toby's yogurt. He twirls his spoon around his bowl, creating a pattern with the purple-red juice.

I love our neighborhood. Oasis Verde is right outside Phoenix and two hours from Pa, a planned community of environmentally green homes and shared spaces built around an urban farm. It's full of earnest hipsters and second-career artists who volunteer at the Montessori school right alongside the vegetarian wives of graduate students here on temporary visas.

We didn't know that the first time we drove into town, after house hunting all day. We just knew we were home. That's what we have in common with our neighbors: the internally induced exhale we all felt when we found the place. If there's one thing I've learned, it's to pay attention when something reverberates in the core of your being.

We didn't even have to talk about it. We just knew. Right then. We parked our car at the farmers' market and grabbed a free neighborhood map. Half hoping we'd be mistaken for residents, we walked up and down every street, our fingers intertwined, looking for the house that would be ours.

Some think Oasis Verde is too planned, even creepy, but we don't mind a deliberate step away from the frantic Adderall-and-SUV mainstream. We like living close enough for Eric to bike to his office. We want to know our neighbors, to have roots. Growing up, Eric went to nine schools in twelve years. Oasis Verde is our version of the village it takes to raise a child.

It's cool today by Arizona standards, but after we finish breakfast, I can't get Toby into long sleeves. We make our way to the park, and his squeal pierces the quiet when he sees his best buddy, Sanjay, near the slide. I pick up the bucket of plastic cars he's dropped and join Lakshmi on a brightly patterned blanket in the shade.

If we'd known each other before kids, we probably would've had even more in common. We both loved our work—Lakshmi in investment banking, me in software project management. We'd both planned to stop working when we had kids. On the surface, our situations are the same, but of course, I had to do it the hard way. Lakshmi got pregnant and didn't return from maternity leave. I got laid off. It took me awhile to regroup before Eric and I decided it was time to start a family. After three miscarriages in two years, I was more than ready to stay home with Toby, but that wasn't an option while Eric was recovering. That year of freelance work zapped whatever meager career ambitions I had left. Now, at home full time, Lakshmi and I agree that we've channeled all that energy into motherhood.

We fall into the easy conversation that comes from seeing each other daily. I tell her about the invisible John Robberson.

"The worst part is that Eric didn't even notice. I must've had the stranger-danger talk with Toby ten times in a row. Do you think I'm being paranoid?"

"Not at all! I would've had the same reaction. He's the supervising adult, right? If this happened to Sanjay, I'd question Nik about it."

I may have my beefs with Eric, but her husband, Nikhil, is even more hands off. He's an engineering professor at the university, very reserved, a true brainiac. I could never imagine him down on the floor, wrestling with his son.

"Does Nik do anything like man-watching?"

"What do you think?" Lakshmi laughs.

Sometimes her mother will join us, sitting in her sari on the rigid park bench. Toby couldn't pronounce her last name, so I suggested we call her Ms. Pushpa. When I explained it was the kind of courtesy compromise used by one of Toby's preschool teachers with an equally difficult surname, she was as delighted as if I'd offered her an ice cream. I can't decide whether she's childlike or wise enough to not allow her years to weigh heavy on her soul.

Our conversations on those days have a different tenor, less personal, more civilized. I don't mind. I'd give anything to be able to spend an ordinary afternoon in the park with my mom. It's been almost four years. She died right after I found out I was pregnant with Toby. I'd had so much trouble hanging on to my pregnancies that I waited too long to tell her the news. At the time, I thought the worst thing would be to get her hopes up again.

I wave as Ms. Pushpa walks up with a picnic basket. We call the boys over and poke straws into their juice boxes. When they finish eating, I tell Ms. Pushpa all about John Robberson—from the winking to the conundrum of the oatmeal cream pies—making Lakshmi listen to it all yet again.

The boys throw handfuls of sand onto the bottom of the slide and take turns sliding into it. I smile as Toby glides on his belly, head first, his arms outstretched like an airplane. Sanjay howls after a bad landing and we look over, still talking. Lakshmi pulls her blue-black ponytail off her neck and twists it into a clip as she gets up to make sure he's okay. We're used to having our conversations interrupted.

Ms. Pushpa blinks her owl eyes and asks in her singsong English, "So if he's not a museum official, what do you make of John Robberson?"

"Eric assures me Toby was just pretending, but he's talked about John Robberson for two days now. I'm thinking John Robberson might be his imaginary friend."

About this time, Lakshmi returns. She isn't familiar with the idea of imaginary friends. She moved to America at age eleven, and sometimes I find these odd little gaps in her cultural knowledge.

I explain and Ms. Pushpa listens with her eyes closed, nodding. Turning to Lakshmi, I ask, "Has Sanjay ever had one?"

"An invisible playmate?" She shakes her head. "But it's cute, isn't it? Shows lots of imagination and all."

"Unless the imaginary friend is a bad influence."

"How could that be?"

I shrug. "Why does Toby want an oatmeal cream pie?"

"Why does anyone want an oatmeal cream pie?"

Ms. Pushpa says, "What is this pie of oatmeal?"

I have to look over at the boys to cover my smile while Lakshmi explains. They jump impatiently at the water fountain. I get up and lift each of them, their squirmy bottoms resting on my hip as they slurp.

I return to the blanket, wiping my hands on my paisley skirt. "I've never heard of a kid whose imaginary friend is a full-grown adult. Toby says John Robberson is as old as Eric. Of course, when I asked if he was as old as Pa, he said yes again."

"Anyone over the age of ten probably looks old to him," Lakshmi says.

Now both boys have their arms out like airplane wings and are flying toward a tree. The afternoon sun seems to dapple through the leaves, mixing warmth with the wind.

Ms. Pushpa says, "It is a common experience, yes, when they see the imaginary friend? How old, again?"

I trap a wayward sandwich wrapper with my foot. "About the age of our boys. Why?"

Lakshmi gathers the trash from our lunch. "If I'm not mistaken, my mother doubts the 'imaginary' part." She says to Ms. Pushpa, "Can I tell her the story?"

Ms. Pushpa nods. Lakshmi describes a boy in a rural village outside New Delhi who began to call himself by another name when he was about four years old. He referred to himself as an adult man with a different name. He spoke of his life as a blacksmith, for example, and gave detailed descriptions about a specific village, where the child said he lived. But the child had never been anywhere except his own home. He didn't know the name of his village, but he insisted on visiting his "other" family, whom he could name.

Lakshmi says, "I'm sure this all sounds superstitious to you, but these details add up. It was obvious to the boy's parents."

"What do they think it means?"

Ms. Pushpa answers, "That the boy is the reincarnation of an older soul. At young ages, the soul is strong in the new body and may retain its memories. When a child is old enough to express himself, it is common for the child to speak of the previous life."

Lakshmi continues, "I think the imaginary friend is an American concept—or Western European at least. In India, the same thing exists, a child speaking of an invisible but friendly spirit. Yet the parents interpret it differently. They assign their own cultural meaning."

"The truth is in the child's experience, not the parent's interpretation," Ms. Pushpa says. "Is it so difficult to believe the soul may speak out of turn?"

I try to ignore the jitters in my gut. "How would one know if it were true? If an old soul were speaking through Toby, for example? What would I look for?"

Lakshmi says, "You'd see signs that the child *was* the deceased person, and he would take on the persona of the old soul. For example, it would be more likely he would ask for living people you don't know, instead of saying he sees someone you don't."

My chest feels heavy as I remember what Toby said about going to see Kay. I can't help seeking visual contact with my son. There he is, flying his imaginary plane into a tree with a loud crash. Sanjay's hand is cupped on the top of his head like a siren, and he wails "woo-woo-woo" as he rushes over to Toby's rescue.

"There is no cause for concern." Ms. Pushpa draws a pattern, a circular labyrinth around a rock, in the ground with a twig. "Perhaps your son is providing you with a tiny glimpse of a universal phenomenon. It is a lovely way to live, to be that open to the soul. If the innocent have access to other spiritual realms, it does not surprise me in the least."

Lakshmi winds her fingers into her mother's hand and brings it to her lips. Ms. Pushpa strokes her hair in response. I have to look away. My mother's hand would've gotten tangled in my hair. We would've been more likely to discuss shampoo than the spiritual access of innocents.

Lakshmi, deep in thought, breaks the conversational lull. "In this case, the parents eventually discovered the identity of the deceased man. Of course, they contacted the family and introduced their son as soon as they could."

"They did what?" From the corner of my eye, I notice Ms. Pushpa has stiffened. Changing my tone, I add, "Sorry. I didn't see that coming."

Lakshmi laughs. "See? It sounds outrageous in this context. But this kind of thing happens all the time."

I try to recap. "Okay, okay. Let's say it's true. There was a man who died; let's call him Joe. And four years later, this little boy starts saying he *is* Joe, so his family's first reaction is to start asking around to see if anyone has ever heard of Joe?"

"Yes."

"And they found Joe? Not any old Joe. The right Joe."

Ms. Pushpa says, "Yes. I understand it was a difficult journey because their villages were miles apart. I believe the entire family traveled in one wagon."

"That's a lot of effort to humor a four-year-old."

"They didn't do it to make the child happy."

"Why, then?"

Lakshmi says, "Put yourself in the other family's shoes. If your husband died and you heard there was a possibility that his soul had been reincarnated in the body of a young boy, wouldn't you want to meet that child? Wouldn't you want to see for yourself?"

I wonder how much time has to pass before I can hear someone talk about husbands dying without my throat closing up. At least I don't cry anymore.

"Yes," I admit. "I would want to see for myself. But the boy's family initiated the contact, right? The dad? The mom? Which one?"

Ms. Pushpa says, "I believe the mothers made the arrangements. To bring peace to both parties."

"I wonder if she had to convince the dad to go." I try to laugh. "Can you imagine Eric in that situation? What about Nik?"

Lakshmi rolls her eyes. "He wouldn't mind, as long as he didn't have to take a day off."

"What a project! I mean, what kind of person has the energy to do what it would take to track it all down?"

Even as I say it, I know I am exactly the kind of person who has the energy for this kind of thing. If it weren't so ridiculous, that is.

"I don't know," Lakshmi says. "Sometimes there are secondary benefits, more material reasons. For this boy, I think the family of the dead husband practically adopted him and his family. They gave him gifts, helped pay for his schoolbooks, even had a big party. The boy has a second family now. It's very nice for all of them."

"Oh. Well."

Ms. Pushpa dismisses this with a wave of her hand. "Take away the money, pfft, take away this idea of superstition, pfft . . ."

Lakshmi strokes Ms. Pushpa's bare arm, calming the clink of bracelets. "And what?"

"Still, there is a child who knows what he knows and a mother who honors that."

Lakshmi turns her head toward me. "Of course," she says. I return her smile and look up to check on the boys.

CHAPTER FOUR

─────────

SOULS SPEAKING

S till thinking about my conversation with Lakshmi, before Eric gets home, I search online for parenting books with "imaginary friend" in their titles. When Toby starts to fuss in his upstairs bedroom, I make my purchase and tend to him while my book downloads.

As soon as I start to skim the chapter titles, I realize I made an impulsive choice. None of the scenarios fit our situation. Toby doesn't really play with John Robberson, nor does John Robberson protect him from anything. Toby doesn't insist that John Robberson is sitting at the table or require that we include him in conversations. And as an imaginary friend, John Robberson isn't exactly pulling his weight. He isn't a superhero. He doesn't show up only when Toby is alone. He isn't very fanciful or imaginative about John Robberson at all. Toby always calls him by his full name. He's completely matter of fact about it. Or him. Or whatever.

The only thing I find about adult imaginary friends is the chapter describing kids who make up someone to function as a stand-in grandparent—or worse, how children of addicts make up the mommies they need.

The book is full of optimistic assurances that imaginary friends are a normal phase of a child's life. Maybe it's the same thing with John Robberson. I close out of the e-book and go online. There's a funny article about a kid in New York City whose imaginary friend was always too busy to play with him. Well, it starts out funny. The longer I read, the lower I slump in my chair. It seems an imaginary friend is a massive defense mechanism, a way to compensate— not, as I originally envisioned it, a delightful display of my child's creativity.

It seems to me that a big part of parenting is explaining how the world works. Toby points to a tree and I say "tree." He points to a dog and I say "dog." He points to his imaginary friend and I say . . . nothing? If I refuse to validate this experience, my silence teaches him there is nothing real unless you can see it, hear it, or touch it. But what about the things you know are real because you feel them? How do you teach that to your kid?

That night as I'm setting the table with Eric, I recount the story of the boy in New Delhi and tell him all the reasons John Robberson doesn't qualify as an imaginary friend.

"Okay. Why are we talking about this?"

"Because Toby keeps talking about it."

He calls Toby to the table, and our conversation is interspersed with the mechanics of eating with a toddler. I'm marinating in my own thoughts, barely participating.

"What's on your mind?" Eric finally asks.

I nod in Toby's direction. "I'd appreciate it if you'd let me know if you see anything weird."

"Weird? Like what?"

I drop my voice. "Like if he seems to know things he can't know. Or talks as if he . . . I don't know . . . has memories. You know, that aren't his."

He sets down his fork. "Oh, please." He looks over at Toby. "Hey, do you even remember John Robberson?"

"Of course he does," I answer. "We talk about him all the time, don't we, baby?"

Toby, trying to make his broccoli stand up like a tree, answers without looking up. "Yes."

"But you know, you never told me," I continue. "What did he look like, Toby?"

He points to Eric.

Toby thinks all grown men look like Eric. "So he's a grown-up like Daddy?"

Toby nods.

"Can you tell me more? What did he wear, for example?"

"Just cwoase."

"Clothes? Like a shirt and pants? Did they look like Daddy's shirt and pants? Or more like a uniform?"

Eric says, "Mannequin, I bet. They had some in old fighter pilot suits there."

"What's a man-kin, Daddy?"

"It's like an action figure, as big as a person. They usually wear a uniform. Like the pilot we saw, with the helmet, sitting in the glass bubble in the front of the plane? He wasn't real. He was a mannequin. It doesn't talk or move; it just stands there."

"John Wahbuhson talked to me," Toby says, mimicking a hushed tone but without the accompanying drop in volume. "He whispered."

I raise an eyebrow to Eric and ask Toby, "What did he say to you?"

Toby, still not getting the volume part of the whisper equation, says, "Do I wike his pwane."

We both smile, over his head. I'm going to cry the day he can say his *l*'s correctly. "Did you like his plane?"

He nods again. "Thud. I seen it. I have one."

"Saw it, not seen it," I say. "One what?"

"Thud," he says. "Can I have dessert now?"

I will never get used to the ping-pong quality of the three-year-old brain. Thud is our dog's name. I choose to ignore that part.

"Yes," I say, "if you eat that last bite and answer one more question."

"Okay." He shoves the broccoli into his mouth.

"Is he real? I mean, if you wanted to, could you touch John Robberson?"

"I didn't want to," he says with a big swallow.

I open my mouth, but Eric holds up his hand. "One question, you said." He pulls Toby's chair out, plucks him from the booster seat, and heads to the freezer.

Eric goes to bed early, anticipating his morning run with the dog. He's been asleep for two hours before I undress in the dark and sneak into bed without a word. Reaching over, I place my hand over Eric's heart, soothed by the lullaby of that familiar beat as I drift to sleep.

Unfortunately, neither of us is a good sleeper. When I reach over again in the fuzzy dark, my hand lands on an empty pillow.

With one eye, I peer at the oversize red digits on our alarm clock. 4:19 a.m. I roll over, trying to regain my grip on peaceful slumber, but my eyelids won't cooperate.

I slip out from between the sheets and prowl the moonlit hallway. A dark, slanted stain appears to be creeping out of Toby's room. When I turn the corner, the angle of the moonlight changes and the stain shortens and takes the form of Eric's shadow. I think he's asleep standing up, at full height, with his legs locked stiff and his arms weirdly inanimate, hanging from his shoulders like unused puppet appendages. He's looking down on our boy, sprawled in sleep, hands over his pillow, his entire body taking up only half of his twin bed. If it were anyone but Eric, I'd be scared to death.

Tiptoeing closer, I hear a low rumble of sleepy whispers. Are they coming from Toby or Eric? Seems like Eric's voice only, but I can't make out any of the words. I step back to allow him this moment of nocturnal male bonding.

I don't know how much later it is when I hear the metallic jingle of Thud's collar, his four padded paws keeping pace with the slow, deliberate footsteps approaching. I'm not surprised. Eric often lets the dog in when he sleepwalks.

"Eric?" I whisper into the dark, testing, but I don't expect an answer. The doctor told me it's better not to wake him.

Without a word, he crawls back into bed and turns his back to me. Thud settles on the carpet on that side of the bed. Eric flops onto his stomach, shaking the entire bed. I place my hand on his back and follow the pattern of his breath. This is the fabric of our marriage—these tiny intimacies and private quirks that become normal between us. Maybe this is the everyday language of souls speaking.

We may not even talk about it in the morning. He doesn't remember anything that happens while he's sleepwalking, so there's no point in asking him what he said. I doubt Toby is aware that anything happened in the middle of the night. I'm the only one in my family who got to see it. I consider it my privilege.

This thought sustains me, and I'm the one who reaches for him this time.

My mom-friends tell me that everyone's sex life gets put on hold after the baby comes and that most of them were grateful for the break. Our situation was different, of course. It wasn't until we finally reconsummated that I realized how truly scared Eric must have been, because his sexual appetite was three times what it used to be. He instantly became more commanding in bed, as if someone had turned his testosterone up to concert volume. Everything was new again. It was exciting; I won't deny it.

Sometimes he initiates sex only after the lights are off, and he won't even talk to me, before or after. Or he wakes me up in the middle of the night, insistent, silent. That might sound bad to some women, but for me, it's sort of thrilling—a little like having fantasy sex with a stranger. Then, there are times like tonight, when he reverts back to the Eric I used to know in bed, slower, more laid back. Sweet. I always soften toward him after nights like this.

CHAPTER FIVE

THE WAY WE WERE

While Toby is at preschool, I let Thud out the back door, retrieve my gloves, and head toward what I call my garden, nothing more than a couple of four-by-four-foot boxes I maintain with the hard-earned rewards of our compost pile. When I need to think, I come out here. It cleanses my soul to get my hands dirty.

Thud joins me, tail wagging, ears up, as I settle in the soil. He pushes his nose under my garden-gloved hand. I pull the gloves off to oblige him.

"Yeah, buddy, that's good stuff, isn't it?" I give him three good pats, our signal that the petting session is over. Good ole Thud. He wasn't my idea, but he's grown on me. For Eric, Thud is nothing but a source of joy, his running buddy. For me, Thud is a reminder of how much Eric has changed, which always makes me think about how he used to be.

We met at work, where I knew how to get through to guys like him. And he was a rock star there, spending his time on a very high-profile project. Our project team used to go out for beers, any of us who were still at the office at ten o'clock. We all worked eighty-hour weeks back then. One of us would get to a stopping point, walk through the cubes making the universal beer-drinking sign (tipped imaginary bottle and a stupid grin), and we'd go to the sports bar next door and decompress. I was the only female most of the time, but I could hold my own.

Our first date, if you can call it that, started when Eric came around making the sign and I was the only one there. I told him he was stuck with me. He looked pretty happy about that. Halfway through the first beer, I declared a moratorium on work talk, and we stayed up until four o'clock telling stories and laughing. Well, I'd tell a story and he'd ask questions. That's how it worked.

I felt listened to for the first time in my life. Like when I complained about my leaky kitchen faucet and he asked so many questions that I drew a map of my apartment on a napkin. I didn't think much of it until the next morning, when he presented me with a toolbox for my apartment. Inside, there were tools and a set of instructions for every imaginable home repair he'd anticipated I might need. He must've stayed up all night.

It was better than a dozen roses.

Everybody knew he was Spock smart and honey-badger tenacious. Everybody didn't know Eric and I had that last part in common. Somewhere between that imaginary-beer-tipping signal and an unexpectedly intense good-night kiss, we turned that tenacity toward each other.

On our first weekend together, we hardly left my apartment. Monday morning, I opened my desk drawer to find a ratchet wrench. And a Ziploc bag with three sizes of nuts and bolts most commonly used in bed frames. And the mathematical formula to predict how many repetitive horizontal shifts would create adequate friction for the nut to separate from the bolt. And a small can of WD-40 with a long red straw and a diagram indicating the precise location to apply it in order to combat any accompanying squeak. Color coded to show where new ones could occur in the future.

It still makes me smile.

He told me he thought I was out of his league. I don't think I was, of course. I think he was just handicapped by his parents' lifestyle. His dad was a turnaround consultant for dying companies, so they moved to a new city almost every year, which meant Eric was always the new kid. The nerdy new kid who was good at science. It's not like the girls were lining up to be his prom date. But Eric hit his stride in college; he found his people in the engineering department. Of course, they were mostly guys.

Eric's not a roses-and-chocolates kind of guy, but once I understood him, I saw the romance in his ways. When he requested a transfer so we could date openly without compromising our work, it was as good as a proposal.

We're a good team. We make a plan. Working so well together and being friends, well, that was just the upper crust. We were drilling down to the magma with each other. Establishing the core. The crust could crack, and we'd still have the core.

Or so we thought until the accident.

Eric was in the rehab facility for almost two months after I brought Toby home. I barely knew Lakshmi then. When we brought Eric home, he was in a lot of pain and sedated most of the time. Entire days passed when I'm not sure he knew Toby and I were in the same house.

He qualified for home health care, which sounded like a good idea at first. I didn't realize that I would end up barely lifting a finger to help Eric's recovery. I'd see him wince with pain, and I'd feel guilty that I wasn't the one making it better for him. I also didn't anticipate how much it would bother me that someone else was in our house all day. I found fault with every aide they sent us and complained more than I should've. I knew he was getting frustrated with me, but when I fired the third one, Eric's response made me realize how much our marriage had changed.

He defended the home health aide and did not even flinch as he suggested that I go back to work. Right away. Put Toby in day care and get out of the house. Like it was that easy. Like the accident had erased his memory of what we'd decided together while I was pregnant. Like it had slipped his mind that the only reason we'd waited to have a baby was to make sure we could make it on one income. His. Like it didn't matter that I knew exactly what I wanted to teach Toby at every developmental milestone that first year. He didn't even acknowledge that we'd ever had a Plan A—much less that this was about Plan Z for me.

It was as if he had spouse-specific amnesia. He knew who I was, but it was as if he'd forgotten . . . well, who I was. I'm not proud of this, but I think I even said "Plan Z" to him.

He shot back, "You think this is my Plan A?"

The old Eric would've said "Shel," in that softer voice, and then I would've hugged him and then he would've said something like, "We're in Plan Z. But we're in it together."

Something like that.

That's not how it went. And as much as I hated it, he was right. Pragmatic and right. One of us had to work and it couldn't be him, and it wouldn't do any good to sit around and pout about it. I couldn't undo this any more than I could bring my mom back to help me.

While I accepted the reality, from that point on, I felt we were out of sync. I kept wanting a do-over, but Eric never looked back. With some money coming in, he would worry less, he said. Having the house to himself during the day would free him up to do what he had to do: focus on making progress he could measure.

After that, I couldn't help focusing on what I couldn't measure: the effect of those eight minutes. Memory loss. Personality shifts.

Like he was tone-deaf emotionally. Out of nowhere, he developed an obsession with getting a dog—and a Dalmatian, to boot! I'd figured we'd have a family dog at some point, but why now? He was convinced it would speed his recovery. But a Dalmatian? They seemed too boisterous. Maybe a lap dog? Please. He wouldn't even discuss it. Only a Dalmatian would do.

It made no sense to me. It worried me, in fact. I tried to talk to him, but he didn't want to hear it. I started a mental tally of any previously unnoticed idiosyncrasies, which I reported on the sly to Eric's doctor.

We got the dog. Eric named him Thud because the darn thing had no idea how big he was and kept thudding his head into the sofa, trying to retrieve a ball that had rolled underneath.

I smile, remembering how goofy and cute he was as a puppy. Looking up from my work in the dirt, it takes a minute before I find Thud's latest hiding place, under the feather grasses near the fence line. He's chewing the cover off a tennis ball with characteristic determination. I guess it runs in the family.

I took a freelance assignment and cried every day when I dropped Toby off at the Oasis Verde day care. It was hard, but we paid our bills and Eric made good progress on his mobility. His doctor was satisfied, yet for months I continued the covert reports of discrepancies in my husband the way he was before the eight minutes and after. One day, the doctor finally stopped me mid-sentence and gave me a referral to a therapist.

I've never been so embarrassed.

I made myself go. Anna let me say what I needed to say without worrying about how ungrateful it all sounded. I really believed I had no right to feel the way I felt. Yet I felt it anyway.

She asked me what he was like when I was pregnant. He was so Eric—in the best way. He went with me to every prenatal visit. We met a doula, or labor coach. She insisted we develop a birth plan and emphasized the benefits of making rational decisions in advance. Eric loved the idea of a birth plan, but he was insulted that I'd even consider a doula. He thought her job existed on the assumption that men weren't capable of assisting with labor. His final contribution to the birth plan? No doula.

Ha.

I told Anna about the night Toby was born. It's not often that you can pinpoint the exact time—within eight minutes—when your marriage fundamentally changed. I was convinced that if Eric and I could unpack those eight minutes, if we could understand what had happened to him, agree on the problem, then maybe we could flowchart a way to get back to ourselves.

Fingers on the linked roots of a nut grass, I chase them to the source and reach for my spade. At least, I hope it's the source. I keep digging.

Eric accompanied me to therapy only once, but the minute he sat on that couch, I knew it wasn't going to work. I realized I must've made him sound like a jerk, because Anna was clearly surprised by what she saw in Eric. He came across as attentive, honest, and admirably determined to recover, still walking with a cane at that point. You see, I have one of *those* husbands. Everybody understands what I see in him. Everyone tells me how lucky I am.

Mid-session, I started to cry. What could I say? He wasn't a jerk. He just wasn't himself. I wadded up the tissue in my fist, and we spent the rest of the hour talking about managing my expectations.

Thud bursts out of the feather grass, shaking the tennis ball cover like he's got a snake in his mouth. When I startle, the root of the nut grass breaks off in my hand. I shake the dirt off the cluster. Maybe I got it all.

Of course Eric's different; he had a life-threatening accident. Of course he's different; he's a father now. I can't expect him to be the same. That's what Anna would say. It's what my friends tell me. It's what I tell myself. I'm managing my expectations.

But those eight minutes changed him. I know what I know.

CHAPTER SIX

THE AIRPLANE GAME

Easter is a bust. For the entire week prior, I try to get Toby interested, painting eggs and talking about the Easter Bunny. If a three-year-old could say "meh," he would. In fact, he's been "meh" about everything except John Robberson and that airplane game. He's got Sanjay hooked on it, too.

Today, I actually forced him to bring a toy dump truck to the park. It didn't work.

"Does the airplane game bother you?" I ask Lakshmi, not taking my eyes off the boys.

"Look at them. Sanjay is following along like an obedient puppy. That bothers me a bit," Lakshmi says. "This is clearly Toby's game."

She's right. It's the same every day. Toby always crashes; it's never Sanjay.

"They should take turns," I say. "I'll talk to him."

"I don't think it will work," she says.

We watch the familiar crash, but this time the boys make such a fuss, we go check on them. Toby is lying on the ground, pretending he has a broken leg. Sanjay can't rescue him, Toby explains, until he gets a cast like John Robberson.

"You have to lay down," Sanjay insists, as he applies the pretend cast on Toby's left leg.

"I am waying down," Toby says, sitting up.

I ask, "Now, Toby, which one is John Robberson? The pilot or the rescuer?"

"Me!" he says, hobbling away. "With a bwoken weg!" Sanjay scrambles after him, and before they reach the slide, both boys have their arms outstretched like airplanes once again.

"See what I mean?" Lakshmi smiles. "He's always John Robberson. It's okay. He can't help it."

"Can't help it?"

"Be honest, Shelly," she says. "You know John Robberson is not his imaginary friend."

She's right again. I do know this much, at least. I raise my eyebrows at her.

"You may not want to hear it," she says, "but I suspect this is like the New Delhi boy. I think Toby is responding to what his old soul is revealing to him."

"I knew you were going to say that." I smile and try not to let on that I've been thinking the same thing. "Okay. Let's say that's true. I just don't get what's being revealed. It's not like Toby has gained this mind-blowing wisdom or anything. All he does is play the same game all the time. What's the point?"

"You need to know more in order to put the pieces together. I'd ask Toby," she says. "The best way to find out about John Robberson is to go to the source."

She must see the reluctance in my face, because she says, "Look, it's all fine and harmless right now, but I wouldn't ignore it. If John Robberson wants something from Toby, don't you want to know?"

We turn toward the boys and watch Toby crash his plane and Sanjay rescue him yet again. From the outside, it looks like nothing just happened, but I feel the sudden shift inside me, as if Lakshmi has swiped back a heavy curtain and I'm squinting against the sun. John Robberson has somehow morphed into more than a remote possibility.

Don't I want to know what John Robberson wants? The longer we sit there, not saying anything else, just watching those boys fly and crash and fly and crash, the more I know I couldn't ignore that question if I tried. My ears are ringing like an alarm that went off way too late. My mind rattles with all the horrible possibilities.

"What could he want?" I blurt, breaking the silence between us. "He can't hurt Toby, can he?"

"Oh, I doubt it." Lakshmi is not only unperturbed, she seems completely unaware of the impact of her words. "He's probably just got some kind of karma that needs to be worked out."

With the urgency I used to feel right before a project kickoff meeting, and maybe a tinge of anxiety, I embark on a fact-finding mission. After Toby's nap, I retrieve my old leather portfolio and sit down with him at the kitchen table. I interview him like a new client, taking care to write down his answers. I read the list back to him, to make sure he agrees.

1. John Robberson is a grown man with a smooth belly who may or may not look like Eric, who may be Eric's age and maybe even as old as Pa.
2. John Robberson might wear a uniform made of a shirt and pants.
3. John Robberson talked or whispered to Toby at the flight museum and asked if Toby liked his plane.
4. Toby likes John Robberson's plane.
5. John Robberson thinks you should wink at girls.
6. John Robberson likes coffee and oatmeal cream pies.

7. John Robberson wants Toby to meet someone named Kay.

"Why does he want you to meet Kay?" I ask him, to clarify this last point.

"I don't want to!" he says, using his outside voice.

I return to my paper and add an item:

8. Toby doesn't want to meet Kay.

"There. I wrote it down. But why not?"

He starts kicking his feet against the chair legs. "I just don't!"

"Okay, okay." I rest my hand against his shins. "Anything else you can think of?"

He leaves the table and finds his bucket. He pulls out a toy plane. "This one isn't the same as John Wahbuhson."

"What do you mean?"

"This is the F-14. Tomcat." He holds it up to me. "John Wahbuhson flew the F-105 fighter pwane. Thud." He fishes around in his bucket again.

"Like our Thud?"

Toby goes to pet the dog while I amend one of the items on the list.

4. Toby likes John Robberson's plane and identifies it as a F-105 fighter plane.

———

Toby knows his airplanes. Ever since the Boneyard, we've read the same mind-numbing book every night. It's closer to an aviation encyclopedia than a bedtime story.

"Daddy will be home soon," I say. "You go play now." On the way to the laundry, I take a tiny detour into his bedroom. My heart thumps like Thud's tail on the hardwood floor when I realize there is no F-105 mentioned anywhere in that book.

Eric, home from work, surprises me in the hallway. "What are you doing with his bedtime book?"

"There's no F-105 in here," I say, flipping the pages toward him.

"Okaaaay." He takes the book from me and closes it. "And why do you find this omission upsetting?"

"Toby says it's John Robberson's plane. Our son has a toy F-105, but do you even know what an F-105 looks like?"

"No. Should I?"

"No. And neither should Toby. How can a three-year-old know something like the name of that plane?"

"He probably saw one at the museum. I don't know." He walks toward our bedroom.

But I know. Toby knows something, and there's no way he could know it. I follow Eric into the bedroom. He pulls a T-shirt from his top drawer and turns toward me, bare chested. I can see the scar under his ribcage.

He says, "Why do you have to read so much into it?"

"Listen to this." I read him my entire list. "What about the oatmeal cream pies?"

He sits down on the bed and pulls off his socks. "What about them? They're a snack. Unhealthy, okay, but it's not like his imaginary friend is telling him to drop a bomb on unsuspecting villagers."

"Why does he keep talking about what John Robberson likes? Why would he do that?" I pick up the socks he dropped.

"For you. The more you ask him about John Robberson, the more he tells you about it. He's humoring you. He knows you want to know."

"What about Kay?" I ask, pointing to the list. "Every time I ask him about Kay, he freaks out. He's not humoring me on that one, now is he?"

Eric rolls his eyes just as my cell phone rings in my pocket. I go to the study to take the call. It's international, which means it's

Carla, which means it's the middle of the night there, which means I should take this.

I'm now two life phases ahead of Carla, my college roommate. She's single and took a consulting sales job right out of school, so she travels all the time and makes tons of money, and we have almost nothing in common anymore. Except that on bad days, we call each other and express how much we wish we could change places. She's in London, sitting alone in her five-star hotel room in the middle of the night, her sleep pattern still stubbornly adhering to the wrong time zone. I'm relieved for the lack of crisis this time. Jet lag. I can deal with jet lag, especially if it's not mine.

I tell her, "Someone told me that jet lag is the time it takes for your soul to catch up to your body."

"How woo-woo of you."

"Eric thinks I'm majoring in woo-woo right now."

"What do you mean?"

I tell her about John Robberson. I hear Carla tapping keys as soon as I say "F-105."

"There's this book I read awhile back . . . here it is. It's written by the parents of a little boy who was the reincarnation of a World War Two fighter pilot."

"Why are they all fighter pilots?"

She laughs. "The kid had ungodly nightmares—like he was trapped in a burning airplane—and he kept talking about this guy by name. The mom believed it right away but the dad refused. Then he got obsessed with it and did all this research, and by the end of the book, they took the kid to the place where the plane crashed so the old soul could have some peace. And it went away and the kid forgot about it."

"So much for the comforting idea of children with old souls."

Carla says, "I know. I hear moms say things like that all the time, like it's a good thing. Like it means they're wise beyond their years. But, jeez, I think it would be awful if your kid really had an old soul—because it means he's a reincarnation, right? And he'd be talking to dead people and obsessed with how the last guy died. Who wants their kid to remember somebody else's death?"

I don't answer, but she stops talking. I hear ice clink in her glass. She asks, "Toby's not obsessed, is he? Having nightmares?"

"No nightmares. But he plays this weird airplane game every day where all he does is crash. Breaks his leg ten times a day."

"But he never dies, right? So it's different." She laughs. "At least you don't have to take him to revisit a crash site."

"And one more thing. He talks about someone named Kay. Not in a good way. Just keeps saying he doesn't want to go see her. Evidently that's what John Robberson wants him to do."

"It's so weird to hear you talk like he's an actual person."

"Well, technically, he's not anymore," I say, dejected. "At best, he's a spirit with a body he left behind."

"And how does that work, anyway?" Carla continues. "What's the lag time between one soul departing and it landing in another body? Minutes? Years? Nanoseconds?"

I hear the chair squeak and realize I cannot stop shaking my right foot. "I'm serious. It's freaking me out. I don't want some lost soul working out his karma on my kid."

She says, in a softer voice, "It's a lot easier to just believe in good old heaven, isn't it?"

It wasn't until my mom died that I appreciated how comforting the concept of heaven is. I remember standing next to Pa at the funeral home. All their old friends repeated these platitudes so confidently that for his sake and mine, I wanted them all to be true: She was no longer in pain. She was in a better place. She would be there to greet Pa when it was his turn. She was watching over me and the baby.

What if they were wrong? What if her spirit, her soul, the very essence of her being had already moved on to someone else? The idea that my mother's soul could shuck her old connections so easily is unsettling.

I couldn't do it, just let my soul drift away. If I died right before my first grandbaby was born, I'd find a way to haunt Toby. Not in a mean way—I'd just want to see.

"What am I going to do?" I ask Carla.

"Um. Google." When I don't laugh, she says, "Start with the plane and go from there." I hear her take a sip from her drink. "Come on, you're slipping, girl. Do your work."

As soon as I hang up, I find it:

Affectionately called "Thud" by its crews, the Thunderchief was the first supersonic tactical fighter-bomber developed from scratch rather than from an earlier design. The "D" model was the most widely used and produced version, with 610 built. The F-105 served throughout the Vietnam War, dropping thousands of tons of bombs on North Vietnamese targets. Thuds continued in U.S. Air Force service until the early 1980s, when they were retired from the Air National Guard.

I bookmark that page and hone my search, looking once again for John Robberson. This time, I try the Air Force website, but I get lost in the jargon. It feels like a maze that could take years to figure out. Finally, I find a site by an amateur Air Force historian that I realize is unofficial, but at least it's clear. Bookmark. There were about eight hundred F-105s built; looks like 395 were lost in battle.

There's a list. A freaking list! "F-105 PILOTS SHOT DOWN." It doesn't get much clearer than that. It's crude, sure. It looks like a Word document. I can just picture some gruff old veteran spending hours on the phone, going to a million vet reunions, tracking all this down.

"Better him than me," I say. "I don't know who you are, buddy, but thank you."

My heart is in my throat as I do a search for Robberson in the document. No result. I try again. Nope. I jump to the end. Total: 443 pilots. Okay. Back to the top. I try again, thinking maybe I made a typo. I alternate spellings—Roberson, Robertson—which returns several entries, but no John. I smile, remembering Toby's insistence on "Wahbuhson." Fully aware that I'm relying on the power of phonetics, I try Robberson again. Nothing. I scroll down the names, which aren't in alphabetical order. Maybe chronological. Not all of them died. It has their status: POW, Rescued, KIA. Nothing. I'm sure it's there. Maybe I missed something. Second time through, same result. I can't believe it. Three times. Nothing.

John Robberson isn't on the list.

I rub my eyes, which are burning. Funny how disappointed I am. I should be relieved. I keep scrolling and clicking until I find the asterisk next to the total count: 395. Crashes, not pilots. My leg starts bouncing.

Footnote: Only 334 Thuds were shot down. Operational issues accounted for 61 crashes. Those pilots aren't on this list.

CHAPTER SEVEN

BACK TO THE BONEYARD

I won't be around on Saturday," Pa tells me over the phone. "I'm taking my lady friend to the Del Sol." That's the casino on the nearby reservation.

"Oh," I say, and manage to compose myself enough to ask if I've met his lady friend.

"Her name's Dottie." He laughs. "She's a pistol. Likes to play the slots till her palms turn black. You know me; I'd just as soon throw my money in the toilet and watch it go around in circles. I told her that, but she likes to sit there for six hours and win two dollars."

The cell phone is heavy as a concrete brick in my hand. The thought of my father on a date . . . I shake my head and regroup.

"How about tomorrow? I'll bring Toby; maybe we'll drive down in the morning and back that same night. How does that sound to you?"

"Sounds like you have something on your mind."

"Maybe we could go to the Boneyard? Toby is still talking about one of the planes there. Are you up for that?"

"Up and back same day?"

"Yeah. He really wants to show me this one plane."

"That's a lot of driving to humor a three-year-old."

I hang up and send Eric a quick text, the best way to reach him at work.

Pa has a lady friend.

He answers back, within seconds, is she hot?

A pistol.

LOL. I can hear him now. Let the old goat live a little, Eric advises.

I tell Eric I'm taking Toby to see Pa at his trailer park the next day but leave out the part about the Boneyard. I'll come clean on it once I have a chance to observe Toby. Maybe I'll see John Robberson. Well, actually, I don't expect to see him. I think Toby will see him. Or hear him. Or turn into him. Or something.

I don't know what I'm doing.

At the flight museum, I ask Pa to take Toby to the restroom so I can interrogate the museum information clerk about the flight history of the F-105. She smiles. She wishes she could help. She offers me a map. She has a brochure. She even recites the museum's website address, *http* and all.

When Pa and Toby return, we walk outside, instantly squinting in the bright sun. There's almost no breeze to alleviate the heat.

"You should've brought your hat," I say as I slip my arm into Pa's.

"I don't see no hat on your head," he mutters.

I'm making a concerted effort to appear as though we are wandering, just taking in the airplanes, as far as Pa is concerned. I smile at his eyebrows creeping out above his sunglasses. He doesn't care. Nothing looks good with those one-piece jumpsuits he wears. He must have one for every day of the week, in varying shades of neutral, all with a big zipper up the front. He calls it his retirement suit.

Just then, Toby takes off running toward a plane with a shark's mouth painted on the front. I read the plaque. The F-105

Thunderchief. I speed-walk after him, leaving Pa behind with no explanation.

I can't leave Toby unattended with John Robberson.

"There it is!" Toby darts underneath the plane to the opposite side. The planes are generously spaced, with no restraining barriers, so he can run back and forth.

There's no museum security guard around, so I let Toby explore. He looks up to take in the shark's teeth and the long black nose. He peeks underneath the fuselage and touches the blue bomb casings strapped below. I see his pudgy hands on the metal casing that once held a bomb.

He is not talking or laughing or crying. I wait, without a word. A bead of sweat rolls down my hairline. After what seems like an hour but is probably three minutes, Toby comes to a stop, mesmerized.

My boy is standing stock-still in his little high-top basketball shoes, his feet wide apart, his legs still kind of knock-kneed. He has his head cocked, with the expression of an inquisitive dog. Even his arms aren't moving. They're hanging there, next to his body. I don't ever think I've seen him stand and not be moving in some way—twisting his torso, swinging his arms, shuffling his feet, wagging his head. I've never seen him so completely absorbed.

Is he in a trance? Is he seeing John Robberson right now? I can't tell. The longer he stands there, the harder it is for me to watch. I'm trying to stare at the invisible, and it's not working.

Because it's not visual. It's auditory. I strain to eavesdrop on the possibility of a whisper, eyes vigilantly scanning to find the source. Nothing.

Out of nowhere, I feel a breeze, as if someone just turned on a fan. It gives me goose bumps, even though the sun is hot on my forearms.

Toby still hasn't moved a muscle. How long can he stay like this? I'm holding my breath. I feel a rock under my left heel and try to move my foot without making a sound.

"What's he doing?" asks Pa in a loud voice, breaking the spell.

Toby runs over to show him the bombs. I follow them, deflated. If there was a moment, it has passed.

"Okay, what was that all about?" Pa asks when we get back to his trailer.

I start at the beginning and, to his credit, he doesn't laugh at me. But it's obvious he doesn't believe one word of it. Pa sits in his recliner taking it all in as I ramble on, not fully considering the ramifications of my words or their impact on my father.

I lean back on the sofa and conclude, probably too flippantly, "I think we really don't know what happens to people after they die. Who knows? They could come back, right?"

He pushes the footrest down to sit upright in his chair.

"Baby girl, I miss your momma more than you do. But she ain't coming back. Her spirit ain't floating around somewhere looking for a little kid to fly into."

"What? I wasn't talking about Mom."

"Is that right?" He rocks back in his chair.

"Oh, Pa. I didn't mean—" I try to explain, and he waves his hand dismissively at me.

I hate that gesture. This is getting old, all these men in my life not taking me seriously. I take a deep breath and see him rub his eyes.

I know. He misses her. "Can I get you something to drink?" I ask.

He shakes his head as I escape to the kitchen.

I miss her too, but my memories are more convoluted. I can't help feeling that we could've found a whole new way to relate if we'd had more time. I would love to talk to her about John Robberson.

I have no idea what she'd say. Now that I'm a mother, I want a do-over with mine. I turn on the faucet so Pa can't hear me sniffling.

In the car on the way home, the late afternoon sun makes me squint, so I reach for my sunglasses. I look into the rearview mirror in time to catch Toby crossing his eyes to focus on the tiny hook of a straw coming out of the juice box.

"So, Toby. Was your friend John Robberson there by the Thud?"

"No."

"He wasn't? It looked like you were—"

"No!" He throws his juice box on the floorboard and starts crying. I pull into the first gas station I see, and we stay there until he settles down. Once we get back on the road, I leave the radio off and he falls asleep.

I take a shower as soon as we get home, and Eric not only plays with Toby, he makes dinner, which is a nice break. Toby is in a much better mood by the time dinner is ready. Eric asks how it went with Pa.

"It was great, wasn't it, Toby? Pa took us to the flight museum. I thought maybe Toby could show me what he saw last time." Before Eric can react, I say, "Tell Daddy what you saw."

Toby's eyes light up. "Thud."

Eric says, "Sure, I remember that plane. The one with the shark mouth, right?"

Toby smiles at his dad. Baby teeth.

I say, in that bright voice adults use when they are actually talking to the children in earshot, "Toby ran right to the F-105 and stayed there, completely still, for a long time. He didn't even move. For a long time. Several minutes. He knew right where to go. I had to read the sign. F-105. Thunderchief."

"John Wahbuhson says Thud."

Eric gives Toby a fist bump. "That's right."

I drop the bright, fake tone and try to get the answer I couldn't get in the car. "Toby, what made you stand so still? Next to the Thud?"

Toby doesn't respond.

"Did you hear anything? Like the last time you were there?" I try to keep my voice light. "How about your buddy John Robberson? Was he there by his plane today?"

"No."

Eric shoots me the grin of a conqueror.

Toby says, "Here."

"Here? Like now?" I hold up my hand to keep Eric from interrupting.

Toby doesn't say anything.

I lean forward. "Please, baby, this is important and you won't get in trouble. Tell Momma. Is John Robberson here right now?"

He looks at his plate. His lip starts to quiver.

Eric offers his hand, palm up, in Toby's direction. Toby holds tight and nods.

"Yes? Toby, are you saying yes?"

"Yes."

It's like a stop-motion blanket falls on the dining room. I can almost feel the ceiling fan slow down. A bird chirps outside. I see dust particles in the sunbeam coming in the window and hear Thud breathing in the corner. I look down at my half-eaten halibut and detect the aroma of pine nuts in the pesto sauce. I steady my fork in my hand and slowly place it on my napkin.

I say, as gently as I can, "Tell Momma. What do you see right now?"

"You and Daddy."

"What do you hear?"

He doesn't respond.

"Tell me. What did he say to you? Tell me." Even before I see Toby recoil, I can hear the pointy steel in my voice.

Eric twists his head so Toby can't see his expression. Stop it, he mouths.

He turns back to Toby. "It's okay, buddy."

Toby's tears, which were about to pop, recede with his father's assurance. "No Kay," he hisses, his eyebrows scrunched together for emphasis.

I say, "Is that what he said? That you have to go see Kay?"

He kicks his feet out, bucking like I've just thrown a spider in his lap. "I don't want to!"

Eric reaches over and lifts Toby out of his chair. "All right, all right. Let's go play." Standing, he says to me, under his breath, "You're freaking him out."

Fine. I breathe. I do the dishes. I can't prevent the flood of possible explanations from polluting my mind. Or the boulder that seems to have settled in the center of my chest.

I pull a load of laundry from the dryer. As Toby plays on the floor, Eric sits near me on the sofa to help me fold.

I whisper, "What happened in there?"

"Toby has an imagination and you don't."

"Or our son just had an auditory hallucination. Have you considered that?"

"Not for one second."

"Eric. Be serious. Have you ever heard about early-onset schizophrenia? Little kids, they hear voices. Voices that tell them to do things they don't want to do."

"Come on. You can't be serious."

"But what if he's . . ." My voice cracks.

"A perfectly normal three-year-old with an imaginary friend?"

"I'm calling the pediatrician."

"Right now? Look at him. He's fine. Can't you wait until morning? This doesn't exactly qualify as a life-threatening emergency."

He's right. I put away the laundry and leave them alone to play until Eric volunteers to give Toby his bath and tuck him in. I slip to the office and quickly find a website describing childhood schizophrenia symptoms. I create a list so I know what to say to the doctor.

1. Onset: three weeks ago
2. Voices: One, but it's not scary to Toby, except when he talks about Kay.
3. Speech: Not disorganized or out of context.
4. Social Isolation: No. He has other friends, real ones.
5. Reduction in Emotional Expression: No.
6. Lack of Motivation: No.
7. Loss of Enjoyment: No.

I read a bit more, browse a few case studies, and finally push back from my desk, somewhat pacified. I'm still going to call, but he's going to tell me not to worry. I return to the living room and overhear Eric reading from that airplane book that doesn't have a Thud in it. Finally, the door closes and I hear his bare feet in the hallway. I intercept him before he makes it to the living room and read him my list.

"Good. Glad you're feeling better about it." He walks around the sofa. "Where's the remote?"

"I don't know if I feel better. Let's just say I can wait until morning to call the doctor." I put the list away. "I would love to know what this John Robberson keeps whispering about."

I pause and watch him change channels in silence.

"And why does he tell Toby to go see Kay? It's like he's sending our kid on an errand."

He's still changing channels and doesn't even make eye contact. "I don't know. Maybe his imaginary friend has an imaginary girlfriend. Toby doesn't like girls yet, so it's not a stretch to understand why a girl doesn't sound like fun to him. I don't see why it bothers you."

Keeping my tone deliberately calm, I let my words come out slowly. "Toby doesn't *like* her. It's almost like he's scared. He doesn't want to meet her."

He matches my cadence. "So he *won't*. We're the parents. We can control this. Create a Kay-free zone."

"Can we? We haven't been able to create a John Robberson–free zone."

"Whose fault is that?"

My face burns.

"Just drop it, Shel." He flips to the sports channel and leaves it there.

"I can't. All these coincidences—what if they actually mean something? What if there really is a John Robberson?"

"There is, Shelly, but only because Toby made him up. Let him have it. The whole thing is harmless."

"No. It's not."

"Yes," he says. "It *is*. Unless you start messing with his head about it, like tonight. You totally freaked him out, jumping all over him."

"I'm sorry. I didn't mean to."

"I know. You couldn't stop yourself," he says. "I just don't get it. Why take a trivial detail and make it scary?"

I'm all jittery inside and have no idea how to articulate it. I say, "Because it's scary to me."

"Only because you didn't think of it for him. Get used to it, Shel. Our son is going to have independent thoughts."

"I know, Eric, but this is different."

"How?"

I exhale a deep breath. "The details are too specific. What three-year-old gets obsessed with a plane that hasn't been flown since

Vietnam? How can he know these things? I can't just pretend he's pretending."

"You can't? Or you won't?"

"I can't."

"Why not?"

I pick up the remote, mute the volume, and turn toward him on the sofa. "Okay, look. I found a list of Thud pilots—don't say anything, just listen. It had the names of all the pilots who were shot down, and John Robberson wasn't on it—don't say it, because it doesn't really mean anything because, Eric, there were 395 Thuds that crashed, but only 334 were shot down."

Eric sighed. "So?"

"So that means 61 went down for operational reasons, and they weren't on that list, so there's still a possibility that John Robberson was a real person and a pilot. Stop. Stop rolling your eyes."

"Want me to close them?"

"I want you to listen." I hit him with a sofa pillow. "I'm trying to be logical and just look at the facts. There has to be an explanation. Here's what I have to establish: One, if there was a real person named John Robberson who flew an F-105. If there was, then he's not imaginary."

I continue the count on my fingers. "Two, find out if he crashed his plane, and three, find out if he died in it. And I'm close. But even if all that is true, it happened, like, fifty years ago. Vietnam. Which would mean his soul has been in limbo since . . . what, 1965?"

Eric picks up the remote and unmutes it but lowers the volume. "So?"

"So then—and this is the thing that's really bothering me—why now, all of sudden, does he appear in Toby's body?"

"Are you listening to yourself?"

"All I'm saying is, even if I can prove John Robberson is real, it doesn't sound like an imaginary friend or a reincarnation."

"Because it's not." He takes my hand. "You know what it sounds like to me?"

"Like a ghost? Or some kind of spirit talking to him?" I shudder. "That's worse!"

"Wow." He shakes his head. "I can't decide if Lakshmi has brainwashed you or you're losing your shit."

"You could decide I'm taking a logical approach to researching a phenomenon I don't understand."

He takes a breath and tries again. "You know what it sounds like to me?"

"No."

"It sounds like a developmental milestone—an indication of maternal separation, which is normal. Maybe it's hard for you to see what's right in front of you—"

"Stop patronizing me. If you have something to say, just say it."

"Okay. I'll say it." He stands up. "Our son is not your personal human experiment. He is allowed to have independent thoughts and dreams. He's three. He gets to pretend without you dissecting it and turning it into a phenomenon. Do you get it? This is not about him! This is about *you*. Get out of his head."

And with that, he tosses me the remote and grabs Thud's leash. "I'm going for a run."

"Why is our dog named the same thing as an airplane? Tell me that."

"I'll be back in an hour."

I know. The dog's name has nothing to do with an airplane. But John Robberson does.

Later that night, I feel like I'm sleeping with a corpse on the opposite side of the bed. I accidently brush up against him, my hand landing on his chest, and he rolls over. As if it repels him.

I don't sleep a wink that night.

CHAPTER EIGHT

I'M THE BOSS

I don't have time to dwell on Eric's coldness the next day, because Toby doesn't understand why he has to go to the doctor if he's not sick. Once we get there he's happy to watch half a movie in the lobby. When they call our names, I let him watch a little longer so I can pull the nurse aside and whisper my concerns before we go back into the examining room.

I appreciate Dr. Moore, our pediatrician, even though we always have to wait. It's worth it because for my allotted ten minutes, he's fully present and focused on Toby.

He reads the chart and tells the nurse to take Toby to be measured and weighed, which leaves us alone. He smiles when I hand him the list I made, but he takes his time to read it thoroughly. His eyebrows pull together when I describe John Robberson's appearance at our dinner table.

Toby returns and jumps onto the examining table. Dr. Moore sits on a wheeled stool and pulls up close. After a general examination, he says, "Toby, Mom was telling me about John Robberson. I'd like to ask you some questions. Is that okay?"

Toby nods.

"Mom says he talks to you. Is that right?"

"He whispers."

"When do you hear him?" Dr. Moore continues. "Does he whisper more in the mornings when you wake up, or at the end of the day, when you're eating dinner, or at night, when you go to bed?"

"I don't know."

"Okay. Does your head ever hurt when he talks to you? Or right after he talks to you?"

Toby shakes his head.

"Tell me about John Robberson's plane."

Toby nods. "Thud. We saw it at the museum. And I have one. In my bucket."

"His toy bucket." I start to explain, but stop mid-sentence when I notice Dr. Moore fails to turn his head toward me.

"Thanks, Mom." Eyes still on Toby, he says, "Does John Robberson ever tell you to do bad things?"

"No."

"Are you ever scared of him?"

"No."

"Do you have other friends, Toby?"

"Sanjay."

I say, "That's his—" but his lifted index finger stops me short.

"Does Sanjay know John Robberson?"

Toby looks puzzled.

I explain about the park and how the boys play the airplane game together. I talk fast, telling him about the crashing and the broken leg. I hear a baby's shriek from the next room. My time is almost up.

I say, "Toby, tell the doctor about Kay."

"No!" He flings his feet in a stomping motion, but he's sitting on the edge of the examining bed, so all he does is crumple paper. Or maybe he's trying to kick me; I'm not sure.

Dr. Moore restrains Toby's legs. "My. That's a big reaction. What's all this about Kay?"

Toby repeats, "I don't want to go see her."

"Ah. This is not your idea, is it? Let me guess. This is John Robberson's idea?"

Toby nods, miserably.

"I see." Dr. Moore nods along with him.

I explain it's the only thing about John Robberson that Toby finds objectionable. It also seems to be the only thing John Robberson has asked Toby to do. Go see Kay.

"Thank you, Mom." Dr. Moore scoots his stool closer to the examining table once again. "Toby, I'm your doctor and I'm about to tell you something important. Are you ready?"

Toby's eyes grow wide and serious.

"You," he says, with his finger in the middle of Toby's little bare chest, "You are the boss of John Robberson. Do you understand what that means?"

He squints. He wants to say yes, I can tell, but he can't. Not yet.

"It means that if you don't like John Robberson's idea, if you don't want to do what John Robberson says, you don't have to. He can't make you."

Toby beams. I can't tell if he's proud or relieved.

The doctor continues, "I want Mom to hear this, so she can help you if you need it. So that means you have to do your part and tell Mom any time John Robberson says something you don't like. If he starts being mean, you tell her. If he has a bad idea, you tell her. If it happens too many times, she's going to come and tell me. Will you do that for me?"

Toby nods.

"Who is the boss of John Robberson?"

"I am," Toby says.

"That's right." Dr. Moore gives little Toby a big hug, another one of those things I like about him. "Now I'm going to talk to Mom outside here for just a minute." He nods to the nurse, who shows Toby a tongue depressor and tries to make it interesting.

Outside the examining room, in a crowded hallway, he tells me he thinks there's nothing to worry about. He sees no clinical indicators but offers a referral to a child psychiatrist in case I want to have him evaluated. I ask what that entails, and when he explains it, I know I won't be making that call. Psychiatric evaluation? Antipsychotic drugs? Not if there's any other explanation.

All I know for sure is that Toby will not be doing the one thing John Robberson wants him to do. Ever. Because I am the freaking boss of John Robberson, effective immediately.

CHAPTER NINE

THE REAL JOHN ROBBERSON

Toby is jumping up and down next to my chair as I check my e-mail one more time before we head out to the park. Still nothing from the Air Force or the guy who keeps the list. If I'm ever going to figure out those sixty-one crashes, I'm going to have to change strategies.

"All right, jumping bean," I say to Toby. "Let's go to the park."

As soon as Toby and Sanjay see each other, their arms pop out into wing position and stay that way for hours.

"They're going to have some great delts if they keep this up," I say, walking up to Lakshmi.

"Well, that's looking on the bright side," she says, patting the blanket for me to sit down. "Was John Robberson at breakfast this morning?"

"If he was, he behaved himself. Yesterday I claimed it. I'm the boss of John Robberson." I fill her in on our visit to Dr. Moore. She's impressed. I also tell her about my argument with Eric.

"What are you going to do with him?"

"I'm going to make my case."

I tell her about my latest discovery: the Division of Personality Studies at the University of Virginia and the work of Dr. Evan Stevenson, who made it his life's work to investigate the past-life claims of small children. I'm fascinated by his research exploring the spontaneous, waking memories of small children who recount dates, names, relatives—intimate details about things the children would have no way of knowing.

This professor of psychiatry, well respected and seemingly legitimate, trotted the globe for over twenty years and interviewed literally thousands of these children. He interviewed the surviving family members of the dead person the child was referencing, as if it were a foregone conclusion, and tried to confirm what they said while identifying things like family bias and the child's perception of pressure. It's exactly what Ms. Pushpa described, only now with a social scientist's validating evidence.

"The only way he's going to take me seriously is if I can quantify it."

Lakshmi offers such encouragement, I can hardly wait to get back to my computer. I've found a hotbed of actual case studies, all involving small children: one remembering the deceased uncle she had never met, another—an eighteen-month-old—who calmly told his father, in the midst of a diaper change, "I remember when I used to do this for you."

I had thought that when I told Eric about it at dinner that night, he'd appreciate Dr. Stevenson's attempts at objectively validating these claims. But no. When I tell him about the boy Toby's age who identified a past-life wife with the matter-of-fact attitude of a forty-year-old, he snorts.

"Come on. A three-year-old talks about his wife?" he asks.

"Weird, isn't it? But you know what I can't reconcile?"

"Oh, please. Enlighten me."

"Never mind." I jab at my green beans until my fork is overfull and I have to use my fingers to pull them off.

"Aw. Don't take it out on your vegetables." He laughs.

"It's not funny, Eric. I want to be able to talk to you about this."

"Okay. I'm listening. What's gotten you so interested in this?"

I whisper, so Toby can't hear, "It's a philosophical question, really. For the sake of argument, let's say the grandfather's soul is in the son's body. Where's the son's soul? Does he not have one of his own? Do you see what I'm saying? If an old soul takes a new body, does it kick the existing soul out? Or did the new body not have a soul? Maybe it only happens at birth. I can't figure it out."

"Huh." Eric turns away from me. "Want some more juice, Tobe?"

Toby holds out his sippy cup. Twisting off the top, Eric lowers his voice. "Could we talk about this later?"

This is code for "Shut up in front of Toby." A flash of indignation tempts me, but I hold my tongue. We've always agreed that we won't fight in front of him.

After Toby goes to bed, I'm dying to get back to my computer, but I don't want to set Eric off, so I watch a basketball game with him in near silence.

After he goes to bed, I have to check. No answer from the Air Force. I send another e-mail to the guy with the list, and this time, I get an instant automated reply. His kids are keeping the website up in order to honor their dad's work, but there will be no future updates. He passed away last month. I was just getting to know him.

What am I supposed to do now? Sit around and wait? Maybe I can work the broader angle. I may have to find all the John Robbersons out there and weed out the ones who didn't fly a plane. It's the long way around, but at least I know where to start. I don't have enough details to use the more popular genealogy sites, and

I'm working toward a search that's specific enough to give me any meaningful results. The best I can do still returns more than three hundred thousand possibilities. I get comfortable in my chair and start to narrow down my search, trying to reduce the entries for John Robertsons and Robersons and Robinsons. Click. Scroll. Scroll. Click. Click. Hours.

At the end of a pretzel of click-throughs, I find myself on a poorly constructed genealogy blog with several Robbersons. My eyes burning from the strain, I somehow get to an entry from a city council meeting in Branson, Missouri, dated five years ago. John Robberson, the fire chief of Branson, announced he was sponsoring a potluck dinner at his home to raise money for volunteer firemen. It noted in the record that his wife, Kay, would be serving her famous icebox pie.

A shiver starts in my jaw, and I duck my chin as it spreads up the back of my head and loops around my ears, into my shoulders, and down my arms. I rotate my shoulders in their sockets, lean forward, and search the obituaries for Branson, Missouri.

There it is.

John Robberson. Survived by his wife, Kay. Preceded in death by his son, John Jr. Air Force Vietnam vet, fighter pilot with a Purple Heart, and the beloved fire chief of Branson, Missouri. Died on March 16, 2010.

Toby was born on March 16, 2010.

CHAPTER TEN

NOW YOU KNOW

I don't wake Eric up to tell him. He leaves for work before I get out of the shower, so I don't get a chance to tell him. I don't even know if he realized what time I finally slinked into bed. I hope he didn't smell the bourbon on my breath, because that's the only way I could dull my senses enough to sleep. I hope he didn't peek into the office before he left, because I'm sure all those notes I scribbled look like the mind map of a bipolar on an upswing. Good thing I didn't have colored yarn and thumbtacks at my disposal.

Who am I kidding? I wasn't ready to tell him. To fight about it. I just wanted to tell someone who would understand.

I practically run to the park today. It all comes out in a jumble, but Lakshmi gets it. She isn't even surprised. She acts like it was just a matter of time before I had the proof in hand. "Now you know," she keeps saying. Now you know. That alone makes me feel more grounded.

"John Robberson is real." I can't stop saying it. Not because I can't believe it. Because I'm so damn proud of myself for finding it. Because I was right. Because it wasn't all in my head.

"Now you know," she repeats.

"But there's still so much I don't know," I say. "If he didn't die in a plane crash, what's the point of the airplane game?"

"It's fun." Lakshmi says, matter-of-factly.

"That's what Eric would say," I laugh.

"No. I'm not being dismissive. Fun serves a purpose. To increase empathy," Lakshmi says. "Maybe the airplane game is just a way to get Toby to let his guard down."

Suddenly, I have a metallic taste in my mouth. "And then what?"

Lakshmi adds, quickly, "If Toby is John Robberson's reincarnation, maybe all he wants is for you to acknowledge him. Maybe it's nothing."

"Now you really sound like Eric."

"When are you going to tell him?"

"Not yet. I know what he'll say, and I have no answer for any of his objections." I lean in. "But I know what I need to do. I have a plan."

It came to me last night. Eric puts no stock in case studies involving people he doesn't know. I have to use Dr. Stevenson's approach and collect objective data on Toby. Firsthand. It's the only way to know if Toby is just responding to my cues (humoring me, as Eric would put it), or if he's responding to John Robberson's spirit. If we can rule out reincarnation, that means we've got some kind of ghost or spirit on our hands. Totally different problems. Anyone can see that.

So, starting today, I am doing the most counterintuitive thing I can imagine. I'm backing off. I will no longer bring up the subject of John Robberson. At all. I won't mention Kay. I won't ask any more questions of Toby so I can be sure I'm not contaminating the process. If he makes a comment, I will make a note of it. I'm now an observer. It's the only way I can be sure. Lakshmi agrees.

It feels good, like I'm reclaiming some distant part of myself. My old self. Even Eric would appreciate my new approach. I'll tell him about it at some point. Not yet.

Down in my gut, I know John Robberson is not good for Toby. I don't know why. I can't explain it yet. My gut is also telling me Kay is at the center of this, but the clouds are going to have to crack open with a message from beyond before I'm going to let my kid anywhere near her.

Now I know.

CHAPTER ELEVEN

TOXIC

Lakshmi's in-laws are in town, so I don't take Toby to the park. He's watching his favorite movie, *Cars*, for the third time this week while I'm at the computer. Again. I'm grinding through books and articles and journals and blogs like a wood chipper. If Toby's a reincarnation, I can learn to accept it, as long as I can convince myself he's not in danger. I decide I have to let it be true in my mind, if just for the afternoon.

One surefire way to confirm that Toby is John Robberson's reincarnation is to do a past-life regression. I don't have to look long to find a multitude of hypnotherapists, all within a half-hour drive, who offer this service. Before I can even start to consider which one to use, the thought of subjecting Toby to deep hypnosis stops me cold. I conjure up the image of my sweet little curly-headed boy lying on some stranger's couch, looking over at me with his puppy-dog eyes, the way he used to when he had to get his shots at the pediatrician's office. That trusting gaze squeezes my heart like a sponge.

I can't do it. Not until I'm sure it's absolutely necessary. Why would I risk triggering a bunch of traumatic memories that don't even really belong to him? No, thank you.

I have to be patient.

As soon as Eric comes home, I turn off that part of myself and make small talk. Sometimes I wonder if he even notices that I'm talking about absolutely nothing. Or worse, if he's relieved.

Toby chatters away at the dinner table, oblivious. He's talking about Mater, the goofy best friend in the *Cars* movie.

Eric says, "That Mater, he's a funny truck, isn't he, bud? How come you're so interested in him all of a sudden?"

"I saw that movie today," Toby says.

"Didn't you see that movie yesterday?"

I say, "It was really crowded at the park. We decided to stay home."

"Did you watch the movie yesterday, too?"

Toby nods and holds up three fingers. "Fwee times."

"You watched the movie three times yesterday?"

"No," I say, "he only saw it once."

"Fwee days," says Toby, using his fingers again.

"I see," says Eric.

When dinner is over, Eric does the dishes and I slide away to the computer, idly reviewing the web pages I visited earlier that day. But I can't focus on any of them. It feels like I'm sitting in the principal's office, waiting for my punishment. When I hear footsteps coming toward the office, I turn in my seat, feeling like I've been caught in a lie.

"What?" I say, unable to dull the sharp edge in my voice.

"You know what."

We look at each other evenly, neither of us breaking eye contact. He speaks first. "You put our kid in front of the television three afternoons this week? You, the Queen of Structured Activity? Little Miss Outdoors? Don't you have a rule: one movie a week?"

He's got me on this one. I don't know if I'm mad at him or mad at myself.

"I've been busy this week, and okay, I let him watch his favorite movie three times. It was hot outside. Sanjay wasn't there. It won't kill him." My voice sounds hollow, even to me.

"I don't care how many movies he watches. That's not the point. It's your rule! If I did that, you'd kill me. I would never hear the end of it! And what are you so busy doing? Because it's evidently not the housework," he says, kicking a pile of toys and dirty clothes that I shoved into a corner two days ago.

What the hell? I'm so mad, I have a metallic taste in my mouth. Thanks to many hours of therapy with Anna, I've learned to recognize this as my cue to not open my mouth and let loose. The real Eric, the one I married, barely notices whether the laundry is done. This kind of complaint, in contrast, is one of those brain farts I used to sneak away and report to his doctors. I will not take the bait. I call for a break, go to the kitchen, and drink a tall glass of iced tea in one gulp.

When I come back, hoping he's had time to cool off enough to have a normal disagreement, I say, "What's this really about?"

"Your little secret. Whatever you're keeping from me. I can only imagine what you're saying to Toby all day. You can't drag him through all this New Age mumbo jumbo. You're interested in it, fine, whatever. But don't try to turn him into some Dalai Lama doppelgänger just because you're bored."

There. He said it.

My theory is that every couple has one toxic word, and every time it's spoken, it pollutes the marriage. It turns into a code word that means every little thing you do wrong is proof of a chronic character flaw. Eric just said that word: "bored."

I don't let him get away with that one.

"Bored?" I hiss.

"Call it whatever you want."

"I call it pursuing my interests . . . with determination and purpose! I call it the very trait we have in common!" I fight off the urge to cram the dirty clothes in the hamper and start straightening the clutter on a dresser instead.

He rolls his eyes. "Really. You're calling it work ethic?"

"I call it having the right to do what I want after I pay the bills and buy groceries and cook dinner every night. And when I cook, I don't make a stupid casserole with cream of mushroom soup; I'm talking about a fresh, nutritionally balanced meal seven freaking days a week, week after week, because I care about our family and I care about what I do, and you have no idea what I have to get done in a day or how much energy it takes to raise another human being and make sure we have the kind of life we both want!"

I throw a handful of loose change into a jar and turn on him, fists clenched at my sides. "So don't you *dare* look sideways at a pile of your own dirty clothes and tell me I'm bored if I decide to spend my time on an activity more intellectually challenging than picking up your sweaty running shorts."

He walks over to the pile of laundry and pulls my bra out. "Does this look like a pair of my sweaty running shorts?" He reaches down, grabs the entire pile, and throws it in the air. The smell is as sour and stale as his voice. "Don't make this about me. Have I ever asked you to do half the stuff you choose to do? If you want to cook everything from scratch, why does that make me your oppressor? If you don't want to stay home, don't! If you want to go back to work, go back to work! But if you stay home, and you want to keep making up a shitload of rules about how Toby can't watch TV, then you can't get pissed if I notice that you're not even living by your own rules. Jeez! That's all I'm saying!"

"That's *not* all you're saying." I bend to pick up the dirty T-shirt nearest me. "At least have the balls to go ahead and say it."

"Fine," he hisses, as he picks up a pair of jeans and throws them back in the corner. He takes a deep breath, and his voice is almost back to normal. "Look. I know this John Robberson thing freaks you out. I don't get it, but it doesn't bother me. I don't feel compelled to fill in the blanks. But you do. And you can't explain why."

With my back to him, I mutter under my breath, "Because I care about our son."

"Oh, that's right. Thank you for that." He stops moving. "I am so fucking clear on that point, you don't need to keep throwing it in my face. Got it. *You* care about our son." His voice is low and even. "And you don't give a rat's ass what I think about anything having to do with him. Got it."

"Because you won't even entertain the idea that something is going on with John Robberson that you don't understand."

"I don't feel the need to understand it because I don't feel threatened by it."

"Well, I do. Need to understand it," I add.

"Look at you, Shel. You're already not acting like yourself. You're freaking Toby out and you don't even notice. You're freaking me out and you don't even care. Get a grip on this."

John Robberson is real, I want to scream at him. *I've got a good reason to freak out.* But I don't say anything. This is not the time. I could produce John Robberson in the flesh right now, and Eric would still deny his existence. I have to play the long game. I stomp into the bathroom and brush my teeth until my gums bleed.

CHAPTER TWELVE

DO CAVEMEN GET REINCARNATED?

On Saturday night, Eric and I go to a party with some of our friends from the old days, most of whom are still single and a few of whom are married but don't have kids yet. Toby is thrilled for a night with the babysitter. I wear a vintage dress with a big skirt. After our argument, things have been tense between us. It's important that we go out and remember who we are.

We head to downtown Phoenix, where our friend Ian lives. It looks dirty and unfriendly. I realize I probably haven't left Oasis Verde for months. We pull up to Ian's new loft and park in a lot that requires a security code.

"What do you think the crime rate is here?"

"He says his next-door neighbor is a policeman."

"Well, I guess that helps. Where would Toby play? He has no grass at all."

"Ian doesn't have kids, remember?" I appreciate his tone of voice. I can tell he's trying. He squeezes me close in a hug as we walk to the door. I press my cheek to his chest, glad to be out with him again, acting like an adult. He's wearing a cool retro-style plaid shirt and khakis and smells good, like sandalwood soap. He even trimmed his mustache, and it's not so bad. For a mustache.

He grew that damn mustache after his accident. At first, he didn't shave at all, and when I finally refused to let his scraggly face near mine for a kiss, he started to shave experimentally. He tried a goatee at first, but I couldn't help snickering at it. I convinced him it was the mullet of the new millennium, one of those trends all those shaved-head guys were going to look back on and regret. So he turned it into a soul patch but said he felt like he was trying too hard. Hipster central. He wanted to be different. Nobody has a mustache anymore, he said, as he shaved off the little tuft under his lip. At that point, I was thankful he'd already shaved off his sideburns, because nobody has pork chops anymore, either.

He talks to it. It's funny; he looks in the bathroom mirror and says things like, "There you go, sport," like it's his long-lost friend. I have to admit, it's a great coppery shade of blonde. The mustache is like Thud—not my idea, but I'm getting used to it.

We knock on Ian's industrial steel door, which has three small, square windows aligned down one side. His doorknob is square and placed lower than a normal doorknob, to line up with the windows. Eric motions to the doorknob and says, "That's Ian for you."

As soon as we follow Ian inside, I realize the door is not the only detail that he's meticulously designed.

"Your loft is great."

It smells like clean, fresh linen. Exposed brick walls, a stainless-steel kitchen with an industrial worktable built into one side, and twenty-four-foot ceilings with exposed air conditioning ducts—black, so it's there, but not in your face. Ian is an architect. He even designed the coffee table and bar stools himself. There's one dividing wall, painted a brilliant shade of cerulean—not too blue, not too green, but perfect as an accent. Tucked away on the other side of the cerulean wall is Ian's sparse, minimalist bedroom. On one side of the brick wall in the bedroom space, I see enormous photographs, some thirty-six inches wide, mounted on foam core, comprising an entire galley of saturated close-ups of plants and body parts and metal toys and vintage detective-book covers.

"Taking up photography?" Eric asks.

"No, that's Mamie's work."

Mamie is Ian's girlfriend. He won't let her move in with him. He tells everyone that she thinks he's too much of a slob, but I don't buy it. Sure looks like everything is in its place. Including Mamie. On display, but could be removed without having to repaint the wall.

"I'm glad to be married," I whisper in Eric's ear.

"I don't like to fight, either," he says. "Let's just have fun tonight."

"That's the idea, honey," I say. Then I turn to Ian. "I need a margarita!"

Ian takes one look at me and makes it extra strong. He calls it a Mexican martini, which seems like nothing more than a giant tequila shot with fresh lime juice. It's made with exceptionally smooth *añejo* tequila, so I'm soon sipping away and catching up on the gossip with a couple of my old, single college buddies. I show pictures of Toby.

I'm glad Carla is here, back from Europe or wherever she was on her latest business trip and looking fantastic. Her only complaint these days is that she doesn't dare date her favorite client, Steve, the only unmarried one she's had in ages. Separated, actually, but the divorce is pending. Her boss is super-strict in his interpretation of their conflict of interest policy. You do not date clients. Ever. So she's hoping Steve will change jobs and not hire her at his new company. Of course, she can't breathe a word of that to Steve. She'll make less money if it happens, but it would give her love life a chance. Once again, I'm happy to not have her set of problems.

By the time Eric and the other guys return from Ian's patio holding a tray of fresh grilled fajitas, I'm finishing my second Mexican martini. I need to get food in my stomach. When I stand up, my brains slosh against the sides of my cranium, which feels as impenetrable as a Neanderthal's.

I tend to ponder out loud when I'm tipsy. Eric says it's more like pontificating. He likes to get me engaged in conversation once I have what we call a "swimmy head." I'm good comic material for weeks afterward, evidently.

Tonight, the image of my brain as soup and my Neanderthal skull as the tureen makes me think of cavemen. Which makes me wonder if cavemen ate soup. No, they ate meat. I wonder if cavemen ever cared about the animals they hunted. Nobody pictures an empathic caveman. A caveman with a soul. But surely a soul would be older than a caveman. Then I wonder if cavemen got reincarnated, which makes me feel bad for the poor stupid caveman with the protruding brow. I imagine he might be relieved to be reincarnated into a more evolved body. Which makes me think about big old John Robberson cramming himself into Toby's little chubby body. I cringe.

"What's wrong, sweetie?" It's Ian, who offers a plate of fajitas and puts his hand on my elbow.

"No, no, I'm fine. I think I need to eat." I steady myself. "Thank you." I feel like one of those people who can't recognize faces because they only see one facial feature at a time. Eyes. Nose. I see Ian's big goofy smile and I'm filled with fondness. He turns his head and I lose his smile. My focus is on the space where his chin should be. His skin hangs in a straight vertical line from his bottom lip to the top of his collar. Poor Ian.

I love the guy but don't find him even remotely attractive. His appeal is on the inside. He's so nice, so civilized. He's like the opposite of a Neanderthal.

Which makes me think how disappointed some floating Neanderthal soul would be to leave behind his muscle tone and wake up in Ian's supple skin. That would be the worst of both, wouldn't it? I can't help a little giggle.

"What's so funny?"

"Do you ever wonder about who we are if we're not our bodies?"

Ian looks at my empty glass and smiles. "Oh, yeah, I'm in. Whatcha thinking about, girl? This should be good."

"I'm serious. Do you ever think about reincarnation?"

"Sure, sometimes. Do you?"

I look around for Eric, but he's heading back to the patio, well out of earshot. I'm relieved to be able to just relax and talk about whatever I want. Ian settles in next to me on the sofa and we start with the caveman question, which evolves into a quasi rant. He hands me a sloppy nacho and another Mexican martini. Two sips in, all I can see is the lime pulp in my glass. My visual field is noticeably shorter, like I'm in permanent zoom mode on the camera. When I turn my head, it takes a second before the sound lines up with the picture. I try to focus.

He keeps prodding me for details, so even though I wasn't planning to, I end up telling him about finding the real John Robberson.

"So tell, me. What do you really make of it? Is Toby a reincarnated fighter pilot?"

"I don't know," I say, trying to have the conversation only with Ian and not everyone who's sitting on the back of the sofa. "I think if he really were the reincarnation of John Robberson, he'd speak differently of him. He'd recount memories, right? But it's a mashup. Toby talks about him like he's a separate entity, but he's replicating pilot memories when he plays. He knows things he can't possibly know. See what I mean? That's when it flips for me. Acting it out is a game. Memories are evidence."

Eric approaches, beer in hand. "Did someone say pilot?" My neck and cheeks flush. I don't know how much he overheard.

"Not just pilot. Fighter pilot, dude," says Ian.

"Don't encourage him." I wave at Mamie. "Come over and tell me what you're working on these days. Don't you have a show coming up?"

I turn my back to Eric and Ian but can't follow what Mamie says. All I can hear is the swagger in Eric's voice.

He leans his head back, sticks out his chest, and says, "You know, back in the day, when it was just me in that single-seater Thud, carpet bombing the Dragon's Jaw, I pulled a high-G barrel roll to get away from the little shit behind me about to gun my ass down."

What?

Ian smiles. "Dragon's Jaw?"

"You know you're in trouble when you pickle the bombs off, pull back on the stick, and instead of a standard pullout, you get snapped into a hard right roll."

Ian gestures to him and nudges me. "Check out the wannabe."

"Do you think he practiced in the mirror?" I force a laugh, determined not to allow him the satisfaction of seeing he's getting to me.

Eric winks at Mamie. "Yeah, I remember when I felt the resistance on that right side, I realized that damn bomb was still in the hole."

"What are you talking about?" Mamie asks, as we turn to face the guys.

"My days back in 'Nam, sweetheart."

She says to me, "Why's he talking like that?"

"He's drunk. How many fingers am I holding up, Eric?"

Eric asks Ian, "Don't you want to know how I got out of it?"

"Bring it."

Gesturing with his hands, he explains. "The weight pulled me right, so I knew the bomb was still there. So what do I do?" He raises his eyebrows, holds the question for a beat. "Reversed the roll-out to the left side, going with the drag of the extra weight instead of fighting it."

Ian pauses, head cocked, lips pursed. "You got the jargon down cold. Truly impressive." He nods and offers his beer as a toast. "Simple physics, right?"

Eric clinks his long-necked bottle to Ian's. "Engineers unite."

"Been reading any military thrillers lately?"

Eric smiles and takes a swig. "Can I get you another beer, buddy?"

CHAPTER THIRTEEN

PARTY RECAP

I leave Ian's with a tiny shred of leftover party mood that dies somewhere in the taxi on the way home. Eric doesn't say a word. We crawl into bed, and I send out the "leave me alone" vibe. In the morning, I go out of my way to demonstrate that I do not have a hangover, despite my dry mouth and radioactive regret. He leaves early to ride his bike downtown so he can retrieve our car from Ian's. It feels like the door sucks the energy out of the room as it shuts behind him, louder than usual, a borderline slam that I hope made more noise than he intended.

It wakes Toby up. You'd think he was the one with the hangover. He's grouchy from the minute his little foot hits the floor, which is unusual for him. I let him eat an entire cantaloupe for breakfast—his favorite—but he throws his fork on the ground before he's finished.

"I don't want any more!"

"Here now, Tobe. That's not the way to act at the table. We don't throw our forks. What should you do instead?"

"May I be excused?" he grumbles.

"That's right. My goodness, what's gotten into you today?"

"I don't want to see her!"

"Right. We talked about this. You don't have to, remember?"

"I'm not going to!"

"That's right."

—

While Toby plays with his planes in the living room, I can't stop thinking about Eric's weird fighter-pilot rant. The longer I think about it, the creepier it seems.

I call Carla to recap the party. She thinks it's nothing more than Eric grandstanding. She says, "Please. He overhears you say memories are evidence, and he makes up a fake memory right there, on the spot, to make his point."

"You didn't hear it."

"True. So ask someone who did. See what Ian thinks."

I text him, since he's at work. He thinks phone calls are rude interruptions left over from a previous technological age.

What was that thing with Eric last night? Was it as weird as I think?

He answers within two seconds: He was drunk. nbd

No big deal? I don't know why I'm asking Ian for insight into an emotionally nuanced situation. Of course he thinks it's no big deal. He thinks not marrying Mamie is no big deal.

I call Carla back. "I need for you to talk me down," I say. "Tell me it wasn't tip-of-the-iceberg weird. That nothing woo-woo happened last night. Convince me."

"You know Eric. He takes everything to its logical extreme. If you say this thing with Toby is more than a game, then he's exaggerating the game to show you how ridiculous it looks. It's like he's daring you to try to make a big deal of it because he knows you'll sound crazy. I think he's hoping you'll realize how crazy it sounds and let it go."

"Do you think I sound crazy?"

"I think you were both drunk and he acted like a dick to make the point that you're overreacting to all this fighter-pilot stuff. So don't overreact to his version; it just proves his point," Carla says. "If it were me, I'd make the point that he shouldn't act like a dick and make fun of me in front of my friends. But you gotta decide whether you want to pick that fight or not."

"I don't want to pick a fight. I just want to be able to talk to my husband."

CHAPTER FOURTEEN

UNDER PRESSURE

Eric and I haven't had a decent conversation all week—not since Ian's party. I think Toby's picking up on the tension in the house. His objections to Kay are worse in the mornings, I've noticed. Where's the kid who laughed in his sleep? I don't think he's waking up in the middle of the night; he's not calling out for me, at least. He says he doesn't have nightmares. In fact, he says he doesn't dream at all. I write it down in my notes. I don't know if he doesn't dream, if he just doesn't remember, or if his language skills aren't developed enough to articulate it yet. I don't know how accurate anyone can be when talking about what happens in their sleep. Even when I catch him doing it, Eric says he doesn't sleepwalk anymore.

I simply don't know. Whatever is going on in my kid's head at night, it's making him wake up as grouchy as Pa used to be right after my mom died. Every morning, he'd have to realize all over again that he was alone.

Today, I decide to try a distraction technique, so we take an early-morning trip to the grocery store. Instead of getting a cart, we walk hand in hand down the aisle. It's a pleasant change, even if I have to keep stopping to replace items kept at knee height. We take our time.

"Shelly?" An almost-familiar face is smiling at me, a woman pushing her squirmy son in a cart toward us. "It's Wendy—from the playgroup?"

"Of course! Toby, do you remember Dylan?"

We'd met at the last neighborhood playgroup. She was new and noticeably more granola than most of the women I call the Other Mothers, the gray in her long hair seeming like a statement. She's going gray without apology or chemical deterrents. I like that.

"He's still on the airplane jag, huh?" she says, as Toby shows Dylan his F-105. "Is his imaginary friend still around?"

That's how I talk about John Robberson. It makes people feel better. Wendy and I make small talk and go our separate ways.

When we reach the bakery aisle, Toby asks me where they keep the oatmeal cream pies. It's been weeks since we've talked about oatmeal cream pies.

"They don't sell them here, Toby. Remember?"

"Why not?"

"I think they're not healthy enough."

"Yes, they awe."

"No, I'm afraid not."

"Thud wants one."

"They're really not healthy for Thud. Dogs like meat. Not sugar."

Toby lets out a shriek that would raise the dead and flings his entire body onto a basket that holds thin loaves of crusty French bread. The basket crashes over, sending the half-exposed loaves out of their fancy paper wrappers and sliding across the newly mopped floor. Toby is grabbing any loaf within reach and throwing it, screaming, "I don't want to!"

It happens so fast, I barely know what to do. I reach for him out of pure instinct, but he clocks me with a long baguette. A small crowd is forming at the end of the aisle.

"Toby!" I wrap my arms around his, preventing him from using any more bread as a weapon. "What is it, baby?"

As quickly as it flared up, it passes. He collapses against me. We're both crying as we sit on the bakery floor. I know my kid. This is not like him.

Wendy and Dylan appear out of nowhere. "Need a hand?" she says.

"We're fine. Just need a minute." I whisper to her, over Toby's head, "Can you get rid of the spectators?"

She nods and rolls her cart directly into the crowd, causing them to dissipate. For a few moments. I can just sit cross-legged on the cold linoleum tiles and rock Toby, shushing his sobs. When he can speak, I ask him if he can tell me what upset him.

"Kay."

I can't be objective and just write this on a list somewhere. I have to say it.

"Oh, baby. Kay's not going to hurt you."

"I don't want to talk to her." He flings his arm, like he's throwing a toy. "I don't!"

"You don't have to, remember? Nobody is going to make you. You're the boss."

He sniffles.

"There. Okay." The other shoppers have returned to their own business, but we're still on the floor together.

"Now that you know that you don't have to see her," I say to Toby, "can I ask you a few questions about Kay? I want to understand why you're upset."

He nods.

"Who is Kay?"

"John Wahbuhson's wife."

I do a double take in the grocery aisle. After nodding to a shop-per who looks disapprovingly at us on the floor, I whisper, "Whose wife?"

"John Wahbuhson's!"

"Okay, okay. What does John Robberson say to you about Kay?'

"We have to go see her."

"And you don't want to see her, I know. But if you're the boss, and you know you don't have to see her, I don't understand why you get so upset."

"I don't want to."

"I know, baby." I kiss his forehead. "But help me understand why not."

Toby's face turns into a little ball of fury, in a split second. "I don't want to!"

"Okay, okay. I'm sorry. No more talk. Let's finish our shopping, and we can get a strawberry smoothie."

Toby's satisfied, but I'm still rattled as we walk into the juice bar that adjoins the grocery store. I see Wendy at a table with three Other Mothers including Pauline, the president of the homeowners association. What are the others' names? Emily and . . . Renee, was it? Remy? Something like that. I order Toby's smoothie and let him join the kids at the other table.

"You okay now?" asks Wendy.

I hold up my drink, a bright green concoction of kale and cucumber juice. "I almost asked for a vodka shot in this one!"

"We've all been there," she says with a laugh.

"How's Toby?" Pauline asks, knowingly.

"He seems to be fine now," I say. "So weird. The oatmeal cream pies set him off."

Pauline looks around the table, eyebrow cocked, before she erupts in laughter. When she speaks, she's not talking to me. "He's afraid of oatmeal cream pies? Shelly, let the kid have a little sugar now and then!"

"That's not it," I say, cutting the joke short. "I actually understand his reaction. That's why I'm a little shaken, to tell you the truth."

"Does this have anything to do with that imaginary friend you were so worried about?" Emily asks.

"Not so imaginary, as it turns out." I blurt it all out, from the oatmeal cream pies to the Thud and how I tracked it down but didn't find John Robberson on the pilot list; and the whole thing about the 395 crashes but only 61 of them being operational; which opens the door to telling them how I took Toby back to the scene of the crime, the Boneyard, and his weird trance and how disappointed I was; and then how Toby heard John Robberson at the dinner table but the doctor said it was nothing to worry about; and how I kept digging until I found a real John Robberson who had actually died on Toby's birthday.

"The very same day," I say, a tad triumphantly, as I pause for a breath.

The Other Mothers exchange a glance, and too late, I realize I've stopped them cold. I take a long sip from my green drink, which is beginning to separate and look unappetizing.

"That's quite a coincidence," says Renee or Remy or whatever her name is.

Pauline asks, "How, exactly, did you put this together?"

Wendy adds, because I think she's trying to help me out, "Oh, you'd be surprised what you can find on the Internet."

"Well, I wouldn't know where to look," Pauline says.

Emily joins her, saying, "I barely have time to check my e-mail, much less track down something like that!" She looks at her watch. "Speaking of time, I've got to run, girls!"

They escape and Wendy lingers a moment longer. "Are you okay?"

"They think I'm nuts." I shake my drink and take another sip. It's awful once it gets warm.

Wendy says, "You know, I just read a memoir by a California woman whose daughter had a mean imaginary friend. The little girl kept hitting the mom and then crying, saying her imaginary friend made her do it. The mom ended up taking the girl to some South American country where everyone assumed she had a demon that needed to be driven out. She went to a shaman or something who told her to do this ceremony . . . or was it a ritual?"

She smiles at my puzzled expression.

"My point is this: I bet all her friends thought she was crazy, too."

Crazy or not, when I get home, I go straight to my list and add this:

1. Toby knows Kay is John Robberson's wife.
2. Toby's temper tantrums are more frequent and intense, which means his resistance to seeing Kay is getting stronger.

I ponder that last entry awhile, my stomach churning the whole time, before I add one more:

3. John Robberson is pressuring Toby.

The worst part about this list is that I can't even show it to Eric. I'm embarrassed about my bout of verbal diarrhea this afternoon. Pauline shouldn't know more than my own husband. I need to sit him down and tell him everything.

At dinner that night, I try. I start by describing the temper tantrum at the store, but he doesn't want to hear about the explanation. He just looks over at Toby and tells him not to do that again. He actually tells our three-year-old that temper tantrums are a sign of weakness.

Weakness? Are you kidding me?

I'm sorry to say I swallow that metallic taste in my mouth and take the bait. We argue about that one, late into the night. And one more day goes by, and he doesn't know the truth.

CHAPTER FIFTEEN

JUST A GAME

The very next night, I'm determined to tell Eric everything. But when he gets home from work, he goes directly to the liquor cabinet and makes himself a Jack and Coke. He sits down on the living-room floor with Toby, the two of them entirely focused on the airplane bucket.

"How was your day?" I call from the kitchen.

No answer.

I step toward the living room and watch as Toby pulls out the metal F-105. He shows it to Eric, holding his palm out flat like it's the floor of a hangar.

Eric says, "You know, when I was a fighter pilot, there was this one time . . ." and he takes the plane away from Toby. Before Toby objects, Eric says, in an animated tone, "I was flying low, following the river." He uses the plane to take a low swoop over the carpet, in a serpentine motion. Toby claps his hands.

I can't believe it. A week after the fact and he's resurrecting his party spiel—with Toby this time.

He keeps going, telling the same story about the Dragon's Jaw, dodging enemy fire, the bomb getting stuck—only at the end, he says, "Is that how you did it?"

Toby, smiling, takes the plane from him, evidently understanding the game without Eric having to explain it. "Fly wight over the bwidge, and . . . awww. Stuck."

"That's right! The bomb didn't release." Eric takes the toy plane back. "I didn't realize it until I tried to pull out. How about you? What do you have to do then?"

I stand stock-still in the kitchen. I don't know which bothers me more—the fact that he's doing this or what he's saying. That fight I didn't pick after the party? It's coming to him.

"You have to woll out, with the bomb," Toby says. "You have to be bwave. Like John Wahbuhson."

"That's right. I was brave, and I rolled out, but you have to do it on the side that has the weight. But you knew that, right?"

"Awound and awound."

I can hear Toby get up, and when I step into the living room, I see him spin with the toy plane in his hand; Thud the airplane flying around Thud the dog.

"And then what?"

Toby looks closely at Eric, then answers, "The smoke whooshed," and he sticks his arms in front of him and swings them toward his chest, in a sweeping motion and continues, "and I jumped out."

"That's called ejecting. You eject so you can get out before the crash."

Toby jumps into Eric's chest, knocking him backward. "Ka-boom!"

They wrestle around on the floor, laughing until Toby says, "Oh! I bwoke my weg."

"Which leg?" Eric asks.

Toby slaps his left leg as he jumps up and throws his body into Eric's. "Cwash!"

I stand over the two of them, not saying a word. As Eric falls backward with Toby, he makes eye contact with me.

"What the hell was that?" I mouth the words, unable to keep from flinging my arms in his direction. If I could shove him over, I would.

"What's up with you?"

"Me? What do you think you're doing?"

"Cwash!" Toby says again.

"I'm playing a game." Eric picks him up and carries him into the kitchen. "And you are overreacting. Again."

I hate Eric's version of the game. Just as I'm trying to observe objectively, Eric goes out of his way to initiate the game with Toby. Carla's right. He's making fun of me; that's all it is. How on earth did I come to be married to a man who mocks me? Where is the logical Eric, the one who can put his emotions aside and have a sane discussion?

Instead of Eric dismissing me out of hand, I'd like him to help me figure out how to protect Toby from otherworldly messages.

For an entire week, Eric comes home and plays the same airplane game with Toby. And every night, I make notes and hold my metallic-tasting tongue.

Finally, while we're brushing our teeth one morning, I broach the topic. Because I'm brave. Like John Fucking Robberson. But I begin with a soft, roundabout approach.

"You were sleepwalking again last night."

"Huh."

"It's the fourth time this week."

"Are you sure?"

"Yes." I spit into the sink and give him the rundown, including the previous night's weird encounter. On both Tuesday and Wednesday nights, I hadn't realized he'd been sleepwalking until he got back into bed. But the previous night, Thursday night, I woke up and the bed was empty. When I got up to look for him, he was leaving Toby's room. I followed him down the hallway and he stopped dead still, like he knew I was there. I stopped, too. He turned and looked right through me. No expression on his face. No recognition, but also no anger. He just started walking toward me, back to our bedroom, so I turned and walked in front of him. We got into bed without a word or a touch.

"Weird," he says, walking out of the bathroom. "But you know I never remember any of it."

"I know. But four times in one week, Eric. Are you stressed? Tense?"

He says, "I'm tense because you're tense. About a stupid game. If you would let it go," he says, "then neither of us would be tense."

But that night, when he returns, he starts right back in again. Before I've even finished eating, he pulls Toby out of his booster seat and takes him to the living room. I put down my fork and shake my head. Unbelievable.

I can hear them wrestling on the floor. "Where's that Thud of mine?" he growls. "I feel like bombing somebody!"

I can't take it.

I storm out of the house without a word. I have my phone with me for the music, not the calls. I don't even look at his texts. Headphones in, I find a good playlist and speed-walk laps around Oasis Verde until it's dark and I'm sure Toby is in bed.

When I return, Eric switches the TV off and says, "Okay. You made your point. I'm sorry."

"All I want is to talk to you about this. Can we do that?"

He nods. "Come sit down. I'm listening. Can you explain to me what it is about this game that bothers you so much? I can't believe you care how I play with Toby."

I join him on the sofa and take a deep breath. "It's not the game I'm objecting to. You know Toby plays it every day with Sanjay. It's not the game itself. I think the game has a meaning. So that's why the part you add, where you act like you remember actually flying the plane—that's what bothers me. It seems ironic that you won't let it go."

"Ironic?"

"You're the one accusing me of keeping John Robberson alive," I say.

"Who said anything about John Robberson?"

"Toby does! That's the whole point. Whenever you play this game, Toby adds what he heard from you to the game, to what he thinks John Robberson said, or knows, or wants."

Eric closes his eyes and squeezes the bridge of his nose. He takes a long time to answer, and when he does, his voice has lost that defiant edge. "I still don't see why this is such a big deal."

"Because there's more!" I grab a pillow and pull it into my lap before I cross my legs and face him. "What about Kay? How can he know about Kay?"

"Jeez. The way you talk about it. He doesn't *know about* Kay; he made Kay up."

"Eric. You have to listen to me. Toby is telling the truth."

"What truth is that?"

I finally tell him about the obituary of the real John Robberson. The Thud pilot. A former fire chief. With a wife named Kay. The date of his death, which happens to be the very same day as Toby's birth.

I've held it back for so long, this actual evidence, hoping against hope that he'd be persuaded. But no.

He shifts his position, crossing his legs and facing me. "It's nothing. A coincidence. You can find anything on the Internet. I'm not convinced that just because there was a guy named John Robberson, who was married to a woman named Kay, that it means that Toby's John Robberson is the same guy. Think about it. Use me as an example: there are probably a thousand different Eric Buckners in the world, maybe a hundred thousand, and odds are that one of them, besides me, is married to someone named Shelly. I really think John Robberson is nothing more than a superman version of me." He shakes his head, almost in disgust.

I can tell I have to use a new tactic. I want to just come right out and say it, but the distance between an imaginary John Robberson/superman and a real John Robberson who died on the same day our son was born—it's a chasm that can't be leaped in a single bound. The room is starting to get dark, and I pause to turn on the lamp. Baby steps.

With Jell-O for vocal chords, I say, "Just for the sake of discussion, let's assume Toby's John Robberson is the same one that I tracked down."

"Okaaaay."

"Either Toby is a reincarnation of John Robberson, or John Robberson is some kind of spirit that talks to Toby."

"Like a ghost? Are you the ghost whisperer?" He smiles. "Like that chick on TV? What was her name?"

"Please, try to listen to me. Pretend for a minute that you don't find this assumption both ridiculous and offensive. Can you do that?"

"Barely. Because, ghost whisperer extraordinaire," Eric says, "there's no way to find out which of your ridiculous assumptions is correct."

"Maybe there is. Remember that researcher? I'm using the same methodology. I'm paying attention to anything he says about John Robberson. I write it down. Does he say he remembers? Or does he say John Robberson told him? What about these temper tantrums about Kay? Because no matter how many times I tell him he doesn't have to go, he still freaks out almost every day."

"Not every day," Eric objects.

"And I write whether he says anything new about John Robberson. Like the thing with him smelling smoke and jumping out. I look at how often he adds details like that."

"Seriously? You have this written down somewhere? Like a journal? Dates, categorization? Direct quotes?"

I feel my neck and cheeks go red. "Yes."

With an affectionate lilt in his voice, he says, "Well, I admire your scientific approach. Impressive. Very thorough. What are your preliminary findings?"

"I think early on, I made a mistake. I may have pushed him too much for details."

He unfolds his legs and changes position, so I can't see the smirk on his face as he says, "Ya think?"

I glare at him. "So now I don't want you to do the same thing. My findings, as you call them, are unclear. At first because of me. But now because of you. You're contaminating the data pool. When you initiate that game with him, when you pretend to *remember* when you were a fighter pilot, he imitates it and adds to the game all the things he knows from when *he* was a fighter pilot . . . Do you see what I mean? I can't tell if he is remembering something, or if he sees something, or if he's playing along with you."

"So, which way are you leaning?" He leans back, hands behind his head. "Reincarnation or ghost?"

"Ghost."

"Okay. Let's say you're right. It's a ghost." He takes my hands in his. "What difference does it really make?"

"The tantrums. I think John Robberson is pressuring Toby to meet Kay face to face. And we have no idea what would happen— jeez. I don't even want to think about *that*. It scares me to death."

He starts laughing. He reaches over and motions to Thud, who rolls on his back so Eric will scratch his belly. Eric obliges the dog, and when he's done, Thud thinks he's going to get to go outside.

He's at Eric's feet with his front paws set apart, his hindquarters in the air, his tail wagging from side to side.

"Okay, buddy," Eric says to the dog. As he stands up, he looks over his shoulder at me. "Chill out. It's just a game."

I sigh and lean back against the sofa. "No, it's not."

CHAPTER SIXTEEN

YOUR MOMMA WAS A BEAUTIFUL WOMAN

Today, Lakshmi and I try out a new yoga class, held in the space behind the Oasis Verde coffee shop. They have child care, which means Toby and Sanjay can play near the urban farm's community garden. After class, we linger over green tea.

"Something has to give," I say. "I need a direct line to John Robberson."

"Well," Lakshmi says, "I don't know what else you could do."

I take a sip of my tea and look around the coffee shop. It's comfortably rustic and familiar . . . except for the guy at the counter. He's in his mid-thirties and wearing a suit, which isn't that unusual. It's his hair. It's unusually thick and slicked back, about a half inch from qualifying as a pompadour. I'm having a déjà-vu moment. Then it clicks.

Eyes still on that hair, I say to Lakshmi, "Have you ever heard of Vaughn Redford?"

"Who?"

"The man who talks to people on the other side. The medium."

"What are you talking about?"

In the midst of a sleepless night several months ago, I was flipping channels and came across an old television show where this thirty-something guy from the Bronx—looking like someone you wouldn't notice on a subway, except he's got the same near-pompadour hairdo as the man at the counter—comes into the audience and brings messages from people who have died back to their loved ones. The show is a live taping of the process. I watched the entire episode, fascinated. Back then, I would've put him in the same category as a street magician. But now . . .

I tell Lakshmi about a woman in the audience whose son had died in a car accident. When he "came through," he told his mother that the wreck was his fault and that she should stop blaming the kid in the car who hit his.

She sees the value in it as a benevolent service to the grieving mother, allowing her to forgive the survivor of the accident and accept her son's death.

I pull out my phone and do a quick search for Vaughn Redford. Not only is he still doing performances, I find his schedule and gasp.

"You're not going to believe this. He's coming to Phoenix. Right before Memorial Day. This could be the ticket." I squeeze Lakshmi's hand. "Will you come with me?"

"Absolutely."

That déjà-vu moment does me more good than forty-five minutes of warrior poses. On my way home, I congratulate myself. That's the ticket, all right. It's my chance to talk to John Robberson without risking Toby in the process. If he's got something to say to my kid, or even through my kid, he can say it to me. Through Vaughn Redford.

Later, in my garden, I start to ruminate on the possibilities of having a real link between this world and the spirit world . . . and, well, I can't help thinking of my mom.

What I'd give to connect with her, to see if she's watching Toby grow up from beyond. I wonder if she'd appear to me. If I go to see Vaughn Redford, it stands to reason that the most likely person to show up for me would be my mom. I can feel my heart swell with longing. I can't believe how much I would like to have seen the look on her face when she met Toby. She would be so proud of him.

I have to bring Toby, of course. Otherwise, John Robberson might not show up.

I stand up and brush the soil from my knees. I stuff the weeds into the garbage bag and spin the bag until the top twists shut. I have no idea how I'm going to break this one to Eric.

We're due for our monthly visit to Pa this weekend. On the way there, I mention Vaughn Redford, but Eric just snorts and we don't talk for the rest of the drive. He doesn't want to hear about it.

On this visit, Toby is learning to play checkers with Pa. Every time we come, Pa has a goal for Toby. Once, it was showing him how to use a screwdriver. He'd sat outside with Toby for hours, with an assortment of screwdrivers ("This here's a Phillips") and a couple of two-by-fours. By the end of the weekend and prior to his third birthday, Toby knew how to use a screwdriver. Pa has no appreciation that Toby might be more likely to poke his eye out than use it correctly. I actually love this about Pa.

But this weekend it's checkers, and Toby's developmental limitations are showing up. Eric rescues Pa from his grandson's short attention span and propensity to make free jumping kings out of his checkers without regard to the rules.

It's cooling off a bit right before the sunset, and Eric decides he'll take Toby to the mall to run off some steam in the air conditioning. This frees me up to talk to Pa alone about the Vaughn Redford opportunity.

I've been thinking about everyone's "most likely person to appear." I figure the more people who show up with the same desire, the better the odds. So if I want my mom to show up, I need to bring who she wants to see, which means I need Pa.

He's thinking about getting new reading glasses. "I'm not getting old, mind you. My eyes are just more experienced now."

I say, "That's what life is all about, isn't it? Experiences?"

How lame. I sound like I'm inserting one of those intentionally chipper segues that morning news anchors use. He looks at me sideways before he answers.

"Well, baby girl, you can't avoid 'em, that's for sure. But I don't have to lay down in front of a tractor to know that it's most likely gonna smash my skull flat. There's some experiences I guess I don't need to sign up for."

This isn't going to be easy. All day, I've been making random statements about life and asking him for advice. He doesn't seem to be suspicious, but soon I'm going to have to say it. Not the part about John Robberson. That would be a deal buster. So I focus on Mom. How do you tell your dad you've bought him a ticket to go see a medium and you're actually very excited about it because you hope, for his sake, that your dead mother will speak to him from the "other side"? So I blurt it out, exactly like that.

About the time I say "other side," he says, "Whoa there, baby girl."

I smile as innocently as I can.

"Want to start all over with that?"

So I say it in slow motion, laying the groundwork, first talking about Vaughn Redford and the TV show. I even bought him a book in large print that tells the story of Vaughn Redford's unusual life. He takes it from me, says thank you, ma'am, and sets it down on the coffee table without opening it.

Oh well.

Working his back molar with a toothpick, he says, "Say your piece." He leans back in his recliner, puts his toothpick down, and makes a zipper motion across his lips. He sticks the imaginary key in the front pocket of his jumpsuit.

I explain what happens on the TV show and tell him my idea about the "most likely person to appear." I think he gets the idea of what I expect when we go. Not that he's interested.

"What if you could talk to Momma again? What if this guy isn't a total fake? What if Momma has a message for you? Wouldn't you want to hear it?"

I take one look at his face and stop talking. I put my hands in my lap.

"You done?" he says.

"Yes."

He makes a big show of pulling the imaginary key out of his pocket. He unlocks the imaginary lock on the zipper on his lips and saves the key. "The thing is, baby girl, your momma was a beautiful woman . . ."

This is how all his memories start. He'll say this beautiful-woman thing, then tell me some story about his wife, his bride, his partner in life, my mother. And at the end, he repeats it again, the same phrase.

He says it as if I never saw the woman while she was alive. She was a beautiful woman. As Pa, the smitten husband, tells it, she was a professional beautiful woman. By this, he means her part-time modeling career. My mom was a model for a local dress shop. The guy had advertising ambition and used her in TV ads and direct mail. It was nothing, small-time local stuff, but she was recognizable. If nothing else, her part-time job set her apart. She wasn't like the other moms. She didn't aspire to be the homeroom mom. My mother had other talents. She was tall and thin, and clothing hung just right on her.

Nobody mistakes me for a model. I inherited Mom's statuesque frame but not her practiced poise or her meticulous grooming.

About the time most girls get interested in those things, I rejected them. In junior high school, when I let my naturally curly hair grow long, into a wild, spectacular mass, it activated a pervasive negative commentary on her part. By the time I graduated from high school, I hated her almost as much as she hated how I looked.

After Toby was born, I regretted the conflict so acutely that I cut my hair into a pixie of soft curls I hoped Mom could see. She was right about the hair. I'm grateful for what I got from her—clear skin and high cheekbones—but I chose not to inherit my mother's ability to put makeup over the chronic disappointments of life. So every time Pa starts a story with the beautiful-woman thing, there's a little part of me that undervalues her perfect exterior finish.

He doesn't. That's the sweet thing about it. He's not being superficial or denying anything. He knew what was underneath and genuinely appreciated her, inside and out.

It was a long time before I realized the way Pa talks about her says more about him than it does about her. I have to admit, there are times when I long for my husband to look past my faults and describe me with such consistent adoration. Hell, I'd be happy if he just stopped making fun of me at every turn.

I refocus in time to hear him finish the story, the one I already know, about how when Mom was sick, she told him she would wait for him in heaven. But he tells it the long way, and it breaks my heart to remember those days in the hospital. Pa and I have never talked about the very end, when she started to say all the hateful things the tumor squeezed out of her. Eric tried to explain the geography of the brain, tried to assure me she didn't mean any of it, but it was hard not to take it personally.

Pa shifts in his recliner. "So, baby girl, if your momma tells me she's gonna wait for me in heaven, then who am I to be summoning her out in order to give me a message? Isn't that kind of rude of me, to pull her away from whatever heavenly activities go on up there, so she can come back and tell me she loves me? I know she loves me. She loved me when she was here, and that don't stop just because she's there and I'm still here. I don't need no damn psychic telling me my business. There ain't nothing he can say that's gonna make any difference to me."

"Okay, Pa, okay."

The next thing out of his mouth surprises me.

"What I can't figure out is why you want to go. What is it your momma didn't tell you? What do you not know? What do you need to hear from her?"

I look closely at him, his crazy eyebrows knitted in concern for me, sitting in that plaid recliner in his jumpsuit. He's getting more and more eccentric as he gets older. And here he is, trying his level best to figure me out like a Sunday crossword. The old goat.

My voice softens and I say, "I want her to see Toby. Then, I guess, she'd really see me."

"Baby girl." He stands up, picks up a nearby picture of me holding Toby as a baby, and sits down on the sofa next to me. "Look at him. Look at you. Did you ever see anything so perfect in all your life? How can she keep from seeing that?"

I nestle under his arm, my head on his chest.

"All right, baby girl, I'll go. For you."

I squeal and give him a big hug. "Thank you!"

Eric and Toby return, and Toby runs to me and gives me a big squeeze.

"Young man," Pa says to him, "do you know that your momma is a beautiful woman?"

CHAPTER SEVENTEEN

THE PISTOL IS A DREAMER

Before you go," Pa says the next morning, as I'm preparing bowls of strawberries with yogurt and granola, "I thought you might want to meet Dottie."

I clank the spoonful of yogurt on the side of the bowl to release the dollop. "If you want us to meet her, we'll be happy to." I hand him the bowl. "If it's important to you."

He takes it and shuffles from the kitchen to his recliner in the living room. He hesitates, then waves his hand at me. "I don't care that much, to tell you the truth. But she wants to meet you. She's been driving me nuts, asking me if I'm ashamed of her, talking like a crazy woman. Last time I saw her, I said you guys were coming down and she kept yakking for a half hour until I told her I'd introduce her to you. You don't have to do it."

So it's not serious, at least on his part. I walk by his chair and smooth the white hair on his head. "It's okay. I'll meet her if it'll get her off your back and things will go back to normal."

Pa takes a bite of strawberry and mutters, "All I did was go to the casino with her on that damn bus they take every week."

"What, did she want to hold hands on the way home?"

He complains about there being so many widows in his trailer park, he can barely say hello without them baking him banana bread and putting on their lipstick every time he comes by. Eric comes into the kitchen with Toby in his arms and says, "Who is putting on lipstick for you?"

"The ladies in the trailer park," I explain with a smile.

"They want a piece of me, I tell you."

Eric says, "You know your problem, Pa? You're a chick magnet."

Pa laughs. "I can fix that. I'm about to break out that deer piss I got left over from hunting. If I wipe myself down with it real good, that ought to nip it in the bud."

Toby wants to play the "jumping game," his new name for checkers, and Pa is happy to oblige. Eric steps outside to return a work phone call and I settle in Pa's recliner to read the paper. I don't see any listing for Vaughn Redford's appearance, now only a week away.

—

We agree to meet Dottie for a late lunch, which in Tucson means one o'clock. When Dottie walks into the restaurant, she's wearing pink Bermuda shorts and a matching shirt with a tiny lizard pin attached to her left shoulder. Not in the front, where people wear name tags, but on the top of her shoulder, tentatively, as if it has only recently claimed its space. I'm trying not to stare at it, but Toby points it out in a way that makes it okay for me to examine it a bit closer.

Dottie, to my surprise, seems to have made no effort to counteract the deep laugh lines around her eyes. A good sign. I like it that her face isn't pulled tight or shellacked with pancake makeup. She has a pink manicure and wears her blonde hair in that once-a-week-at-the-hairdresser teased-up kind of style, the one that makes women buy satin pillowcases so their hair won't get messy while they sleep.

"You must be Dottie. So nice to meet you," I say, finding it easier than I thought it would be to see Pa escorting a woman.

I order for Toby as soon as we sit down. He'll do a lot better sitting here in a booth for an hour if I get him fed quickly. I dig in my bag and pull out a travel game that has plastic cars, buses, and trucks in a puzzle, and Toby entertains himself.

The adults make polite conversation about Tucson. Dottie orders a margarita and tells Pa about one of their neighbors in the trailer park who had a heart attack.

"They ride the casino bus together every week," Pa explains.

Dottie launches into a detailed description of her last slot jackpot. I keep an eye on Pa the whole time Dottie is talking. He interrupts her often, and she talks right over him. When he pokes fun at her, she laughs. They argue about whether she can make more money playing slots than he can at the poker table. Pa maintains that Texas Hold'em is a game of skill that can be learned. She shrugs her shoulders. That little lizard pin catches my eye. It seems animated by Dottie's movements.

It occurs to me that a habitual gambler might not be the best companion for Pa, who I can picture standing with her in line at the ATM in the lobby of a casino. My mother would've never set foot in a casino. I visualize Dottie's manicured hands turning black from handling coins and fight off a grimace.

Toby finishes his macaroni and cheese, and Eric agrees to split a chocolate shake with him. Toby crawls under the table to sit in Pa's lap, which puts him next to Dottie. He touches her shiny pin with one finger, almost petting it.

"Liz-uhd."

Dottie laughs loudly. "Isn't he cute? He's my little reminder."

"Reminder? Of what?" I ask.

"Oh boy. Here it comes."

Dottie gives Pa a playful poke in the ribs.

He says to me, "If you didn't think she was loco before, now you're going to know it for sure."

The waiter returns with the milkshake, and Toby scrambles back under the table to Eric. Between spoonfuls, Eric makes a scribble on the back of the kiddie menu, and Toby draws around it to turn it into a figure. They call this "the scribble game," and it works in restaurants. As long as they have paper, Toby will sit and draw. It's good, but it means Eric is completely disengaged from our conversation.

"Lizards are a symbol for your dreams," Dottie explains. She goes on to tell us she's one-sixteenth Navajo so she's an expert on totems.

Pa interrupts, "I keep asking her where the hell in Arizona her people found a big enough tree to carve a damn totem pole."

I suppress a smile.

"Totems don't have to be ten feet fall. We don't see too many now, but we keep the spirit alive. We have oral traditions, passed down from generation to generation," Dottie continues, unde-terred. All animals stand for something, and all of us have a totem pole of animals that define our lives. At the top of Dottie's totem pole is a lizard.

"It means I'm a dreamer," she says, petting the rhinestone liz-ard, "and it never fails. Whenever I wear the lizard, it catches the eye of the person I dreamed about."

I sincerely hope I'm not the reason for the lizard pin. Surely this lunch—meeting Pa's daughter—isn't a part of her dream. I'm begin-ning to feel like an unwilling co-conspirator.

She reaches across the table and puts her hand over mine. I don't pull away, mostly because I don't know how to do it without seeming impolite.

Toby announces that he has to potty. I pull my hand away from Dottie to allow room for Eric and Toby to leave the booth.

"Are you talking about me?"

"Close. Guess again." Then, turning to Pa, she says, "She'll figure it out. She's a smart one." She swipes the salt from the rim of her glass, licks her finger, and takes a shot-sized swallow of her margarita.

"Who?" I ask, clearly not wanting to guess.

"Him. The little squirt."

The air conditioning is cold, and I rub my bare arms to settle my goose bumps. Striving for carefree, I ask, "What about him?"

"He has a special talent, doesn't he? For seeing things you don't?"

I'm not about to talk to this woman about John Robberson. I pause, then say, as nonchalantly as I can, "Oh, I don't know about that."

"Yes, you do."

I stop rubbing my arms and cross them in front of me.

She says, "You've never dealt with dreams, have you? Don't worry. I'm not pushing anything on you. I'll just tell you what I dreamed, and you can decide for yourself what it means."

I look over at Pa, but he's cleaning his fingernails with his pocketknife. I can't believe he can tolerate this woman.

Dottie takes my silence for consent. "Okay. In my dream, I'm underwater and all of a sudden he's there, the little one, scared at first, but you know how when you fall in the water, you go down awhile, then at some point, you start going up again? Right when he hits that point, right before he starts floating up again, he hangs there in slow motion for a spell, then he looks right past me and I can feel it, he isn't scared anymore. Then, whoosh, he's gone."

"Hmmm," I say at the pause, but she's not finished. My heart is pounding in my ears.

"You know how in dreams you can jump around? Well, boom, just like that, I see boats all lined up in a marina, but it's like I'm overhead, looking down on it. This little guy is lying faceup on the dock, his hair plastered down on his forehead. I can hardly see him; there's a bunch of people standing around, and they're all worked up while one guy bends over him. Not sure who that is, but it doesn't matter. Then, boom, the dream jumps again, and I see everything like I'm lying on that dock right next to him. An airplane flies overhead, and it drowns out the crowd for a minute. He opens his eyes and sees it, then he gets flipped over and everyone is in his face, and all he wants is to tell you something real bad."

"What does he tell me?"

"That's when it fades out, so I don't know. That means it's not for me." She takes another sip of her margarita. "So, when it happens—when, not if—I'd listen if I were you." She settles back into the booth. I can picture her blowing smoke from the barrel of a recently fired handgun.

"Wait," I say, glad Eric's not at the table. "You can't tell me my son is going to drown and not tell me how to prevent it."

"Calm down, sweetie. I didn't say he was gonna drown. I see him on the dock. The dream is about what he says afterward."

"No offense to your dream, but I'm not about to let Toby flounder around in the water, unsupervised, just to see what he's going to say right after he almost drowns."

"Hate to break it to you, sweetie, but it's not up to you." Dottie digs in her purse for her lipstick, which is the exact shade of her Bermuda shorts. "Or even about you. Everything happens for a reason. If one day that little guy ends up in the water, you can bet there's a reason. I'm betting it's bigger than you. I'm betting it's not about you being a bad mommy. And I'd bet a jackpot that you know more than you're letting on." She pops the lid back on her lipstick.

"Remember, the first thing he says after he sees that airplane—that's the message you've been waiting on. You'll know what to do."

Eric and Toby return to the table and Pa says, "Glad you're back. We need another level head at the table. These two can't decide which end of the crazy bone to chew on."

CHAPTER EIGHTEEN

WHERE THERE'S FIRE

Toby had another tantrum today, this time right in front of the broccoli bin at the market. The mention of Kay's name sends him to a dark place, and while I'm still the boss of John Robberson, I can't control how much pressure he puts on Toby. I also can't wait until Vaughn Redford comes to town. It's the only thing I'm looking forward to these days.

I call Carla on a whim and make her promise to distract me the next time she's back in town. Turns out I only have to wait two days before she's off for Memorial Day. We catch an afternoon yoga class and go straight to happy hour. Two glasses of wine and we decide to catch a twilight show—some silly chick movie—and we laugh the whole way through. We both needed a day off.

I get home before Toby goes to bed. As soon as I open the door, Eric says, "How was your night out?"

"Fun. Yours?"

"Fun."

Toby runs to me for a hug. "Daddy let me jump off the monkey bars!"

"Come on, Tobe," Eric says, and I catch a glimpse of his shushing gesture.

Toby steps away and claps his hands over his mouth. I bite my lip as Eric explains it's nothing, just a small adjustment to the game. It had to change, they both agree.

"It was jacked up," Toby says, giggling.

"The crash angle," Eric explains.

"Did he just say 'jacked up'?"

"He meant to say inaccurate," Eric says.

I'm still stuck on why Eric feels it necessary to teach a three-year-old the phrase "jacked up," but he's busy explaining the aforementioned inaccurate crash angle.

"Since the plane was coming in from above, it can't crash laterally into a tree, the way Toby's been doing it," he explains, using that animated voice that keeps me from yelling in front of Toby. "The plane crashes from the sky, somewhere closer to a forty-five-degree angle. But," he says—as if the distinction he's about to reveal will change my mind—"the pilot ejects first and lands on a tree limb. From above."

"So you're playing the game again?"

He says, "We couldn't climb the tree in the park, so we used the monkey bars."

Those monkey bars are a full five feet above the three inches of gravel on the ground. I make Eric recap—give it to me one more time, describe exactly what they did, in detail. He helped Toby climb on top, encouraged him to stand up and straddle two bars, held his hand until he got his balance, then caught him when he jumped into Eric's arms, both of them screaming "ka-boom!" the whole time.

"John Wahbuhson had to jump out of his pwane," Toby explains. "I was bwave like John Wahbuhson."

"And what happened to John Robberson? He broke his leg," I practically shout at the two of them. "No. No more brave." I shake my head and finger in unison. "You hear me? No more jumping from the top of the monkey bars."

I hiss at Eric, "You should know better. How do you think this one's going to end?"

I turn to our son. "Come on, Toby. It's bedtime."

"Goodnight, bud," Eric says to Toby as I carry him up the stairs.

As I pull his T-shirt over his head, Toby says, "Are you mad, Momma?"

I take a deep breath. "No, baby." I rub his little tummy in a circle, like he's a Buddha. He giggles. "I just don't want you to get hurt jumping off the monkey bars."

The bedtime routine—the book, the hug, the tuck-in—relaxes me as much as it does Toby, so I linger longer than usual. His breath slows to a rhythm, but I stay and stroke his back, smoothing his monkey-printed pajamas, more for my benefit than his.

My peaceful moment is pierced by an ear-splitting siren.

Thud starts barking like there's an intruder. Toby jolts into my arms, legs clamped around my waist. We rush downstairs, me holding him and him holding his ears. Instead of quieting Thud, Eric opens the curtains so we can all watch the fire truck turn on our street and pass right by our window.

Toby jumps up and down like a cricket.

"Let's go!" Eric whips Toby onto his shoulders, tells him to duck when they reach the front door, and leaves me to restrain Thud and jog behind them for three blocks.

I don't get a chance to wonder whether it's a good idea to take our son to a fire. Who knows what he'll see?

We aren't the only ones following the smoke and sirens. I see a couple of the Other Mothers. Pauline is the only one who waves back to me. We join about fifteen of our neighbors on the well-manicured lawn and driveway of Mrs. Gilliam's house, a seafoam-green clap-board cottage with dark shutters that happens to be right across the street from the fire.

Eric calls out, "Hey, good lookin'," to Mrs. Gilliam, whose husband died right after we moved in. She's the first person we've known who lost her life partner, and when we met her as newly-weds, we felt protective toward her. Eric fixed her dishwasher when he found out she'd been washing dishes by hand since her husband died. She baked him cookies when he was hurt. She offers to babysit Toby, but I'm afraid he'd wear her out, so we drop by often instead.

I tuck my arm in Mrs. Gilliam's and join Lakshmi, Nikhil, and Sanjay, standing beside Eric. Toby is surprised the fire truck is yel-low, and we all have to discuss that as we stand together and watch a surprising volume of grayish smoke billow from the formerly white shutters on a vacant house that used to be a pretty robin's egg blue. It's been empty for almost two years.

Pauline fills us in. Rumor has it that a California investor bought it, the first of many houses he planned to buy low and sell high. All the neighbors laughed about it. Our property values are too stable for that kind of speculation. Evidently, he figured it out, because we haven't seen him since. The general consensus emerges: he set his own house on fire. I'm just glad it was empty and there's not a family being displaced.

The fire truck in Mrs. Gilliam's neighbor's driveway has obscured our collective view, but someone points out the first flames licking at the bottom floor windows. Within seconds, we see the drapes catch, and the fire seems to take a breath and sprint up the side of the house. The firefighters get to work and motion the crowd back. There's still a lot of smoke.

Mrs. Gilliam looks a bit disoriented. "Is it Thursday, dear?" she asks me, under her breath.

"No, it's Wednesday. Why do you ask?"

"Well, on Thursdays, that nice young man comes by in his van." She pops her forehead lightly with her hand. "But he wouldn't be here this late."

"What young man?"

She tells me he drives a white van, the kind with no windows, with nothing written on the side. He comes by once a week like clockwork, on Thursday afternoons between two and four. He always pulls all the way into the driveway along the side of the house across the street, she reports, and uses the back door. She thinks the owner hired him to water the plants and bring in the mail.

"Something funny is going on in that house," Lakshmi says to me in a low tone.

Sanjay and Toby are now riding on their fathers' shoulders, trying to get a better view of the fire truck with its lights still flashing blue and red, in a circle, penetrating the dusk. Toby holds Eric's hair with both fists. Sanjay leans over Nikhil's head, clasping him under the chin. His little arms barely reach. They shriek and wiggle, leaving their fathers to dodge their bare feet. I can't remember being that excited about anything. It's contagious.

Eric mumbles to Toby. I shift my weight so I can hear what he's saying. He points to the fire chief.

"John Wahbuhson was the fire chief."

I'm glad Eric can't see my expression. I've never told Toby about John Robberson's other career. Another item for my list of things Toby knows that he should not know.

Eric and Toby move away from Sanjay and Nikhil, a step closer to the scene, deep in conversation, pointing and commenting on the firefighters' technique. I see Ms. Pushpa making her way down the sidewalk, and Lakshmi goes to meet her.

Wendy walks up late and waves to me despite the lopsided tug from her son Dylan. I get the impression this was not his idea. He's trying to sit down and looks as bored as he did when the playgroup went to the science museum.

I introduce Wendy to Mrs. Gilliam and she turns toward us, unconcerned that Dylan is now lying on the sidewalk, and has her back to the firefighters as they do their job. After a bit of small talk, Wendy pulls me aside and we sit on the curb together. "You know, I've been thinking about you. I wanted you to know, I think your focus is insane."

She sees my expression. "Insane—like in a good way! Your focus. I mean, wow. It's so cool. You're paying such close attention to your kid. You're really tuned in to him. I find it inspiring, I really do."

"You may be the only one. My husband thinks I'm making something out of nothing."

"What does he know?" She pats my hand. "This is textbook mother's intuition. If there's a threat, we moms feel it, way before it makes sense, way before we can explain it."

I look up and see Eric, with Toby on his shoulders, sneaking even closer to the burning side of the house. They have identical trance-like expressions on their faces.

She says, "I would feel it if it were Dylan. You just *know*." She smiles. "You're his mother. Give yourself permission to trust your intuition."

"Wendy, I can't tell you how much I needed to hear that." I give her a one-armed hug before we stand up.

"It's out. The flames are gone." Eric and Toby walk back toward the group. "They should be coming out the front."

Our group politely applauds its thanks as two firemen file out of the house, laughing. They call the chief up to the front door. He sticks his head inside, then closes the front door, and one of the firemen tapes the door closed with yellow Keep Out tape in a crisscross pattern. The chief approaches and tells us it's all over, everything is under control, there's nothing to see here. He makes a point to remind the moms to keep our kids away from the house.

As we make our way home, Eric talks about the crime-scene tape, explaining that it's standard procedure. "To make sure there's no looting," he says with authority.

I mention Mrs. Gilliam's comment about the man who comes on Thursdays. "Lakshmi thinks there's something funny going on in that house."

"Oh no!" He puts his hands up to his cheeks in mock horror. "Does she think we need an exorcist?"

I don't answer.

"Hey, Shel. I have an idea. Let's live in the real world, instead of the invisible one you and Lakshmi keep making up. In the real world, here's what happened: an empty house caught fire."

—

The very next morning, Pauline interrupts my breakfast to inform me the police are in hazmat suits right this minute, confiscating what's left of four hundred marijuana plants from the empty house that caught fire. She rants about how we all could've gotten poisoned from the smoke. She's afraid her kid may have gotten high last night by accident. Eric overhears my attempt to assure her that the firefighters have it under control. He gestures at me until I ask Pauline to hold.

"Tell her you can't get high from burning raw marijuana plants. They burn entire acres of it in California all the time. Those guys are in hazmats today because they're handling the remnants."

Eric, always the expert. What does he know about hazmat cleanup? I relay the message to Pauline.

"Tell her she should worry less about the cleanup and more about how the grow house got here in the first place," Eric says.

I cover the mouthpiece while Pauline keeps talking. "I can't listen to both of you at once," I whisper to Eric.

"Tell her they should do a seminar on how to spot grow houses."

"Do you want to talk to her?"

"No, I'll be late for work." He finishes his orange juice and rinses his glass in the sink.

He won't admit it, but on this one, Lakshmi was right. It wasn't just an empty house that caught fire. There was something fishy going on, but Eric was so caught up in mansplaining the real world to me, he refused to see what was right in front of him. And as soon as we find out the truth, he acts like he's known all along.

The very next night, Eric changes the game with Toby. No airplane crash. Now he takes on the role of the firefighter, and Toby plays right along.

I refuse to engage in this fight in front of Toby, so I don't say a word about it. I take notes. I listen. I do not comment when Toby takes all the airplanes out of his plastic bucket and puts the fire trucks in. I make a note on the day he and Sanjay start playing fireman. They run into a burning house and rescue each other. The game may change, but Toby still adds the John Robberson commentary.

"John Wahbuhson says a buhning house can faw down on you."

"Wook out for booby twaps!"

"Pee-yewww! Rotten eggs!"

All these seeds sprout in Toby's mind while Eric's at work. I don't know if the two of them make up new details when I can't hear. All I see is Toby acting out a more elaborate fireman story each day: full cautionary checks for booby traps, with dogs trapped inside and rotten egg smells. Smoke. Roofs that collapse. No more plane crashes. No more broken legs.

I don't remind Eric that the real John Robberson was a fire chief. I don't tell him that I've never told Toby about the real John

Robberson. There's no way Toby could know he was a fire chief. I don't tell Eric how completely, totally freaked out I am by this turn in the game. I have no idea what's coming next. So I just listen and take more notes.

One night, after dinner, I flip through a magazine while Eric, on his fourth beer of the night, explains the two-by-two method, which means that no firefighter should enter a burning building alone. If there are two inside, he says to Toby, there have to be two outside, backing you up in case the roof collapses.

"The house can faw down."

"Right."

"Kay's mad about the dog."

"Oh, please." Eric's voice has taken a bitter tone that causes me to look up. "That's just stupid. You want to tell her something, tell her that."

Toby screams, "I don't want to!"

Thud startles from his corner, his dog tags clinking as he shakes himself awake.

"Eric," I hiss. "What are you doing?"

"How can anyone get mad about saving a dog?" Thud thumps his tail on the floor and comes over to Eric, ready to play. He ignores me and talks to the dog. "Isn't that right, big guy?"

He rubs Thud's head before he gets up to throw his beer bottle in the trash.

Toby starts crying.

"Come here, baby." I put the magazine down and crouch down to Toby's level to receive his chubby arms around my neck. I whisper in his ear, "Daddy's just being silly. He doesn't know what he's talking about. You don't have to do anything you don't want to do. I'll make sure. Who's the boss of John Robberson?"

"Me?"

"That's right." I pick him up. "Let's go upstairs." I can't be in the same room with Eric right now.

After I put Toby to bed, I've calmed down enough to ask Eric, with the most neutral tone I can muster, to explain what he's doing with the game.

He finds ESPN, mutes the TV, and answers, matching my tone, explaining that he changed the game on purpose, after our last talk, kind of like a test. He wanted to see if Toby would follow him. It worked. Toby followed him, so he thinks that proves there is nothing to it.

"Why's he talking about rotten eggs? What do rotten eggs have to do with anything?"

"Sulfur. It's a sign of a chemical fire. Means you have to use hazmats."

"And booby traps?"

"It's nothing."

"Eric."

"Meth houses. Those guys don't want anyone poking around, so they rig the house with booby traps. Sometimes first responders get caught in them."

"Meth houses? You're teaching a three-year-old about meth houses? He plays that game with Sanjay. Yesterday, they were on the playground, yelling about booby traps. How am I supposed to explain that?"

"Ah, come on, I don't tell him why they have booby traps. He doesn't know what he's talking about."

"Are you kidding me?"

"All right, maybe I went too far with that one," he says. "I'm sorry. But it perfectly makes my point."

"Which is?"

"There's no way Toby knew about any of that stuff, no way. But when we play, he acts like he's known all along."

"I'm still stuck at the part where you teach our three-year-old about meth houses."

"I'm not . . . I'm just giving him details . . . to prove a point. To you."

"Which is?"

"John Robberson has nothing to do with it. I told you this before. He's just an amped-up version of me. I take him to a flight museum, and John Robberson was a pilot. I broke my leg, so Toby says John Robberson broke his leg. We see a fire truck, and all of a sudden John Robberson was a fire chief."

"John Robberson *was* a fire chief."

"So?"

"You've gone too far." I can't stop my frustrated tears, but I control my voice. "Stop the game."

"I would if I thought it was hurting him."

"What if it is? Think about that. What if it is actually hurting our son, and you just won't acknowledge it?"

"I would never hurt Toby."

"Not on purpose, no. But what if you weren't so sure? Why keep doing it?" I ball my fists over my eyes to compose myself. "You made your point."

Finally, I pull his face back toward me. "Search your rational, logical brain and explain it to me. Give me one reason you are determined to keep playing the game. Why it's so important for you." I let go of his face. "If you can't do that, I have to conclude the only reason you keep doing it is to piss me off."

He looks at me a long time before he speaks. "I don't know why you feel the need to make this about us. But it's getting old, Shelly. Really old."

He grabs the remote and pushes the volume key, extinguishing the silent static between us as the room fills with television chatter. We watch a miserable half hour of the local news. He flips me the

116

remote. Over his shoulder, on his way to the bedroom, he says, "Okay. You win. I was out of line about the meth house stuff. I'll stop playing"—he makes air quotes—"the game."

The air quotes make me mad, but I feel we've had a breakthrough.

CHAPTER NINETEEN

THUD

The less we talk, the earlier Eric runs. But I don't say that, because he would say it's because we live in the desert and do I have any idea what it feels like to run six miles in the ninety-degree heat? Do I want him to drop dead from dehydration?

The next morning, he wakes up with the first beam of sunlight in our window. He says he has to complete his five miles before eight o'clock or it will be too hot. Thud's leash jangles, and I can hear his doggy toenails on the tile floor. That dog loves to run.

When they return, Toby and I are having breakfast and it's almost nine. "What took so long?" I say. "Everything okay?"

Eric ignores me. "Come on, buddy," he says, as he gets Thud some fresh water in his bowl. The dog's back is arched, and he's moving like an eighty-year-old man. On top of that, he's wheezing. He won't lie down. He ignores the water.

"Is he okay?"

Eric explains that everything was fine until he stopped for a restroom break at the sports complex nearby. He tied Thud's leash to the water fountain while he went in and didn't notice anything was wrong until about fifteen minutes after the break, when Thud was slowing down and struggling to breathe. The dog wouldn't run anymore, and Eric could barely get him to walk the rest of the way back home.

Thud is making a painful wheezing noise with each inhale. The poor dog pushes his head down toward the floor with every breath, almost like a gag, almost like he's trying to cough out a hairball but doesn't have the energy.

Toby hops down from the breakfast table, and I stop him. "No, baby, I think you need to leave Thud alone for now."

Thud makes a short, low harrumph, almost like a cough. He steadies himself, front legs in a wide stance, head down, like he's going to puke.

I whisper to Eric, "He looks terrible."

"I know," he snaps. "Where's that twenty-four-hour animal hospital?"

I tell him the intersection and push him out the door. "I'll call the office and tell them you'll be late."

"Is Thud okay?" Toby asks in a shaky voice.

"Daddy will take care of him. The doctor will take care of him."

I call Eric's office and tell one of the engineers, an old fart (judging from how he sounds), that we've had a dog emergency this morning and that Eric should be in before noon. He asks me if Eric knows about the conference call he's supposed to be on, and I ask him if he's ever owned a dog and hang up before he can answer.

As soon as they leave, I ask Toby to help me load the dishwasher. We bring a step stool to the kitchen sink so he can see how I rinse everything before loading it. I'm taking my time and we spend a long time at the sink, and still, no word from Eric. My she-bear is kicking into gear on behalf of the dog.

My phone rings, and I answer without looking. It's Pauline, still worked up about the grow house. She heard about Mrs. Gilliam's man in the white van, and now she wants to do background checks on new homeowners to keep this from happening again.

I launch into a way-too-detailed explanation of why that is a horrible idea. Logistically impossible. Not just impossible. Fundamentally wrong. Maybe illegal. I'm talking too fast and my heart rate is up, so I take a breath. Toby is getting restless, my dog is sick, and I can't think about this right now. I tell her as much, and at least it gets her to shift gears. She launches into a me-too story about how the vet saved their schnauzer.

Still no word from Eric. Toby decides to work with his watercolors, so I set him up on the back porch, laying newspaper everywhere. I keep him company while he paints with his brushes, then the sponges, then his fingers. Finally I join in, and we paint pictures of the dog, using our thumbs to make the black spots. Toby's pictures have Thud on a fire truck. Thud barking at a burning house.

"He'd better be careful," I say, pointing to how close he's drawn the dog to the fire.

"I know," he says, "because if he goes in the house, he'll die."

"Let's put the watercolors away now, all right?"

My phone is in my pocket, and I keep checking it. When Eric finally calls, his words come out in a rush.

"They think he swallowed a bee. Maybe he was messing with it around the water fountain. The vet said it wasn't the running that got him; it was the time it took for the sting to start to swell in his throat. Thud was really struggling for the last mile. I should've carried him." His voice cracks, but it holds together, like high-impact glass that shatters but retains its shape.

I walk with my phone to the bedroom and close the door behind me so Toby won't hear. "You didn't know. As soon as you realized—"

"I should've noticed earlier."

"He's going to be okay, right? What did they do for him?"

"He's in an oxygen tank, and they loaded him up with an anti-histamine. Now all they can do is watch him and make sure it's working. If they can keep the swelling down, they can keep his air passage open and he should be okay. I had to sign a form saying they could do a tracheotomy if they needed to."

The cracked glass in his voice finally seems to give way, as if the word *tracheotomy* sends it crashing to the floor.

I manage to say, "Do you want me to come up there and wait with you? I could drop Toby off."

He clears his throat. "No, I'm still in my shorts. I had that conference call, which I've already missed, and there's a lunch meeting. I have to make that one. I have to present the schedule for phase three and talk about—" He hesitates, and I can hear the weight on his vocal chords. He sighs. "Anyway, I can't miss it. There's nothing to do here. They say they'll call me and give me updates on his condition. It won't do any good to sit here."

"Are you sure? Seems like one of us should go and sit there."

"They won't let you see him, and it doesn't make any sense to go to the vet's waiting room and sit. They'll call."

"Is there anything I can do?"

"Tell Toby we're taking care of him. Is he okay?"

"He's fine. Are you okay?"

I can hear him straighten and can picture him pulling his broad, freckled shoulders back, bracing himself. "Be there in a few."

Maybe ten minutes later, Eric explodes through the door, shucking his sweaty T-shirt into the laundry bin as he hops out of his running shoes. I hold Toby in my arms to keep him from darting underfoot. I hear the shower water running and Eric's cell phone ringing. The shower turns off.

Silence.

I have a bad feeling about it and strain to hear. It could be someone from work. Or a wrong number. I'm hoping it's anything, anyone except the call I already know it is. I feel a nudge and look behind me, but nobody's there.

"Maybe," I say out loud, "maybe it's good news." But as soon as I say the words, I can almost hear a loud buzzer in my head: no, wrong answer. On that hunch, I take Toby outside to check on the garden, walking on queasy knees and talking too cheerfully. I don't tell Toby that Thud is okay, because I'm pretty sure he's never going to be okay again.

I realize I feel worse for Eric than I do for poor old Thud. It's as if some nasty mess has landed in my house and all I can think about is how to clean it up. My mouth is dry and my hands feel shaky, but when I check, my outstretched hand looks still. I wish I were one of those people who can cry as soon as something sad happens, but I'm not. I look for something to fix. Nothing sinks in with me until there's nothing left to do about it.

The next thing I see is Eric standing in the patio doorway, and I know by the look on his face that Thud is gone. I point at Toby with a shrug and he holds up a finger, indicating he needs a minute. He turns back inside, and I can feel his sobs in my chest. When he reappears on the patio, I try to hug him, but he shrugs me off to blow his nose.

"Come inside, Toby, let's go talk to Daddy. Inside."

We explain it to Toby in simple terms, that Thud's body stopped working.

"Why?"

Eric kicks into a way-too-long explanation about throats and lungs and how everyone needs air to live. As Toby starts to try to hold his breath for as long as he can, I interrupt.

I tell him about the bee sting, how it swelled up and made it so Thud couldn't breathe on his own anymore. Eric adds that the vet thought that maybe Thud was allergic to bees because he had such a strong reaction.

"Not all bee stings mean you can't breathe," I clarify.

"Most bee stings," Eric is quick to add, "you get a swollen spot, and it hurts, but you're okay." He takes a deep breath. "The problem," he explains, "is that Thud's swollen spot was inside his throat."

"But why didn't the doctor make it better?"

I explain that the vet tried, but Thud was too sick and couldn't get enough air for the medicine to work. "It was too late."

Toby nods. I'm not sure if he accepts this so easily, or if what actually happened simply hasn't sunk in. I watch him carefully.

We're sitting on the floor of the living room, with our backs leaning against the sofa, the soft carpet cushioning the blow. Toby comes out of my lap and goes to Eric, who is sitting cross-legged and heartbroken. I doubt Toby has ever seen him look this miserable. He sits on his daddy's right thigh and put his hands on the side of Eric's face.

Eric crushes him in a hug.

Toby wriggles loose, stands up in the circle of Eric's legs, and faces him. Even though Eric's eyes are dry, Toby kisses his daddy's right eye with a gentle touch and a soft "mmm," then kisses his left eye, like we always do for him when he cries.

"All better, Daddy?"

"Not yet, buddy, but you showed me you love me, and that makes me feel better. I'm super-duper sad about Thud. I'm going to miss him."

My eyes spill over, watching Toby display such empathy. This is the best lesson Toby can take from this. Thud was part of our family. Eric will miss him the most, and Toby somehow understands.

I put my head on Eric's other shoulder. "Thud loved you as much as you loved him."

He puts his arm around me and pulls me close. It's the first gentle gesture he's made in a long time. My eyes spill over with tears of longing as I snuggle into his neck.

Eric says, "Toby, I need to talk to your mom. Can you play in your room for a few minutes?"

Toby complies without a word.

"Are you okay?" I ask.

He breaks down and sobs, his arms clinging to me as he yields the weight of his entire body to our embrace. "I'm here," I say as I cry right along with him, wondering if his grief about Thud is triggering something else. "I'm right here."

When the first wave passes, he wipes his face with the backs of his hands. I hand him a box of tissues and take a couple for myself.

"Feel any better?"

"I'm a wreck," he says. "Sorry about that."

"You have nothing to apologize for. It's good to let it out," I assure him. "I'm glad I could be here for you."

He nods. The air between us feels heavy, expectant. "I've never cried that hard," he finally says.

"Do you want to talk about it?" I ask, as gently as I can. "Sometimes it helps me process the emotion if I can put words to it."

"I can't believe I didn't realize what was going on with him." His voice breaks. "How can I be that tuned out?"

"What do you mean?"

"It's hard to explain. I just feel . . . I don't know . . . disconnected."

I nod.

"It's not like me, not to notice how much he was struggling."

"Eric. It's not your fault. You did everything you could do, once you realized . . ." My voice trails off. "Even if you'd noticed earlier, I'm not sure there was anything you could've done. You were still a long way away."

He says, "I feel like I'm a long way away from everything in my life."

I hug him. "Come back, then."

Eventually, Eric says he has to get to work, so I offer to pick up Thud from the vet. I call Lakshmi to see if she can watch Toby for a few minutes so he won't have to see the body. Getting our pet's corpse from the vet is the kind of thing I can do dry-eyed, as long as I do it quick and don't have to talk to anyone. I don't argue about the bill, even though it seems inordinate to me. I sit in the waiting room—the one I didn't go sit in earlier, when the dog was alive. Soon, the vet's assistant appears, and I don't know whether he's being polite or rude, but he loads the cardboard box in the back of my car without speaking.

After making such an unexpected connection with Eric, I don't feel quite as sad as before. I turn on the radio on the way back home, feel guilty about it, and ride the rest of the way in silence. Good ole Thud. Even on his way out, he's had a positive effect on our family.

I wonder where Thud's spirit is right now, and think about what I will say if Toby asks me that. I'm going to stick with heaven as the right answer, I suppose.

When I return, I place the cardboard box that holds Thud's body on a low shelf in the garage. Toby and I make a list of all the things Thud liked to do and gather up all his doggie toys. We make a trip to the home-improvement store to buy some wood to make a grave marker.

I barely remember the daze of making funeral arrangements for my mom, except that it gave us tasks to perform while the reality sunk in. I'm hoping this will be true for Toby, that by doing the rituals with him, it will become more real for him.

When Eric sees our handiwork that night, he hugs Toby and tells him how much it means to him. He invites Toby to watch as he goes into the backyard to dig a hole for Thud's grave. When he's ready, I help him retrieve Thud's body from the garage. Standing over the grave, I read aloud our list of the things Thud loved to do and the reasons he was a good dog. Eric talks about how much he and Thud loved to run together and tells stories of when Thud was a puppy. With a thick voice, he tells Thud he's sorry he didn't know about the bee. I finally cry at that one. Eric gets choked up, but Toby seems fine. Who knows what he's thinking about right now?

Toby holds Eric's hand and says with finality, "And he wasn't in a fire."

Only he says "fi-wah." I ruffle his curly hair and refuse to ruminate on what the hell a fire has to do with anything.

We put the dog toys on top of the cardboard box in the ground, and Eric starts filling up the hole. When it's full, Toby tamps it down with his bare feet, and I put a big sunflower on top.

That night, Eric and I make love for the first time in weeks. That's when I really have a good cry.

CHAPTER TWENTY

DOGS IN HEAVEN

I take Thud's leashes off the hook in the garage and give his dog food to our next-door neighbors, who have a cocker spaniel. When Toby asks, I tell him we might get another dog, but not yet. Eric keeps blaming himself. I want to make sure he has his bearings before we try to replace Thud.

Ms. Pushpa is in the park today, so she follows when Toby wants to show Sanjay Thud's grave. We walk out to it. Sanjay asks why he's under that pile of dirt.

Toby says, parroting what we've told him, that Thud's body is in the ground, but his spirit is in heaven with Grandma.

Sanjay has never heard of a grave and looks puzzled when Toby talks about Thud going to heaven. Lakshmi explains to the boys the difference between what happens when an Indian dog dies and an American dog dies. Ms. Pushpa nods her approval. Toby holds Ms. Pushpa's hand as he tries to absorb the idea that an Indian dog's body gets burned up, on purpose.

"In a fire?" he asks.

"Yes, but it doesn't hurt. It's a good fire, with smoke that floats all the way to the heavens."

"Kay would still be mad," he says.

Lakshmi and I exchange a glance.

"Toby," Ms. Pushpa says, bending over to meet his eyes, "why would Kay be mad?"

"Because of the dog in the fire."

I brace myself for the outburst, but it doesn't come. Sanjay pulls Toby's hand away from Ms. Pushpa and they begin running laps around the yard. "But she shouldn't be mad!" Toby yells back toward us.

Ms. Pushpa nods, as if this makes sense.

"What do you make of it?" I ask her.

"He has something to say." She registers no concern. "Listen to him."

"That's exactly what I'm trying to do. But . . ."

"Be patient," she advises.

CHAPTER TWENTY-ONE

TALKING TO DEAD PEOPLE

Finally, it's Vaughn Redford day. We arrive on time, but already there's a long line waiting for a lime-green wristband that proves we've all paid our $150. Pa has his "I'm humoring you, baby girl" look on his face as he checks out the crowd in line with us.

"You said it's sold out, right? How many are supposed to be here today?" His fuzzy white eyebrows merge together in the middle. He wore that damn baby blue jumpsuit today. It's the worst one.

I see a sign that tells me the capacity of the hotel conference room is 350 people, and I cringe when I say it to him, because I know he's doing the math in his head. Now that he's asked, I can't help doing it myself so I can control my expression when he explodes about it being over $50,000 for one hour of work and goes on to ask how many shows Vaughn Redford is going to do that week. I hand him the schedule and let him figure out the answer is three, and I wait for him to snort with disbelief that we are actually doing this.

I'm trying hard not to feel I'm being taken advantage of. When I think about how I lied to Eric about the cost of the tickets, my face gets hot. We fought about my going at all. Eric's voice got low. Mine got loud. Eventually he relented, since going was more important to me than my not going was to him. I guess I didn't really think I'd won that one, because when he asked me how much it was, I told him $150 and let him think that was for all three tickets (mine, Pa's, and Toby's).

I'd worked it out, foregoing my summer haircut (there's $50 right there), eating more chicken and less salmon, that kind of thing. We do all right, but it's not like we have an extra $450 every month that either of us can spend without the other noticing.

I'm carrying a burden heavier than my thirty-pound toddler. I shift Toby from one hip to the other. He starts to squirm, so Lakshmi—who made good on her earlier promise to go with me—takes him by the hand and walks to the gift shop while we hold our place in the line.

Pa tells me he went to the casino with Dottie again, and I nod and ask if he had a good time. He starts to tell me about their winnings. The conversation seems freakishly normal. Like people who end up laughing in the church foyer after a funeral. Is that disrespectful to the person they are supposed to be grieving?

I look around and realize the woman directly behind us is holding a square box of tissues. She came prepared. All I have in my purse is baby wipes.

When we get nearer to the registration table, I wave Lakshmi over, and Toby runs ahead of her with a squeal. The grandmothers in the line all smile at him and whisper to each other, nodding. The two young women behind the registration table are not amused. The one with dull shoe-polish hair and a pierced eyebrow notices my nose piercing and smiles at me, but her companion, the heavy one in a black concert T-shirt, is formal and stiff. I give her our tickets, and she pulls a paper out of an accordion file and explains that, of course, she expects the child to be removed from the room if he becomes disruptive. I nod.

She hands me the paper and tells me I have to sign a release. To ensure I understand this is for entertainment purposes only. To make sure I understand that if anything Toby is exposed to during the show is upsetting to him—if there are any psychological problems later, any kind of disturbance—we can't sue Vaughn Redford. That I will take responsibility for bringing him here.

My legs feel heavy and thick. What am I doing? Pa doesn't want to be here. Toby would rather be on a playground. I should've come alone, or with Lakshmi. I pull her aside.

Lakshmi asks, "Everything okay?"

"I have to sign a release."

"It'll be okay. I'm willing to walk around the back with Toby. That way, he's in the room in case John Robberson shows up. And you can sit up closer with your father in case your mother shows up."

Like a suspicious smell coming from inside a wall, the idea seeps into my consciousness: she is completely confident there are going to be spirits "showing up" today. Her only concern is which ones.

The shoe-polish-hair girl calls out, "Doors close in three minutes."

The hotel conference room smells like moldy carpet and manufactured air and reminds me of the large training sessions I attended for my old job. Same beige walls, same cheap plastic contemporary chandeliers, same green hotel banquet chairs, lined up in rows, facing a platform stage with one lonely chair and two faded ficus trees at either side. It's the seminar equivalent of a traveling carnival. The room crackles with anticipatory static. I can almost feel my hair standing on end as if someone has rubbed a balloon on my scalp.

We have to settle in the middle of a row, which worries me because if Toby gets loud, I'll have to climb over people to get him out of the room. I get him settled and he ends up sitting on the floor on his knees, facing the chair, which he converts to a table. He begins to draw on the sketchpad I brought, with colored pencils he selects from my hand when he's ready for new ones. He'll be okay here for a while.

This is the part of motherhood that makes women forget themselves. I embarrassed myself in my striving to attend, and now that I'm here, I'm disconnected from the very experience I sought out. All I can do is focus on the same things I'd have focused on if we were home. So why am I here?

Vaughn Redford comes out to a standing ovation that he quickly dismisses. He makes a few comments and fields the first questions, mostly the verbal equivalent of fan mail. A woman in a black-and-white geometric-print blouse, mid-thirties, with a good haircut and manicured nails, asks, "If a person dies before he can speak, before he learns to talk, then how does he communicate with you? How would he come through?"

My heart sinks.

Pa leans over and says, "Ain't too hard to figure out why she's here."

I slap him on the leg. "Hush."

Vaughn Redford says, with admirable empathy, "They're all spirits, so it doesn't matter what they can do with their bodies here." He goes on to tell a story about a different woman, at an earlier reading, whose child died in surgery. That's all she said. He explains that he had made a point of asking her not to reveal the child's age at death. He predicted age seven. When he started her reading, the child referenced many things that were current for the mother—things like the type of vacation the mother had recently taken, a picture hanging on a wall. So the child's spirit was still watching the mother, closely.

According to Vaughn Redford, the main reason the child came through was to tell the mother not to feel guilty, that she was okay. The mother said, "She?"

Vaughn Redford is quiet in both voice and posture when he delivers the punch. The mother said she hadn't even known she was pregnant but had an emergency appendectomy, with no time for a pregnancy test before, and the seven-week-old fetus died in surgery, before she even knew about it. So she was thrilled to discover it would have been a girl.

The crowd gasps.

I swallow the clot of sorrow that has crawled up from my heart to my throat.

"So," Vaughn Redford says, "the spirit is present, even if the body never even makes it to this world."

"Damn. He's good."

"If you don't stop talking, I will choke you with my bare hands."

Pa snickers.

I turn my head away from him and can feel hot, prickly tears seeping out. All I can think about are the three miscarriages I've endured, and I can't help wondering if I'm going to get a message today. Can it be true that my unborn children are spirits around me? I viscerally want to believe it. I reach over to Lakshmi, who squeezes my hand. She's so short, she can barely see, so she's sitting with one leg curled beneath her as a booster seat.

Pa whispers, "Hey, squirt."

Toby looks up from his coloring book.

"You let me know if you spot your grandma, all right?"

I swallow hard, knowing that Toby has never seen his grandma.

Then the session actually begins. The air in the room feels crowded and crackly, much different than it did when we first walked in. I smell mold, but I feel something else . . . that I can't quite articulate.

Vaughn Redford indicates he's feeling some energy from the left side of the room, near the middle section, with someone with an *M-G* name, like Maggie, Margo, Marguerite . . . He points to the middle seats and says, "See that lady with the pink shirt? Raise your hand, ma'am. Her. It's coming from right behind her."

I twist in my seat as the two women sitting behind me, one older and the other who looks like she could be the daughter, whisper with their heads together. The black-T-shirt girl is making her way over with the microphone. The younger woman says, "Marge?"

He says, "That's an *M-G* name, all right. Stand up, please."

Marge is the older woman's sister, the younger woman's aunt, and she died over a year ago—and evidently, according to Vaughn, wants to come back and tell everyone she loves them.

It means nothing to anyone except those two women. I am somewhat intrigued to realize what a bystander I am to the whole process. All I can think about are those miscarriages, and in spite of myself, I find myself praying that my babies will show up.

I've always thought they were all boys, all three of them. I'd love to know if I was right. We agreed not to name them. So for me, they're First Baby, Second Baby, Third.

Vaughn Redford is already on to someone else, and this goes on for a while. Each time he swings his arm around, walks over to one side of the room, and calls out a letter or number or other cryptic clue until someone responds.

This is exactly what makes people skeptical. While I was researching him, I found that most critics believe this process is the most objectionable part of Vaughn Redford's alleged psychic skills. Some describe it as "fishing" for details, proposing that in a room of three hundred people, the odds are that someone will know someone who died and who had a name starting, for example, with the letter *D*. Other critics charge that he uses the Q&A period to gather information about people. Then, conveniently, those folks are the ones who get readings. I can see the logic in this, and it was persuasive to me at first. In fact, I'd convinced myself not to go, when I ran across a study by the University of Arizona. Vaughn Redford volunteered to be tested by a psychological research group, which confirmed that on blind readings, where he didn't see the person being read, he was 80 percent accurate about the information he provided. Details like who died, how they died, even specific little things like pictures or jewelry keepsakes the dead people referenced in their communications; the research team concluded that he was actually seeing something. I didn't doubt the study, and it was one of the things that made me feel better about coming here today.

But now that I'm here, all that logical proof stuff—it doesn't matter at all to me. I'm not thinking about Kay or John Robberson or any of that. All I want is to see my babies.

I put my hand on Pa's knee and wonder if he feels the same pull in his heart, if he is sitting there praying that Mom will show up. His fuzzy eyebrows are moving up and down as he follows the psychic bouncing ball of Vaughn Redford's focus. I think he's paying closer attention than I am.

Toby has been almost miraculously quiet. He stopped drawing a few minutes ago and climbed up into the chair. Lakshmi is playing a little hand game with him to keep him occupied, all the while keeping her eye on the front of the room. I wonder if he can feel the energy, or emotion, or whatever it is in the room. Maybe he sees it, and all I can do is feel it.

The next thing I know, the black-and-white geometric-print lady is standing up and saying, yes, we have a *P* name. Patrick.

Pa gets a cynical smirk on his face, which I catch. He squeezes my knee and says, "Here we go." Vaughn Redford provides some mundane detail, which triggers the grieving mother. She chokes out the story of her eighteen-month-old who fell down, hit his head, and lapsed into a coma for eight months until he died. They celebrated his second birthday in a hospital room with nurses who dutifully ate cupcakes on his behalf. He never regained consciousness. I can picture that hospital room—all clinical and white, with pathetic balloons tied to the metal bedrails—and a teeny-tiny boy on the bed, asleep and asleep and asleep. I hope to God nobody stuck a damn pointy hat on his head.

My throat feels thick again, and my nerves are going crazy, sending out hyperjittery messages to the rest of my muscles. My leg starts twitching. The woman's husband is sitting next to her, still as a stone, while she stands up and sobs out her story. Vaughn Redford assures her that Patrick is happy and running around, with none of the limitations he had on earth. I can see Eric in that husband, and I can't help wondering if the boy was hurt on his watch. It would make a difference. Eric blames himself for Thud's death.

I take a deep breath to settle my shakiness. Vaughn Redford shifts to someone else, which I don't quite follow, so I startle when the woman one row in front of us drops her purse as she turns in her chair to look at me.

Toby looks up at the commotion as Vaughn Redford describes the husband who passed. They do their thing, and I am feeling ridiculous that I thought this would solve anything.

Then, out of the blue, Toby looks up from his book and says, "Thud!"

The people around us titter with laughter. I shush him quickly.

Almost as an answer to Toby, Vaughn Redford says, "Yes, that's right, that's what I'm getting. Thud? Is that a name, or a noise, or what? Does that mean anything to you?"

He points at me. "You. The kid's mom. Can you stand up?"

Lakshmi pushes me to my feet, and someone hands me the microphone.

"Me?"

"Does Thud mean anything to you?"

"Um, Thud was our dog?"

The crowd laughs.

"You named your dog Thud? What kind of name is that?" He looks to the audience and shrugs as he walks toward the front of the stage.

"He kept running into the couch when he was little." I smile, playing to the crowd.

"Okay. Has Thud passed?"

"Yes."

Vaughn Redford explains he's getting a feeling of tightness, thickness in his throat. He tells me (well, the whole room) that Thud suffocated. "He loved to run, and he's in no pain now."

The crowd murmurs, but I'm left standing there like a fence post. I still can't believe he's talking about Thud like he knows him.

Then the weirdest thing happens: I smell the dog. I smell Thud's doggy breath, the dirty hot scent of him as he barged into my kitchen every morning after his run with Eric, to slop water all over my tile floor. I smell it, exactly as if he were rubbing up against my leg as I stand here with 350 people I don't know, including poor Patrick's mom, in a moldy beige conference room with a microphone in my hand. I look at Vaughn Redford. It's as if he's at the end of a long tunnel. I have the sensation that he and I are the only ones in the room.

I sneeze.

The black-T-shirt girl reaches out for the microphone, obviously annoyed now that she has to wipe it down. I didn't actually want the microphone in the first place, but now I'm not ready to give it up. I turn away from her.

Frantic, I ask, "What about the fire? Is there a fire?"

"No, it's a throat thing." Vaughn Redford pauses and cocks his head as if he were listening. "Now I'm getting a double *J* name. JJ?"

"John?" My heart does a flip-flop.

"I'm not getting that. It's a double." He looks at me. "JJ."

"No. There's a John."

"Am I stuttering?" The audience laughs. "This one's not ambiguous. It's not John. It's JJ. You don't know what that means?"

"No," I say, not bothering to hold the microphone to my mouth.

"Maybe this part isn't for you." He waves his arm in my direction. "Are you here with your dad?"

"Yes."

"Sir, does JJ mean anything to you?"

"No." Pa reaches for the microphone. "Excuse me. I want to make sure you got that. That's a *hell no*."

Everyone laughs.

"Okay, fine. But somebody back in that section needs to hear this," Vaughn Redford says. "JJ is very insistent. He's telling me to say 'let go.'"

Pa snorts.

Vaughn Redford looks at me. "Maybe he'll listen to you, then. Tell him to let go."

I want to shake him, to get him off this JJ thing. "What else does he say? Anything about Kay? Do you know about Kay?"

"That's not how it works." He launches into a long discussion about why he can't take questions; it's not like placing an order. You can't just summon spirits from the other side. They have to want to come, whether we want to acknowledge the connection or not, blah, blah, blah.

I hand the microphone off and sit down.

Pa says, "Can we go now?"

"I'm sorry about that."

I can't make sense of any of this. The whole Thud thing is weird enough, but then this Redford guy pulls a *J* name out of his hat? And then argues with me?

Lakshmi asks, "What the hell is up with JJ?"

"I have no idea," I whisper to her, "unless John Robberson stutters now."

I pull Toby into my lap and breathe in the smell of his hair to clear my nose. What about the smell? I smelled the dog. Not any dog. Thud.

Toby squirms in my lap, and I'm more than happy to be the one who steps outside with him. Pa follows me, but Lakshmi stays for the rest. We wait at the registration desk outside the conference room, and Toby draws pictures of Thud.

CHAPTER TWENTY-TWO

DEFINE OPEN-MINDED

On the drive home, Lakshmi wants to recap our Vaughn Redford experience, but we can't make any sense out of the JJ thing. There's so much I want to tell her, but not in front of Toby. The most lingering emotional effect of the experience, for me, comes from the unexpected longing I felt about the miscarriages. I can't quite carry my end of the conversation. Soon, she asks if I'm disappointed that I didn't hear from my mom. I can't answer that one, either. I guess it depends on what she would've said.

After my mom died, I heard her voice in my head for months. At the grocery store, every time I'd say hello to the checker, her thoughts echoed in my head, even though I didn't share her opinion. *Dreadful tattoo. On such a lovely girl.* Walking around the neighborhood. *Look at those flowerpots. Now, someone there cares about her home.* Often, when I looked in the mirror. *You have such beautiful eyes. Now why would you let your hair cover them up like that?*

To be fair, my mom was wonderful when I was a little girl. I have sweet memories of her playing and pretending with me. Maybe each mother has a sweet spot, an age range that suits her best. Some moms are great with teenagers. Others are great with babies. Mine wasn't great with anything past puberty, so we fought until I left for college. By the time I came back, neither of us knew the other very well. I blamed her for that.

But really, I had no idea who she was, either. That's what I miss: the chance to be friends with my mom. So I settle for hearing her voice, and sometimes—right before I wake up, or when I'm day-dreaming, in that lucid but inattentive state of mind—I feel it. My mother nudges me, a slight physical sensation. A little push on my shoulder. A knowing, supportive nudge.

I always try to find the meaning in them. When I was worried about losing my job, her nudge didn't mean I wouldn't lose my job. It meant that I was going to be okay even if I lost my job. When the layoffs came, I realized she was right. I guess I've gotten used to the idea that a spirit can interact physically with the living.

But I've never smelled her.

Before Eric and I met, I read a study somewhere that said that the olfactory function, the sense of smell, was the single most salient trigger to the brain's memory banks. As soon as I learned this, I stopped changing perfumes every day. I picked one and wore it from that point on.

When we get home, Toby immediately blurts out that Thud was there. Eric laughs. I decide right then. There's no point in men-tioning the stupid JJ part. It would just take away from what hap-pened with Thud. Maybe tonight, Thud is going to be the thing I can use to get Eric to listen to me.

After I get Toby to bed, I ask, "Can I talk to you about what happened today?"

"If you want to."

I start to tell him the whole story about Vaughn Redford—well, everything except the actual ticket price and the JJ part, but I do include the message that Thud's not in pain. Eric doesn't roll his eyes or anything, which I take as a good sign. When I tell him I smelled the dog, actually *smelled* him, Eric gets really quiet. Maybe I've pierced a hole in his rational, cognitive veneer. It's an opening, or at least I want it to be.

I sit up on the bed, my back to the headboard. I pull the covers up to my armpits and tell him about the woman with the *P*-name baby, Patrick, and how I pictured birthday balloons. My eyes fill. I remember what my due dates would have been for every single one of our babies, whether they made it or not. First Baby. Second Baby. Third.

"So this made you think about babies," he says.

"The ones who didn't make it. If they had 'come through' or whatever, if I'd found out some weird detail about them . . . I might be more skeptical. I might be able to explain it away. Like my desire or my intention sent out some kind of vibe this Vaughn Redford character picked up. If that had happened, I'd always believe there was some hocus-pocus to it."

"But now you don't? Because you were thinking about babies and not expecting to hear from our dog?" He stifles a smirk.

"It proves I had nothing to do with it, right?" I ask. "See what I mean? And he knew Thud suffocated—how could he nail that? Not only does the name have to be right, the information has to line up. If Vaughn Redford had called out my mom's name, told me how much she loves me, or that she sees Toby—it just wouldn't sound real. I'd know he was a fake. If she showed up and told me my hair *still* looks like shit, well, maybe that would've been convincing."

I look down at my hands, because it's not funny. "But that would've made me really sad, too. That she still doesn't see who I am."

"Her loss, Shel. I tell you that all the time."

It's my loss, too, but he doesn't get it. I can't explain it, either. There are some things I wish I didn't know. But I've been to the canyon of grief. It's like you're standing on all the things you're so sure of, until the pain drips and drips like battery acid and eats holes into the cliff you've been standing on your whole life. So you fall into the dark, and you stagger around until your eyes adjust, and when you climb back out, you can see the shadows in everything. You can't know that until you've been there.

A lot of the time, I feel dumb around Eric. He's got a brilliant mind. I'm no slouch, but we both know he's smarter than I am. But his cognitive certainty is a luxury position, born of the things he hasn't had to learn.

Like how it feels to ride the roller coaster of hope and let yourself fall in love with a tiny person you can't even see. I know how disorienting it is when your otherwise dependable and healthy body defies you. I know exactly when the roller coaster goes downhill and you start to believe there's no place inside you soft enough to hold a baby, because you've failed at the one job that's supposed to come naturally to you—one time, two times, three times. I know that finally, you have to learn that maybe it's not up to you.

I know how it feels to outlive your mother, which doesn't sound all that horrible because at some level, you think that's how life goes. But I know how hard it is to look back and realize I spent almost half my life arguing with her about my freaking hair. And I know how helpless it feels to not be able to get to know her at the time in my life when I actually want to do that. I know how much I wanted to find a reason why we both got stuck with a brain tumor that brought out the worst in her and how hard it was not to take it personally, as if there was something more fucking true about what she said when she didn't have control of her facilities. I know that's bullshit, and I also know how it feels to be neck-deep in it.

I know how sickening it is to realize, one day, that she's in a coma before I can make it right. I felt my heart shatter every time I reached over and held her unresponsive hand up to the bump in my belly—one month, two months, three—so I've come at it the hard way, but I know that eventually even I can learn to be grateful for intangible, illogical things like nudges and smelling my damn dog. I don't want to know these things, but I do.

How can Eric know what he doesn't know?

"Something weird happens when we get too close to that line, between this world and the other. It feels like I was there today." I check his reaction. "Do you know what I mean?"

"Shel."

"Even when . . ." I shake my head and don't finish. "I just can't help thinking about your accident. You were right on that line. Where do you think you went? For eight minutes?"

Even before he says anything, I can tell I've ruined it.

"Really? When are you going to let that one go?"

I sit up straighter on the bed and pull my pillow into my lap.

"You want to know where I went?" He moves away from the headboard, squaring off to face me. "Nowhere. I've told you this all before. I laid there on the table until the medical intervention worked and my heart started beating again and the oxygen returned to my brain . . ." and his voice becomes a blur in my head.

He doesn't remember anything about the eight minutes. Or the ambulance ride. Or the accident. Or leaving work that day. Or even going to work that day. Or the day before. He has a weeklong black hole in his memory. The doctors said that was to be expected. One of his doctors told me he thought it was God's grace to survivors, to not remember the trauma.

I didn't understand at the time.

I bought Eric a book about near-death experiences. It provided detailed accounts of people who saw the tunnel of light and felt the floating over their bodies, the wash of contentment.

Eric doesn't remember a floating sensation, but if it happened, he thinks it's because that's what happens when blood flow is reduced to the part of your brain that controls spatial sensations. He says he doesn't have any memory of a tunnel of light, but it wouldn't surprise him because that's what happens when your retinal nerves are compromised.

After he finished the book, he told me he thought that self-report was possibly the worse scientific evidence in the world. It's based on memory, with no physical evidence. There's no way to quantify it, and worse, everyone who is self-reporting is doing so at times when their brain cells are misfiring like crazy and maybe even shutting down. Not exactly a reliable resource. As everyone knows, memory is notoriously fickle and highly open to suggestion. So there's no way to know if everyone sees a tunnel of light because we've all read about how you're *supposed* to see a tunnel of light. Well, Eric was never going to play along with that.

There's nothing spiritual about it for him.

He concludes, "So, sorry to disappoint you for the millionth time, but nothing happened in those eight minutes."

"But Eric, what if something happened and you just don't remember it?"

He snorts. "What if nobody remembers it? What if one guy made it up and wrote a book, so everyone has read the same book since the seventies, so now there's a whole generation of people who expect to see it? What if nobody actually remembers anything of his own experience? Has that ever occurred to you?"

His condescending tone, painfully familiar, seems to glide past that metallic taste on my tongue, slide down my throat, strangle my empathy, and pluck my vocal cords, until it finds the one that will produce the most defensive note in my voice.

"Nobody remembers anything? Because you don't?"

"When we don't have all the data, there's a human tendency to fill in the blanks. So maybe they report what they thought they were supposed to see. Maybe they want it to be true."

"What if it is true?"

"Maybe it is for some. But the uniformity of the reports leads me to believe . . ." He stops, searching for the right words. "I think it's very hard to think for yourself. To have an open mind."

It's my turn to snort. "Like you?"

"Yes, like me."

"Just because you're smart doesn't mean you're open-minded."

He crosses his arms. "Define open-minded."

"Really?"

He says, "The way I see it, you think you're open-minded because you are willing to seriously entertain every idea under the sun. As if you can try it on and assume it's true until you are proven otherwise. And sure, there's something to that approach. But here's the issue: you think I'm not open-minded because I have the ability to observe something I don't understand, file it away, and refuse to jump to an early conclusion. I am actually more open-minded than you, because I don't have to force a hypothesis to be fact. I have the patience to know when I need more data. I can tolerate the ambiguity of not knowing."

I'm struggling to keep the defensiveness out of my voice. "But Eric, you don't *feel* what you don't know. We can't even talk about this, three years later. You won't allow it. You refuse to allow your personal experience to override your cognitive beliefs. That's why you say you don't remember. You're so afraid your experience might validate something you don't understand."

He looks me in the eye. "No. I'm just not willing to force my personal experience into somebody else's theory. Particularly if I experience things I don't fully understand."

"Like what?"

There's a long pause. Too long. "It doesn't matter," he finally says.

It feels like my throat just collapsed. I choke out, "It matters that you think you can't tell me anything."

"I don't tell you things because lately, there seems to be no limit to your ridiculous interpretations. I'd be throwing gas on a fire."

I break down once again. He sits on the side of the bed, just watching me like I'm a stone that's inexplicably leaking, inconveniencing him. Finally, I say, "Eric. Please. I'm so tired of arguing. I hate this . . . distance between us."

He waits a long time before he responds. I reach for his hand, but he pulls away. "Well, I'm glad you said it." He sighs and drags his fingers through his hair. "This seems like the right time to say it. I have something to tell you."

"What?"

"I went to see Anna today."

"Therapist Anna? Why?"

"I wanted to get an objective opinion."

"About what?"

"About our marriage."

My stomach does a ten-story runaway-elevator plunge. I'm sure all the color drains out of my face. I stare at him, but he won't make eye contact. My ears feel like they're being bricked off. I can't feel my feet.

"Are you okay?" he asks.

"I need a minute."

I close the bathroom door behind me, sit down, pull off a way-too-long stream of toilet paper, and use it to cover my mouth in case I make any sound while I cry. With shaky hands, I wipe my tears, flush the toilet, and wash my hands. I lean into the mirror and take a deep breath.

When I come back, Eric is sitting on the edge of the bed. He's pulled the bedroom chair over so it faces him.

"Sit down," he says, patting the chair.

I can't figure out how to just crawl in bed on my side and go to sleep. Maybe if I just go to sleep, he won't say whatever horrible thing he is about to say.

"I'll sit down," I say, "but don't make me say yes to fifty logical conclusions first. Just come right out and say whatever you're going to say. What are we talking about here?"

"The distance. Between us." He shakes his head. "It's too much. We're getting too far apart on too many things."

"So let's close it, Eric. That's all we have to do." I keep my voice even. Logical. "Things ebb and flow. It's good you said something. We're too far apart; okay. We know what to do. We close the gap."

"Shel. It's not just ebb and flow. It's so wide now—like an abyss. I don't know if we can anymore."

I can't stop the hot tears or the tremble in my voice. "That's why you went to see Anna? Because you're having doubts about our marriage?"

"Yes."

"What did she say? She told you we could fix it, didn't she?"

"Yes," he admitted. "But I told her, just like I'm trying to tell you, I'm not sure we can."

My mouth is so dry I can barely swallow.

He says, "Look. I know why you really went to see that psychic guy."

"You do?"

His tone is even and measured. There's no judgment in his voice. "You were trying to contact Kay, weren't you? Or John Robberson. Right? So you can ask him why he wants Toby to go see her."

I nod.

"That's what I mean. You couldn't even tell me that. Instead, you come home crying about miscarriages and your mother and talking about smelling our dead dog . . ."

I feel as if he's slapped me in the face.

"Anyway. That's not my point. You can't tell me the real reason, but you and Lakshmi are totally together on this, aren't you? It's all you talk about."

"You can't be jealous of my best friend. I get to have friends, Eric."

"I'm not saying you shouldn't have friends. But you have to admit, right now, you're closer to Lakshmi than you are to me. Doesn't that bother you?"

"It's different."

"How? You confide in her. It's like your little secret world, and I can't get in. You keep your true thoughts and feelings from me and spend all your time trying to sell me on your latest theory. Do you care what I think about any of this? No. Anytime I try to tell you my opinion, you get all defensive and we get into a fight about it."

"But—"

"I even tried to objectively demonstrate how misguided you are, how much weight you're assigning to random acts of imagination. That was the whole thing with the game, which you blew way out of proportion. I'm trying, but what do I get back? You smelled the dog? Do you hear the words coming out of your mouth? But if I don't pick up a fork and eat an entire plateful of the shit you're dishing up, you think I'm attacking you. I can't win."

"What if—"

"Look, Shel. I see where you're going. I see what you want to believe. Maybe it has to do with losing your mom, or the miscarriages, or whatever . . . We're not on the same page anymore."

"Is that it? We're just not communicating? We can fix that, Eric."

"I wish it was that easy. I'm sorry, but it feels like our belief systems have shifted." He makes the same hand motion that weathermen make when they're demonstrating how tectonic plates shift in an earthquake. He jerks one hand toward him, the other toward me, until they're barely touching on the sides.

I flinch.

"I'm over here," he says, indicating the hand closest to him. "And I can't get to where you are, over here." He pushes his other hand even farther in the other direction.

He takes a breath before he continues. "Hear me out. I can't bring myself to respect what you're doing. I realized the other day, my entire picture of you, of who you are, has shifted. You were always so smart and reasonable . . . You used to see the world the way I do. And now . . . Shelly, you're chasing a ghost. The widow of a ghost. And you think it's your motherly duty. And you're so convinced there's something there, you don't give a rat's ass if I like it or not. You're hell-bent on pursuing this. It's like you can't *not* do it."

He's right. I can't say anything in response.

"I just don't know if I can spend the rest of my life with someone who believes something so far away from what I know to be true."

"Eric, lots of couples have different beliefs. I don't understand why we have to believe the same thing." I reach for his hand.

"Because of Toby." He pulls away. "I refuse to teach him to believe his imaginary friend is more important than his real life. I can't support you teaching our son to believe in a ghost, to assign some cosmic significance to the games he plays on the playground. What you believe about John Robberson is so fundamentally ridiculous, I literally cannot believe what comes out of your mouth anymore. I have to force myself not to think about it just to get through the day, and I dread coming home and listening to your latest speculation. You're caught up in this thing that only exists in your own head."

I blink, stupidly.

He rakes his hand through his hair. "Haven't we been through enough? Why are you doing this to us? To Toby?"

"I'm trying to protect Toby."

He shakes his head. "I know you don't want to listen to me, but see if you can hear this: I will not allow you to drag him into this. You are not protecting him. But I will." He looks at me, his eyes even and cold. "Is this sinking in with you? I will do whatever it takes to protect him. Even from you, if I have to."

My ears are ringing, and I'm not sure if I can speak. We have just crossed a line that I never thought we would. We haven't even been married ten years, and this is the most dangerous conversation we've ever had.

Careful.

My armpits are clammy with sweat, and my heart feels all revved up, like that toy car of Toby's where he yanks a plastic handle through the center of the engine, its teeth catching on the gears, causing it to scream. Vrrr! I close my eyes and shudder, picturing how he keeps stabbing that plastic spear into the heart of the engine, just to see how loud it will roar before he lets it go. Vrrr! Vrrr! *Vrrr!*

"Shel? Did you hear me?"

Breathe.

I roll my lips together in a tight line and hold up my finger, silently asking him to give me a moment. I choke back the fear that's flooding me right now. I know how much the next words out of my mouth matter. I can't dissolve. I can't lash back at him. I can't say anything I will regret. I have to stand up and let the wave crash into me. It doesn't have to knock me down. I won't let it.

Recap.

"Yes. I hear you." I take his hands and visually strip every strand of sarcasm off my tongue. "Let me assure you, there's no reason Toby needs for you to protect him . . . from me."

He opens his mouth.

"I hear you," I continue. "I hear you saying I'm responsible for creating distance in our marriage because I won't ignore this John Robberson thing."

He nods.

"You think my friendship with Lakshmi is keeping me from confiding in you. And your feelings are hurt because you think I'm not taking your perspective into account."

"Yes."

"You are worried, very worried, about Toby and how this affects him. And, I guess, you're disappointed in me, because you think I'm being gullible and irrational. Do I have that right?"

"Yes."

I exhale shakily.

"But you're not saying, are you, that you don't love me anymore?" My voice cracks at the end, and I hate myself for it.

"Shel."

I wipe my cheeks with the back of my hand. "Right? I don't hear you saying you're ready to give up on our family, do I?"

"No. Not yet."

"Okay."

This recap thing works. I can see why men get good at this; it's a relief to compartmentalize it. You can't think and feel at the same time. I'm choosing to think because I can't afford to uncork everything I feel. Not in this moment. I can do that later. Right now, I have to force myself to say everything from his point of view.

"So, bottom line, you're saying that my interest in John Robberson is out of control."

"Yes."

"You're . . . rather offensively . . . suggesting that it's more than an interest—that it's some catastrophic shift in my fundamental"—I make the tectonic-plates movement with my hands, now making him cringe—"belief system." I glare at him. "Do I have that right?"

He nods.

"So. If you see that I *can* control it, if I stop researching, stop talking to Toby about it, draw a boundary with Lakshmi, tell you the truth about where I am with it . . . basically, you need to see that I've got it settled in my mind."

"Shel."

"Just tell me: if I can do that, will it resolve the issue?"

He says, "That's why I went to see Anna. I don't know if you *can* get it settled in your mind, Shel. I mean, come on. You thought you smelled our dead dog tonight. And you think that holds a hidden meaning. So I don't know."

"I'll get a grip on it. I promise."

"Maybe we need some time apart—"

"Don't." I hold his gaze and force myself not to cry any harder.

He's the one who looks away. "Fix it," he says. "If you can."

"I can."

"I'm not so sure."

"Give me time. You'll see."

He goes to sleep in the guest room. Our marriage bed feels like one of those overhyped mattresses where one partner's setting is ninety degrees lower than the other's. His side is now at zero. Instead of being comforted that I can have it my way, all I can feel is the resulting hump in the middle, a barrier that keeps us apart. Tears run into my ears as I lie flat on my back, hollow and anxious, the full weight of our conversation pressing on me until I can almost feel the slats of the box spring on my spine.

CHAPTER TWENTY-THREE

MAD ABOUT THE DOG

S orry we're late," I say to Lakshmi as I join her on the blanket spread under the tree. I wanted to cancel our standing play date but felt it wasn't fair to Toby. The boys head off toward the slide and I turn away, not allowing myself the opportunity to notice what version of the game they will play today.

"So, I want to hear! What did Eric say?"

It feels like I've aged twenty years since Vaughn Redford asked me about my dead dog.

"He didn't believe me . . ." my voice trails off.

"Are you okay? You don't sound like yourself."

I smile but feel my eyes rim red. She squeezes my hand and waits.

"We had a horrible fight last night. Somehow we got from Thud, which I thought would make him feel better, to my mom, to talking about his accident, and the next thing I know—"

"He tells you you're crazy." Lakshmi finishes for me. "That's his default position, you know, when you don't agree with him."

In the past, I've felt I could tell Lakshmi anything, but I've never needed to tell her that my husband left my bed, that he loves me less today than yesterday, that the connection with my soul mate might be less eternal than I want to believe possible. If I fix it, I don't actually have to say that out loud to anyone. And maybe it won't be true.

"Why is he so defensive about this?" she asks.

I rub my eyes in an attempt to camouflage my involuntary tears. If I start crying out here in the park, I may never stop. "Gawd! I just want John Robberson to go away."

"You know what to do. It's a puzzle with only one missing piece." She twists her hair into a ponytail, a gesture as familiar as her tone. "John Robberson wants Toby to go see Kay. Obviously, he's using Toby to get a message to her. I know you don't like it, but that's all he's wanted for weeks."

"I know."

"Then give him what he wants! Have you ever thought of this from his perspective? Put the pieces together. You've got an Air Force fighter pilot who survived a plane crash in Vietnam. Voluntarily or not, he leaves the military and becomes a fire chief. This man spent his life with a front-row seat to trauma. He's seen and done worse things than you can imagine. I'm willing to bet he's no rank-and-file follower, Shelly. He's used to taking risks, and he's used to getting his way. He's a spirit with unfinished business with his wife. If you help him with his marriage, maybe it will help you with yours."

Or destroy mine. The involuntary tears again. I dig in my bag until I find something to throw away.

On the way to the trash can, I look over at the boys and see they've added a new twist to the fireman game. Sanjay is on all fours, barking like a dog, inside the plastic cube at the top of the connecting slides.

"I'm coming in to get you!"

155

Toby climbs up the ladder of the closest set of monkey bars, fighting off imaginary flames on the way. It comes to me like an echo in my head: Kay gets mad when you go back for the dog.

I turn my back and walk over to Lakshmi, so I don't see Toby jump or fall or trip or get shoved by an angry spirit or whatever happens next. All I hear is a dull whack, a splay of gravel—and silence.

Sanjay calls out, "Mommy!" and points to Toby lying facedown under the monkey bars.

We both turn. In an adrenaline sprint, I reach him while he's still inhaling his scream. His face shudders, trying to find a recognizable place for the pain to land, but he's in unchartered water here. He's moving. He's conscious. I see him curl up, roll onto his back. With one hand clamped to his mouth, his eyes search me for an explanation.

"Let me see, baby."

I pry his hand away from his mouth. Through the bloody drool running down his chin, I see a gooey gap where his baby teeth used to be. Before I can tell him not to look, he sees, for the first time, his own bright red blood, mixed with dirt and slobber, a shocking gory mess, dripping from his fingers down his wrist. He thrusts his sticky hand in my face, shaking it, saying, "Bwud! Bwud!"

I cover his hand with mine and bring it to my lips. I kiss his palm and say, "It's okay, baby. Breathe."

He collapses into me. Lakshmi offers a package of moistened baby wipes and a makeshift ice pack.

Keeping my voice calm, I inspect him systematically; I test his pupils, his bones, his skull. He's surprised that even though his hand has blood on it, it does not actually hurt. His lip is starting to swell. His tooth is gone. A baby tooth.

I know it was going to fall out anyway, but just for today, I need for John Robberson to give me a fucking break. More than anything, I wish I could believe this was a harmless accident. Against my will, my eyes once again fill to capacity with tears. I blink them away.

"Did you see what happened, Sanjay?"

"I was the dog, and he was saving me from the fire."

Toby says, "Don't be mad, Mommy."

I hug him and shake my head.

Lakshmi says, "Don't be silly. Why would she be mad, Toby?"

"Kay gets mad about the dog."

Lakshmi raises her eyebrows and lowers her voice. "See what I mean? It's time to get him to say that to Kay. Whether he wants to or not."

She has no idea what that would cost.

CHAPTER TWENTY-FOUR

THE GOOD WIFE

Eric hasn't gone for a morning run since Thud died. He's taken to riding his bike instead. I'm glad for his early morning routine because it means I haven't had to explain to Toby why his dad is sleeping in the guest room.

Every day this week, as soon as I hear Eric leave the house, I make up the guest bed and vacate our room so he can still shower there. If he moves his clothes into the guest closet, it's going to make me sick.

Every day so far, I've had a smoothie ready for him when he returns. Strawberry banana, made with mango juice and that expensive protein powder he likes. He's polite, says thank you and all, but he doesn't acknowledge that I've gotten off his back about the protein powder. We both act like we don't know how hard I'm trying.

Once I noticed that if Toby is downstairs when Eric leaves for work, he gives me a peck on the cheek. But when he's not, I get the same good-bye I'm sure he gives to the guys on his project team. I try to make sure our son is eating breakfast at that time every day.

I put my John Robberson notebook away. After all, I don't need to keep collecting evidence. I don't tell Eric what Toby said about

Kay being mad at the dog. I don't tell him what Lakshmi said about the possibility of John Robberson getting impatient. I certainly don't tell him I'm worried she might be right, or how much it scares me to think that my son is blocking the goal of a military-trained spirit. But I can't keep from ruminating about it all day long.

And I've been avoiding Lakshmi the last couple of days. Yesterday, I took Toby to the science museum but couldn't find the energy to engage with him once we were there. I just let him play while I sat on a bench and spun on my speculations. Today, we're going to an afternoon movie.

When we come out of the theater, Toby jabbers about the airplanes he saw as I turn on my phone and check for messages. I don't know whether to be happy or nervous when I see a text from Eric. I click on it.

do we have plans this weekend?

No, I type back.

Scott invited a group of us to his lake house to go tubing. Says to bring the whole family. I need this. Project budget not approved yet.

I almost hear angels in my head, singing the "Hallelujah" chorus. This is exactly what we need. I worked with Scott. Scott loves me. I can help Eric get his funding.

I'm so excited!! Want to send me your proposal? I can take a look at it if you want.

My thumb hovers over the "Send" button. Too much, I decide, and I backspace it away. I wait for my heart rate to slow as I think about how to strike the right balance between nonchalance and cooperation. Less is more.

Sounds great.

Immediately, he answers: I'll set it up then.

At dinner that night, we talk to Toby about what he can expect. He's never been boating before. I smile as I listen to Eric describe tubing to him, of course starting with where inner tubes come from, detouring to the difference between an inner tube and a tire, and finally ending up with how much fun it is to ride in the tube behind the boat.

When I come downstairs after tucking Toby in bed, Eric clicks off the TV and asks, "Can we talk about this weekend?"

"Sure. I'm really looking forward to it." I sit in the armchair and turn to face him on the sofa. "What time do you think we need to leave?"

"I don't know. I'll check."

"Friday after work? Or are we driving up early Saturday morning?"

"Shel. I don't know." Eric fidgets. "Sorry. Look, I'll get the details and make sure you know all that. I just don't have it yet. That's not what I want to talk about."

"Okay."

"I don't want what's going on between us to be . . . you know . . . an issue. I don't want you talking to the wives about it."

"It? Meaning our marriage?" I ask. "Eric. Of course I'm not going to talk to women I barely know about our marriage."

"Or John Robberson. So if Toby says something, just let it go. Don't react. Don't drink too much and start talking about ghosts or airplanes or fire chiefs or anything. Don't"—and he waves his hand, that dismissive gesture I hate—"just don't."

I bite my metallic-tasting tongue and pause before I answer. "Stop." I attempt a feeble smile and reach to find a tone of voice that will pass for reassuring. "I get it, Eric. I told you I could control it. You'll see. I can be the good wife."

"It's important. Scott can't think I'm off my game. Distracted by my home life."

"I know," I say.

I don't say that I know damn well Scott is not the one worried about Eric being off his game.

We wake up right after the sun rises on Saturday and make the half-hour drive to Saguaro Lake. Toby and I try to identify all the watercolor shades of the morning sky, yellow and pink dissolving into a blue so pale it barely qualifies as a color. As we get closer to the lake, I'm happy that Eric joins in and points out the striated shades of the rugged desert cliffs, orange and brown and beige.

We find Scott and his wife, Jenny, at the marina, tending to the boat. As we load our bags, Scott explains that both Marcus and Lin bailed at the last minute. Eric pretends to be disappointed, but I know he's glad to be the only one who showed up.

Jenny and I team up to glob sunscreen on every inch of Toby. I cover his nose with zinc oxide, making it a shiny white button on his face, while she squirts a quarter-sized portion into her palm and reaches for Scott's back. I follow her lead and turn my attention to Eric, who looks lean and strong in boardshorts riding low on his torso. He stiffens at first when I apply sunscreen to his shoulders. It's the most physical contact I've had with him in a week. When I'm finished, he says, "Thanks, hon," as if he calls me "hon" on a regular basis.

The boat is white with blue and yellow stripes and blue seat cushions. Its nautical intent stands in stark contrast to the green and gray slosh of the lake, making it seem almost cartoonish. Toby seems nervous, so I'm glad when Scott insists on life jackets. We all make a big deal of strapping into our bright orange vests.

Eric and I watch without a word as Jenny gives Scott a hug from behind while he steers the boat out of the marina waters. I wonder if Eric misses us as much as I do.

As the boat accelerates, Jenny turns on the stereo. Toby pushes his head under my arm so he can sit closer. I explain to him exactly what we're going to do. He's not so sure.

I volunteer to go first. Toby howls when he realizes I am actually going to get out of the boat and into the inner tube. Despite my efforts to prepare him, the shock of seeing his mom in what he considers a dangerous situation is evidently testing his resolve.

The boat starts slow, and I smile bigger than I should, trying to make it okay for Toby. I swallow plenty of lake water before he seems to realize I'm in no danger. I bounce from wave to wave, my legs flopping every which way, and it takes awhile before I can stop worrying about him and enjoy it. I remember to wave to Toby, and he responds by squealing with delight. Eventually, I give the slow-down signal, a thumbs-down. There's no graceful way to exit an inner tube, so I squeeze and squirm and finally squirt myself free. When I get back into the boat, I'm still laughing.

Eric is next. I keep telling Toby, see, Daddy likes it too. Over and over, Eric gives the thumbs-up signal for Scott to go faster, faster. The boat makes a few sharp turns, which pull Eric across the wake, and we all cheer when Scott successfully flips him into the water. By this time, Toby has the hang of it, so he's happy to see his daddy fall into the water.

"He's bwave," Toby concludes.

Now Toby is begging for his turn. He wants to ride with his dad. Scott promises me that he'll drive like a turtle.

I keep my eyes on Toby the whole time. He has the same expression as when we swing him in our arms—one, two, three, whee. He keeps his mouth wide open with delight until he swallows a lungful of water, which makes him cry. I signal for Scott to stop the boat, and I can see Eric coaching Toby through it.

"Ready to come back in?" I call out.

Eric waves me off. Toby gives the thumbs-up and they try again, this time with Toby's lips clamped tight. He's sitting on Eric's lap. Eric presses himself far into the tube to make room. He uses his body to situate the tube to absorb most of the bump from the meager wake. Toby, quiet at first, becomes more animated as his confidence grows. When they finally crawl back into the boat, Toby's giddy, but Eric seems more subdued than usual.

Scott cranks the music and the boat's speed when it's Jenny in the tube. She belts out good-natured hollers with each big bump. She's short and chunky, so I'm surprised that when Scott flips her out of the tube, she dismounts with the elegance of a gymnast. Once she's back on the boat, she grabs a beer before she dries off.

Toby, completely encased in a thick towel, squirms on my lap. Eric sits across from us, not saying a word. His smile looks forced as he turns down both a beer and an offer to drive the boat. I accept the beer so we don't come across like a buzzkill couple and try not to look as relieved as I am when Jenny puts hers down before she takes the wheel.

Relax, I tell myself. I look over at Eric. Something's not right.

During Scott's turn, Eric moves to sit by my side and admits he's been the recipient of a king-sized lake enema and is not feeling a hundred percent.

I don't dare laugh.

We've been on the water less than an hour, and I can already tell Eric is finished. It's going to be a long day on the water for him. I get another beer from the cooler and accidently-on-purpose spill half of it into the lake, then hand it to Eric to use as his cover.

"Go up front with Scott," I whisper to him. "I'll be the designated tuber."

Jenny is not shy when it comes to driving the boat, and she keeps Scott out there a long time, laughing and accelerating every time he says he wants to come in.

"Who's next?" she calls out when she finally allows Scott back on the boat.

"Ready, Toby?" I ask, in a shiny happy voice, and off we go. I make a point of not pressing myself too low in the tube, so we fall off early and often. Toby likes it.

By lunchtime, I've taken so many turns in the tube, I'm sure my butt cheeks look like raisins. I don't mind. Eric still doesn't look well, but at least he's getting his chance to talk to Scott. I smile between bites of my chicken-salad sandwich as Jenny teaches Toby how to tie a square knot.

After lunch, we head back to the marina. When we get the boat secure in the dock, Scott and Jenny walk over to talk to another couple they know, which gives Eric a chance to rush away to find the restrooms.

I take my time gathering our belongings from the boat. Toby walks barefoot on the blue seat cushions toward the back of the boat. Along the dock, there are several families around in various stages of coming and going, loading and unloading their respective boats.

The marina smells like dead fish and gasoline. As I search for my sunglasses case, I glance at the mossy water and wonder how many hundreds of thousands of parasites are in it. I'm in the front of the boat, busy straightening the orange life jackets we'd taken off and shoved under the seat cushions, when I hear a dull thump that sounds like someone dropped an ice chest. Then a splash.

"Ooh, that's gonna be gross. I hope that wasn't someone's lunch," I say, turning around to smile at Toby.

He isn't there.

"Toby?"

"Toby!'"

I don't think twice about the green muck as I charge in after him, but I'm surprised at the depth of the water. I dive too steeply,

and the time it takes me to surface is excruciating. My ears are ringing like an alarm. Eyes open, I realize I made a splash that pushed
Toby farther out. I've made it worse. I can see his face in the water,
eyes closed and arms floating away from his body. I have a surge of
superhuman strength and lunge toward him under the water. I miss
and have to come up for air. On the second try, I touch him and he
feels rubbery. I feel around for a place to anchor my feet but find
none. I've never been a good swimmer, and I have no idea how to
rescue someone, but my panic has given me tunnel vision.

When I reach him, Toby is limp. I surface and immediately
turn his face up to the air. I'm about ten feet away from the dock,
directly behind the exposed propeller of the boat engine.

Suddenly, Eric is there in the lake with us. He wrestles Toby out
of my arms, and I go under. He leaves me in the water to crawl out
on my own. Scott extends a hand and pulls me up onto the dock.
When I get my bearings, Eric has Toby laid out flat on the dock,
and by this time, several other people are crowding over them, yelling instructions. The sound of my own shallow breath is replaced
by a cacophony of voices, filtered through the crackling anxiety in
my ears.

Jenny's voice: "Stand back! Stand back!"

"Is there a doctor here?"

"Give him room."

"Is he breathing?"

"CPR! Who knows CPR?"

Eric checks Toby's breathing, tries to rouse him. When he
doesn't respond, Eric uses his finger to clear Toby's mouth and bends
over him. He begins chest compressions, firm but not too firm. His
face is calm as he counts to himself. He leans over and breathes into
Toby's mouth. Somehow, he knows exactly what he's doing, and I
love this man so much.

I step aside and let him do the right thing. "Back off! Will you all just back off?" I stand next to Jenny and Scott, my arms outstretched, the three of us creating a frantic circle around Eric and Toby, me never taking my eyes off my baby.

The crowd steps back. They start explaining it to each other, in lower tones.

"What happened?"

"The kid fell in. This guy came sprinting outta nowhere. He must be a paramedic."

"Is he bleeding?"

He's not. Eric lays Toby on the dock, checks his pulse again, and assures me he feels a heartbeat. I needed to hear that, but Toby still isn't conscious. His brown curls, plastered down on his forehead, make him look unnatural. I push them up, out of his eyes. His little face is slippery under my hand.

Eric's ear is on Toby's little chest, so the top of his daddy's head is probably the first thing Toby sees when he opens his eyes. He coughs and sputters, and Eric flips him over in case he throws up. Toby twists to clutch his dad and says, "Kay."

My heart stops.

Eric laughs, crazy with relief, and says, "Okay, buddy. You're okay."

"See? He's okay!" announces Jenny.

Toby crawls over to my lap. The three of us sit on the dock, dripping wet, while Scott makes sure the crowd disperses and Jenny tells me I should get Toby checked out by a doctor.

I'm checking him for bruises, looking at the pupils of his eyes. I can't keep my hands from shaking.

I know what I heard.

Eric keeps saying, "Okay. It's okay, buddy," until Toby motions for me to come closer. He cups his hands around his mouth, pushes his self-made megaphone to my ear, and whispers, "Momma. Kay."

I hold his head between my hands and look into his eyes. He returns my gaze without blinking. I tell him with my eyes that I understand. I know exactly what he means.

I nod and put my finger to my mouth, shushing the pounding of my heart in my ears, made worse by the noise of an airplane engine overhead.

I look up. Dottie's dream comes rushing back to me. I'm paying attention, all right.

Jenny has our bags hoisted on her shoulder like a sturdy mule. "Come on," she says. "Everybody up. We're heading out. Let's get this little man to the ER. Scott, you're driving. I'll follow in our car."

Just like that, we all stand up and do what she says. I envy her superpower.

CHAPTER TWENTY-FIVE

SOMETHING IN BETWEEN

At the emergency room, under the bright, nervous lights, the nurse tells us first, and then the doctor says the same thing, repeating it until we're sure: Toby is all right, it's nothing more than a bump on the head for him and a scare for us. We did the right thing and acted quickly, so the doctor won't even call it a near drowning. Even when I say it, he smiles tolerantly and says, no, no, nothing like that. Jenny and Scott leave only after the doctor confirms one more time that there's no concussion, no reason for our son not to get a good night's sleep.

I don't object when Toby falls asleep in the car, and I let Eric carry him to his room. We stand at the foot of his bed, neither of us saying a word. I allow myself the tears I've held back all day.

When I turn to leave, Eric follows me to the bedroom, breaking the silence. I know he's trying to make me feel better when he assures me that it was an accident, that it's not my fault.

I don't correct him. I can't find a way to explain how clearly I know that it was no accident. Nothing random about it.

I can't tell him that as I held Toby's hand on the way to the hospital, I whispered a promise to our son: *We will go see Kay.* I can't describe to Eric the validation I felt when Toby immediately calmed down and sat like a little Buddha in his car seat.

I've always believed that the slippery, porous boundary between consciousness and unconsciousness, between the physical and spiritual worlds, is most prevalent at times when we transition between states. That not-quite-awake, not-still-asleep feeling. The meditative hum of stillness like a lucid daydream. A here-but-not-here condition that only happens once we surrender the daily chatter in our heads.

How can I make Eric understand that when Toby regained consciousness, it was like returning from that in-between state, and Kay's presence must have been palatable to him? I can't tell him this nonaccident—this, too—is about John Robberson. I can't tell him that John Robberson must have finally figured out that Toby needed to be unconscious to gain full access to him.

Don't you see? I want to tell him, *John Robberson got to Toby. I was right there, and John Robberson got to him anyway.*

I can't say any of that. It doesn't make any sense, I know. I can't even tell Eric that at some level, I'm relieved. That I was wrong. That maybe the best thing was for John Robberson to finally be able to convince Toby that it's okay to talk to Kay.

There's no way to communicate how important it is that Toby has finally agreed to do what John Robberson wants. This is a game-changer.

I go into our bathroom and stare at myself in the mirror, look myself in the eye, bore past the green and yellow flecks in my pupils, and tell myself the truth.

What I really want to say to Eric—to the old Eric, the soul mate who used to listen to me—is that I'm trying not to let it hurt my feelings that the first person Toby asked for wasn't his own mom.

If I could tell him that, maybe he would understand. I have to get him to see that we have to make room for the possibility that there might be something bigger than us going on here. Something I don't completely understand. Something in between.

"Shel? Did you hear me?"

"Sorry. What?"

"I said, do you need anything?"

"I'm exhausted. Are you coming to bed?"

He takes a step backward and my heart sinks. "In a few. Thanks for . . . you know. Today. And Toby's going to be fine. Don't worry." He looks down at his feet, his hand on the doorknob. "Try to get some sleep," he says as he pulls the bedroom door shut behind him.

Around three o'clock, I jolt awake from a murky green dream and make my way to Toby's room, relieved to find his hair dry. He's breathing air instead of water and doesn't have a fever, and when I pull back the covers, his belly button is still an outie. When I check on him again a few hours later, I see he's rotated himself to the foot of the bed as usual, and I smile.

I know what I need to do now.

I settle the jitters in my stomach and make myself smile before I knock on the door of the guest room, as lightly as if the door were made of the eggshells I'm walking on.

Eric cracks open the door. "How's he doing?"

"He seems fine. Still sleeping." I nod and try not to show my discouragement that we're talking through a crack in the door. "Want to join me for breakfast? Before he wakes up?"

"I was going to get a smoothie on the way in. I told Scott I'd meet him early today."

"Oh." Recovering, I say, "That's a good sign, right? That he wants to meet on Sunday?"

"Hope so." He opens the door, and I see he's already dressed. Neither of us moves.

"Tell Scott I thought yesterday was fun. Minus the drowning and all." I smile. "I liked Jenny a lot. Didn't you?"

"Sorry, but can we talk about this later?"

I don't move out of his way. "Real quick. I was thinking maybe it would be good for us to do things like that more often. Get away together, you know, take our mind off things. So I thought today, if you're okay with it, I'd look into finding us a family vacation spot, maybe over the Fourth of July weekend?"

He pauses. I can see the wheels turning in his head. Finally, he makes eye contact.

"I'm trying, Eric. You have to try, too. You said you would. It's only fair."

"You're right. Okay."

"Good luck with Scott," I say, stepping out of his way. "Be sure to tell him how much we appreciated the invite."

But Eric doesn't even know how much I appreciate it, because without knowing it, Scott bought me the modicum of goodwill I needed with Eric to do what I need to do for Toby.

That night, I present Eric with a few vacation options, careful to steer him where I need to go. First, the too-expensive beach resort in the Caribbean. Then the Disney cruise I know he won't choose. So when I mention the Ozark Mountains, he's amenable. It doesn't take long to agree on a two-bedroom condo with fishing access on Table Rock Lake. I don't point out the lake's proximity to Branson, Missouri. For the first time, I'm relieved that Eric showed so little interest in John Robberson that I never got the chance to mention his hometown.

Fourth of July weekend.

We're going to drive and stop and buy fireworks along the way. We'll go fishing and hiking and make s'mores in a campfire near the lake. I can tell Eric I have to run an errand. Toby won't pay attention to the roads. I won't even have to say anything—I'll just take Toby and let him say to Kay whatever her husband needs for him to say. I'm not leaving until she makes John Robberson go away, once and for all.

Eric doesn't have to know why we're there. Once John Robberson is gone, it won't matter. I promised him I'd control it, and I will. Truth be told, he doesn't want to know the details; he just wants the result.

So we're on the same page, really. If you think about it.

CHAPTER TWENTY-SIX

INDEPENDENCE DAY

I like car trips. I play Slug Bug with Toby, which he likes a lot, mostly because it breaks my usual "no hitting" rule. I go out of my way to sing along to the radio and count the cows we pass. Eric is in a better mood. He tells me he's optimistic that Scott will approve his budget and he will be able to hire two new guys. We seem to have forged a tentative peace, an unspoken agreement that we're going to try. We fill any conversational lags by taking turns entertaining Toby. When it's not my turn, I work out my plan to find Kay.

I'd love it if I could not only find her but also hang out long enough to figure out where she goes on a regular basis. Maybe she eats breakfast every day in a diner. Maybe she leaves work at the same time every day. Maybe Toby and I could "run into" her in a public place. That would be best. But it means a lot of legwork on my part, and I'm not sure I can do it without Eric being suspicious.

All I have right now is a highway and a box number. The address doesn't register on our GPS. I can't find it on Google maps. The closest I get is a satellite map that shows a two-lane highway with mailboxes along the sides. I'll have to figure it out when we get there.

Southern Missouri is unexpectedly beautiful, with verdant hills and crystal-clear streams. Almost simultaneously, Eric and I roll down our windows, a shared unspoken instinct to stick our arms out and make waves in the wind current. When we finally arrive in Branson, the hills are obscured by the town's attempts to be an entertainment mecca. I can't help chuckling at the log-cabin font used to advertise everything from souvenir T-shirts to big gospel churches. The cars are packed on the road as tight as a tourist's bulging belly in a golf shirt.

I pick up a listing of the shows that made Branson famous. Eric wryly observes that he'd have to reach a certain level of intoxication before he'd really appreciate the Baldknobbers Jamboree. Not a viable option with Toby, so we ditch that idea. In the front seat, I point to an ad for Silver Dollar City, the amusement park, and Eric looks at me as if I offered him a chocolate-covered cricket.

Our condo is tucked into the woods, and our unit has a clear view of the lake. My shirt sticks to my back, and my hair frizzes in the humidity. In the back of the building, we discover a rock path that leads all the way down to the water, with a marina right there on the property. We agree on this point: we are not renting a boat.

Eric suggests we buy groceries at the marina store, but when we see it, we both know that's not happening. There's no fresh fruit or produce of any kind. I feign disappointment, but I'm relieved. This gives me an excuse to run an errand on my own.

"Toby, do you want to come with me to the store?"

He shakes his head from side to side, twisting his entire body.

"Come on, Shel, don't make him get in the car again." Eric grabs Toby and turns him upside down in the air. "We're going exploring!"

"You guys go ahead. I'll feel better once I get the food issue settled. Then I'll join you."

I pick up a map of the lake and surrounding areas and locate what appears to be the largest grocery store, thinking it will be my best bet. I head in that direction and stop at the first gas station I see. The cashier—a rail-skinny grandma with yellowed fingertips—is happy to show me how to get to Route 76 but adds, "It's a big-ass road, sugar; I hope you got more than that."

I tell her the address and she assures me she's terrible with directions. "I'd lose my fool head if it wasn't screwed on."

"Do you have a phone book?"

I find six Robbersons. Carl . . . Fred . . . James . . . No John. No Kay . . . Two Williams . . . Steven. There's nobody on Route 76.

Damn.

I thought I'd be able to find Kay in the phone book and set an appointment. I had even rehearsed how that conversation would go. I guess I should be glad there are only six entries. I'm too close to the cashier to rip the page out of the phone book, so I take a picture of the page with my phone, making sure I can read the phone numbers for every Robberson listed. It's a long shot, I know, but before I traipse all over the Ozarks, I need to rule out that the number I have is a PO Box. So I ask where I can find the post office.

The cashier tells me it's in downtown Branson, smack dab in the middle of all that traffic. She looks at her watch and says, "It idn't no use, though; they're gonna be closed by the time you get there."

Ten minutes later, I cuss at the Good Samaritan in a Ford F-350 pickup who keeps letting other people enter the line of traffic, which causes me to miss another green light. I want to honk, but he has three shotguns on his gun rack.

By the time I find the post office, it's been closed for twenty minutes. I make a note of where I am. I decide to give up for the day, navigate my way to the grocery store, and find fruit and yogurt, chicken breasts, ripe tomatoes, and fresh sweet corn. On the way back to the condo, I time myself so I can make another post-office trip tomorrow. I'll ask them how they deliver to Kay's address. Mailmen know that kind of thing. I may have to make a dry run to figure out how long I need to be gone before I get Toby (and not Eric) to join me. It starts to dawn on me how difficult that might be.

The next morning, on Independence Day, we wake up early and go fishing as the sun rises. We do pretty well, except when Toby slips near the edge of the water and the mud sucks his shoe right off his foot. He says it felt like it grabbed him and wouldn't let go, and he cries until I splash knee-deep into the water and wash his shoe off. When we start walking again, his shoe squishes and makes farting noises as he takes each step. There is nothing funnier to a three-year-old boy than a farting shoe.

We find a suitable fishing spot, and before long, we catch a few respectable crappies. We release most of them, but Eric makes a big deal out of catching our lunch, so he sets the biggest one aside and lays out some newspaper so he can gut and clean the fish. Toby is fascinated. I didn't even know Eric knew how to clean fish, but he seems right at home.

We make our way back to the condo to fry the fish for lunch. Eric shows Toby how to roll the filets in cornmeal first. I slice the reddest tomatoes I've seen in a while and serve the corn on the cob, which Toby turns into a kernel mustache. I can't even watch Eric replicate it, purposely letting the corn stick into his mustache. They think it's hilarious.

That night, we walk down to the marina and watch the fireworks as patriotic music plays over a fuzzy loudspeaker. I look over at Toby sitting in Eric's lap, both their faces lit up by the synchronized explosions in the sky, and I feel an inner nudge.

I know, Mom. It's going to be over soon. For better or worse, at least it will be over.

Eric and I take turns in the shower, which gives me time to think. When he comes out, I tell him he can take the bed tonight, and I turn away before I can see the disappointment on his face. I pretend I'm offering in an effort to be fair. I pretend I don't realize I may be throwing away the first opportunity to share my bed in weeks.

When he protests out of chivalry, I insist. I tell him I can find a comfortable place in Toby's room. I tell him I'll be asleep before my head hits the pillow.

But I'm telling two more little lies. I'm not going to find a comfortable place, because I know I am not going to sleep tonight.

I sit in the beanbag chair in Toby's darkened room in the rented condo and listen to him breathe. It is a beautiful sound, his little boy sighs permeating my awareness as I work out the details of my plan.

I regret my failure at the post office. I hope what I have is the rural equivalent of a street address, the number of a mailbox in front of a driveway, in front of a house. I don't even know if I'll see it from the highway.

I open the closet door about two inches, turn on the light, and move my beanbag closer so I can see the map in the illuminated crack. The light jags across the floor, up the wall, and over the flat bedspread on the foot of Toby's bed. He's so small. He only fills the top half of the bed, so the light doesn't even touch him. My throat closes up, remembering that tiny body lying motionless on the dock.

I study the map until I'm satisfied. I stand up to stretch and bend over Toby's face, close enough to feel his breath on my cheek. I tiptoe down the hallway to trace my steps in an attempt to get out of the house without waking Eric.

I sneak into the bedroom, where Eric is fast asleep, to dig my list out of the side pocket of the suitcase. Feeling I've been away from Toby too long, I return to his room to pack a backpack, tucking granola bars, my wallet, and the rental-car keys inside. The map. I pick it up from the carpet near the closet. A flashlight? Found one in the kitchen. I fasten the backpack, settle into the beanbag, and watch Toby.

I do not sleep.

I ruminate about how the plan will work. I'll leave before sunrise, to give us enough time to locate Kay's house. When I've exhausted the possibilities and dug a rut in my mind about this, I allow myself to think about what happens *when* I find her. Not whether I can find her.

All I have to do is introduce Toby to Kay and watch. See if he looks familiar. See what happens when she looks into his eyes. The windows of the soul. I will not interfere with whatever is going to happen between them. With my heart pounding, I wonder, will she see John Robberson in him at first glance?

Even if she doesn't, I can picture how it will go. We'll knock on the door. I'll hold Toby up and see if anything clicks. If not, I'll introduce him. She'll invite us in for some coffee and we'll talk. She'll know exactly why Toby keeps asking for her. She'll explain it to me and I will finally understand and maybe we'll even laugh about it.

John Robberson will finish his business.

John Robberson will go away and leave us alone.

We'll get back to the condo and bring bagels for Eric, who will forget that he's mad, and I will be relieved because now he has nothing to be mad about. Even if Toby tells him about it, it will be over, so it will be okay. Maybe we'll even laugh about it.

We will be free of John Robberson. It really is Independence Day.

CHAPTER TWENTY-SEVEN

WINDOWS OF THE SOUL

I don't think about myself or about how I look after being up all night. Even when I walk past a mirror, the visual image doesn't fully register. I'm in faded tie-dyed yoga pants that ride low on my hips with wide legs and an intricate Middle Eastern scroll around the legs. I forget I haven't put on a bra. My ribbed knit undershirt is not adequate coverage for public view, but I don't want to risk going in for more clothes and waking Eric up. I pull my hair away from my face with a couple of bobby pins to hold my bangs tight to one side, which leaves the curly part in back to splay up like a sunburst coming from the middle of my head. While I sit in the dark, I pick at a blackhead on my chin until it's a hard red bump.

I'm on a mission bigger than my own petty concerns. I am the vessel Toby needs to make this connection. In the beanbag, an unfamiliar wash of spiritual awareness falls on me. I ask Mom if she's there and wait to see if I will get a nudge. Whether it comes from my mother's spirit or my own, something makes me stand up and say "It's time" at 4:59 a.m.

I scrawl a quick note to Eric: "Woke up early. Went to the grocery store for breakfast food. I have Toby with me." I leave it on the kitchen counter, near the coffee machine. That will buy me some time.

I gently rock Toby. "Come on, baby, you can stay asleep. Momma has to do a little driving so we can go see Kay, but you can sleep in the car, all right?"

He doesn't wake up. He flops over and rolls out of his covers, so I can pick him up. He's wearing pajamas with bulldozers and yellow hard hats on them, and his hair is flat on one side. He's thirty pounds of dead weight, and I kiss his head as I cover him with a square blanket, hoist the backpack on my other arm, and open the door to his bedroom. The condo hallway is darker than Toby's room, with the single slat of light coming from the hallway closet.

I squeeze the door silently into the doorframe behind us. The night air is cool and feels good on the back of my neck. Toby almost wakes up when I roll him into his car seat, but I flip off the overhead light. He stops squinting. I prop his head up against the cushioned side of the seat and stay there, still as a statue, until his breathing is regular again.

I throw the backpack in the front seat, put the car in neutral, and roll backward out of the parking space before starting the engine. I wait to turn on the headlights until I'm out of range of the parking-lot lights and reach down to dig the map out of my bag. Turning left past the marina, I head toward Route 76. About ten minutes later, after passing the bait shop, the Dairy Queen, and the gas station, I turn left again, onto the poorly maintained two-lane road marked by a "76" sign pocked with buckshot.

"Some big-ass road," I say aloud, remembering how the gas-station clerk had described it. "Looks like somebody took target practice on that sign."

I fall quiet, considering for the first time that the people who live on this road might—no, probably—have guns at home. As if to confirm the need for them, my headlights catch the shiny eyes of a possum in the road. Shuddering at its oily, repellent shape, I slow and watch the critter scurry across the road.

I look in the backseat. I'll tell him about the possum later. He'll like that. I wonder if I need to wake him now so he won't be cranky when we get there. I'll wake him when I see the mailbox. We can sit there a bit before we go inside. Besides, the sun is not due up for another hour, at least.

The numbers on the mailboxes are heading in a predictable and ascending order. I slow when I pass one or a group of mailboxes, once even getting out to read the names on the sides. Most of the mailboxes are standard-issue black like an old-fashioned workman's lunch box, but some are shaped like mallard ducks or have messages written in hand-painted letters with big dots on the ends. Some have the name and the number; others only the number.

I pass one crooked stake and slow down as my headlights discover the bunged-up mailbox lying in the ditch, freshly decapitated. I get out, and the morning air is cooler than expected. There's no number on that box.

I get back in the car and drive to the next intersection. No signs. The sky is changing colors. I have sweaters on my teeth and bad breath. I go straight but have no idea if I'm on the right road now. No marker of any kind. The mailbox numbers have a B in front of the number and have jumped backward in sequence.

Finally a Y-shaped intersection appears, and a pockmarked "76" sign jig-jogs back into view. I turn again and my headlights reveal mailbox numbers in ascending order again. I'm on a two-lane asphalt road with tall grasses growing in the ditches on either side and lone mailboxes separated by one-acre lots, each with its own long gravel driveway. There are plenty of trees, but none of them look like they've ever been trimmed. Some homes have fences; some have toys in the yard. Every home I pass now is a double-wide trailer, a mobile home disguised so it doesn't look mobile at all.

The sun isn't quite over the horizon. I creep along as the numbers top 500. 520. 548. On the other side of the road, 551.

Then I see it: Robberson.

White hand-stenciled letters on a black mailbox. No mallard mailbox for the Robbersons, evidently. I stop, hardly believing we're really here. Staring at the address in my hand, with the metallic taste of adrenaline on my tongue, I confirm it one more time before I pull the car to the side of the road. I get out and look closer, the morning air a fresh shock.

Robberson.

John and Kay.

Box 584.

I crawl into the backseat, next to Toby. "Hey." I rock his shoulders and give him a kiss on the forehead. "Time to wake up, baby. There's someone you need to meet."

The sky is purple, down low. Pink, if I look up. Mostly strange, unfamiliar shades of military blue and deep gray. I can't see the sun yet.

I unlock Toby's car-seat buckle, and he starts to stretch and rub his eyes. He crawls out of the seat and into my warm lap. I rock him back and forth in my arms, bringing him to the morning. He snuggles his soft hair under my chin in a way that I know I'm going to miss. When he grows another two inches, he won't fit in that little spot anymore. I kiss his face again and again, saying, "Good morning, sleepyhead."

When I can feel his body respond, I offer him some Juicy Juice, which does the trick. He's awake now and looking around.

"Where's Daddy?"

"He's still asleep. But guess where we are."

"Where?"

"We're going to see Kay. We're at Kay's house. See, right there on the mailbox, it says John Robberson. And Kay. This is where Kay lives."

I'm acutely aware that I'm repeating myself, and it sounds manic, even to me, so I stop.

He nods his head, his straw full of purple juice. I wipe his face, brush my hands through his hair to fluff up his curls. I want him to look nice.

"Toby?"

"Yes."

"Can I ask you about John Robberson?"

"Yes."

"What did he tell you to go say to Kay?"

"He doesn't want her to be mad anymore."

"Why is she mad?"

"Because of the dog."

"Thud?"

"No, Momma, the dog in the fire. She's mad because he went in for the dog."

"So you're going to tell her not to be mad about the dog? Is that what you're going to say to Kay?"

"Yes?" and he looks at me to see if that's the right answer.

I shake my head, sorry I'd pushed too far. Again. "Tell you what. I'm going to take you to meet Kay, and you can say whatever you need to say. Okay?"

"You do it," he says.

"No, baby. John Robberson wants you to do it. But I'll be right there with you, I promise."

We get out of the car. Toby comments that it's nighttime. I don't consider what Kay might be doing right this minute. I assure him it's going to be fine and point to a light coming from a window in the house.

We walk hand in hand up the gravel driveway with grass growing in the middle, between the tire tracks. I'm getting used to the crispness in the air but wish I'd thrown on a sweatshirt. The dew on the grasses smells fresh and reminds me of the urban farm at Oasis Verde.

We walk past a dirty white Chevy sedan parked near the house. It doesn't quite fit inside the covered carport, which has boxes and gardening tools stacked high. A folding card table in the middle of the carport is piled with silverware and knitting supplies and craft materials. I can't resist a nosy peek inside the car. The backseat has wadded-up fast food bags on the floorboard and library books strewn across the seat.

The sidewalk from the driveway to the front door is paved with bricks stuck into the dirt in an uneven curve. The gravel crunches under our feet. I shift my weight in my flip-flops, trying to keep them from clopping against my heels. Toby's light-up shoes glow orange neon with every step. The porch light is off, but I can see in the front window. It looks like a lamp near the door is on. It's probably a night-light, designed to give the impression the owner is home. In one way, it's too early for us to be here. In another way, we're way overdue.

I knock on the metal screen door. It's cold and hurts my knuckles. I knock again, louder. My fist is in midair, ready to knock again, when a light comes on in the back part of the house. I squeeze Toby's hand. He reaches for me and I hoist him up.

Another light comes on, in the living room now. I stand straighter so Kay won't see me peeking in through the window.

"All right, all right. I'm coming."

I hear the firm *chunk* of the latch, the loose rattle of the door-knob, the *chink* of the porch light flipped on, an audible expression of the visual sensation of moving from the dark to the light. In one split second. One little *chink*.

I shuffle Toby on my hip. The wooden door opens, but the screen door remains closed.

"What is it? Do you know what time it is?"

I don't know what I expected, but my prior conception dissipates. I didn't realize I had conjured up a version of my mother in my head, so it's all I can do not to gasp at how short Kay Robberson appears.

She's easily in her seventies and stands before us in a pale blue housecoat snapped up crooked at the top and pulled closed by her arms, crossed in front of her. She's five foot nothing, heavyset, with wispy gray hair the consistency of cotton candy. With the light shining behind her, it looks a little like a halo. It reminds me of Pa's eyebrows. Kay's eyelids are swollen and she squints, which pulls her features tightly around her nose, with soft puppy wrinkles all around the outside of her face. I can tell she was pretty once—before the cigarettes and sun and hard knocks took their toll.

"Well?" Her voice is not unfriendly, but it isn't exactly welcoming, either.

With some effort, I don't say anything and hope she understands. I look at Toby expectantly and shuffle him off my hip to hold him in front of me. He dangles there like a marionette puppet.

"Look, it's pretty darn early. Whatchu need? Is he sick or something?"

I've vowed not to interfere with whatever spiritual interaction needed to happen, but I have to shake my head to answer her question. I straighten my arms and hold Toby out toward her. At least toward her screen door.

"Darlin', do you speak English? Are you okay? Don't drop him, now. What do you want?"

Please. Look at him.

I force myself to say nothing. I know it must look really strange, but I'm begging her with my eyes to see past the strangeness.

"Take that boy home. Go on, now."

And with that, Kay Robberson shuts the door. When the porch light flips off with a decisive *chink*, I whirl into action.

"No!" I step off the porch, toward the front window, stumbling over the peonies planted underneath, feeling the soil grind between my toes. I lift Toby as high as I can. The bottom of the windowsill is about chest height as I stand in the flowerbed. I rest his little bottom on my shoulder so he's in full view.

"Do you know this boy?"

No answer.

"Do you? Do you know him? Look at him, will you? Just look at him!" With my hands under Toby's armpits, his little nose practically touches the screen on the windows. Toby squirms. He really looks like a puppet now.

"Tell me! Look! Just look!"

The porch light comes on again, and the next thing I know, Kay steps out on her front porch with a twelve-gauge shotgun. She motions with the barrel of the gun and hollers, "Git!" She barks at me over and over, like she's calling a bad dog. I pull Toby toward me and fall down in her flowerbed. Toby lands on top of me, now crying.

"Now you're crunching my flowers!" Her face is red and her voice is shaking. I can't tell if she's scared or mad or drunk with power because of the gun in her hand. She stands over us. I fumble around in the soil, a pungent mix of manure and chemicals.

I experience a flood of adrenaline that starts low in my brain stem and crashes in an enormous wave of instinct and defensiveness I didn't know I had. My yoga pants scrunch down, and half my butt is showing. Toby howls, manure mud on his face. I don't even know if Kay can hear me.

I'm not exactly sure what comes out of my mouth. All I know is I have to disarm this old woman. I have to get my child out of that chemical manure pile. *Go, go, go.*

I lunge toward her.

The next thing I know, I'm holding the shotgun, and Kay Robberson is splayed out on her back in her front yard. Her nightgown flaps up obscenely in the fresh morning sunlight, and I can see varicose veins on the insides of her knees. She moans and rolls over, clutching her back.

I scream "Get down!" and whiplash-shove Toby into the weeds. His wails rise and fall like a siren. With adrenaline pumping, I sprint to the shotgun, put a death grip on its long, cold barrel, and spin three times, grunting as I catapult it like an Olympic discus thrower.

I grunt and stagger backward, dizzy and disoriented. My pulse pounds against my temple. The shotgun whoosh-whooshes through the air like a sluggish propeller. Toby howls in the background, the squall reaching me in slow motion.

I hear, "Duck!" but it's a lonely bellow from a deep well, far away. I am cemented in place. The spinning rifle, after being suspended in air for what seems like hours, finally breaks the spell as it hits a tree with a crack. It clatters to the ground.

I scoop Toby into my arms and bolt down the driveway, jiggling and crying, limping when I lose a flip-flop. We collapse in the backseat of the car. He burrows his head into my neck, reminding me of an ostrich. I hug him, desperation hammering through my veins.

I don't think I've ever been more ashamed of myself. It's one thing to lose it. It's another thing to lose it in front of your kid. What if that gun had gone off? Not only have I knocked an old woman to the ground, but I've left her there hurt.

What's wrong with me?

I look at Toby's light eyes—Eric's eyes. I can barely stand what's reflected there in his tears. He's scared of me. He's scared of his own mother. I close my eyes and breathe. My scalp prickles with the sensation of a curtain drawing back, a receding of the waters, a tide washing back out to sea. I don't want Toby to get caught in the undertow.

I have to get a grip.

How can I fix this? I do my best to comfort Toby. I wipe my eyes, shake my head, and fish around in the backpack for some baby wipes. I clean his face and knees. I find a granola bar, break off a piece for him, and say, over and over, everything is fine now. We're safe. I find his juice box.

I'm kicking myself that I clammed up when she answered the door. If I diagrammed the problem on a flowchart—well, that would be the point at which events departed from the expected path. It was a mistake to think I wasn't going to have to explain something. I should've said something right away—put her at ease.

Now I know.

I've come so far. I can't just sneak back into the condo without waking Eric. What am I going to say to him? No. I can't be this close and not get what I came for. I'm only going to get one chance.

I hug Toby. "I was wrong, baby, and when you're wrong, you have to apologize. So now, I think we have to go back up there so I can tell Kay I'm sorry."

"No." He shakes his head. "I don't want to."

"I'm not looking forward to it, either, but it's the right thing. If you do something wrong, you have to go and apologize and ask what you can do to make it right."

"A do-over?"

"Yes, something like that."

As I'm walking back up the driveway, I find my flip-flop. Fifteen minutes after I knocked Kay Robberson on her backside, I rap on her door again.

Immediately, she throws open the inside wooden door, obviously expecting someone. I can see she has an ice pack on her back.

She retreats, pulling the door halfway closed. "Good God almighty. You better get outta here. Ernie's gonna be here soon."

"Please. Let me apologize. I've never done anything like that before. I'm so terribly sorry. Are you all right?"

"No. I am not all right. Do I look all right?"

"Do you need to get to a doctor or something?"

"If I do, I'll get there myself, thank you."

"I'm so sorry."

"Yeah. You said that."

She starts to close the door the rest of the way. I block it with my hand. "Please. I had to come back and make sure you're okay. I'm embarrassed. I don't know what got into me. I'm here trying to find out something that is extremely important—"

"What can be so important that you need to wake me up at the crack of dawn, come at me like that, throw a loaded gun, and then run away like a nutcase?"

"I know. There's no excuse for my behavior. I am *so* sorry. Please, if you'll listen to me for five minutes, I'll go and never bother you again."

Kay doesn't say anything, which may be as good as I'm going to get in this situation, so I take a deep breath. I pick Toby up before I start talking. She stands behind the screen door and shifts the ice pack to her other hand. I'm sure I look crazy, there on the porch with manure on my face, fertilizer beads in my flip-flops, and a big wet muddy smear on my left hip.

"My name is Shelly Buckner, and I live in Arizona. This is my son, Toby. He's three."

I hold him up to her, and he buries his face in my neck.

"A few months ago, he started talking about someone I think you know. At first we thought it was his imaginary friend, but now I believe that this person might be real. He talks to my son."

I pause, waiting for some kind of response.

Nothing.

"You see, I believe the person who talks to my son is your husband, John."

She narrows her eyes.

"John Robberson," I say.

Slam.

I knock again.

"Go away!"

"Please, please, Mrs. Robberson. Kay. Toby says that John told him that he needs to come see you." I raise my voice. Toby is on my hip, and I have the screen door propped open with my shoulder. I rest my forehead on the wooden door.

No response.

Is she on the other side?

I whisper, "Isn't that right, Toby? Am I getting it right?"

Toby nods and I turn back, putting my mouth near the seam at the doorframe.

"Please!"

Toby and I stare at the closed door.

"John Robberson says Toby needs to talk to you. About a dog. I don't know what that means. Please, can't you, won't you open the door?"

I stand in silence on Kay Robberson's porch for a long time. I'm prepared to stand here all day if I have to.

A white patrol car pulls up the driveway. I turn to see a tall, stocky man with a gray crew cut striding toward me. He says, "Something I can help you with, ma'am?"

The front door opens and Kay calls out, "Ernie! This is the one." She breaks down crying, the words coming out in gulps. "This girl's crazy or something, coming out here on my property, talking nonsense about John to me, and . . . and . . . she knocked me down and took my gun . . . and . . . and . . ."

"She has a gun?" His hand moves to his belt.

"No, she threw it at the trees!"

"Yep. I'm here, Kay. You go on inside now."

Even thought I am watching him, Ernie creeps toward me. In the final three yards, he lunges, grasps me firmly by the elbow, and forces me off the porch. "Okay. We're all done here."

"Let go!" I try to twist my arm away, which makes him clamp down harder. He leads us to his squad car and opens the door. "Why don't y'all get in the back there?"

I'm still holding Toby but shift him to the opposite hip. My body is tense and hard. I know Toby can feel it. "Fine. We'll leave. I have a car right here. We don't need a ride."

Ernie whispers in my ear, "Come on, little momma. You don't want me to make a fuss here in front of your boy." Then, louder, he says, "I'll give you a lift to your car."

Defeated, I get in the backseat of Ernie's patrol car with Toby. I say "Hey!" as he drives past my car, realizing that I don't have my wallet, my cell phone, or anything with me. "Can you turn around? I need to get my backpack out of the car."

"You shoulda thoughta that earlier."

I try to argue but stop when I realize I'm only making Toby cry and Ernie even madder. I start crying. I can barely remember the name of the condos where we're staying but tell Ernie anyway. I'm sure Eric is awake by now and probably freaking out. I'm exhausted and overcome with despair and embarrassment. I cannot stop crying. I try to tell Toby it's okay, but he clings to me like a drowning rat.

From the backseat of the squad car, I look up and realize we are heading the opposite direction of our condos. "Where are you taking me?"

"We'll head on over to the police station, and you can tell me the whole story there, in private. Then we'll see if Miss Kay wants to press charges against you, then we'll let you call someone to come and get you, all right?"

"Press charges?"

"Yes, ma'am."

"Am I under arrest?"

"Oh, no, nothing like that. Kay's got a good heart but a quick temper. We're gonna let her calm down a bit and see what she wants to do. That sound all right to you?"

"No, it does not sound all right to me," I hiss at him.

"Guess you shoulda thoughta that before you started beating the living daylight outta a defenseless old lady, huh, momma?"

"Stop calling me that."

I don't ask what will happen if she wants to press charges. For what? Trespassing? Assault? Can they throw me in jail? What have I done?

"Don't cry, Momma." Toby looks at me with concern and puts his hands on the sides of my face. He kisses my eyes, and it slows my pulse. I have to get out of my emotions and use my head. I have to pull it together, for Toby's sake. I hope he won't remember this later.

I wipe my eyes with the backs of my hands. "I'm okay now, baby. We're going to take a drive with the officer here. He's going to show us where he works, okay?"

"I want to go home."

CHAPTER TWENTY-EIGHT

EVERYTHING HAPPENS FOR A REASON

The Branson police station is located on the ground floor of City Hall, a beautiful old stalwart in the middle of downtown. As the morning sun shines down, I realize I'm walking into a government building with my nipples clearly visible in my tank top. I pick up Toby and hold him to my chest. We both smell vaguely of manure. I have never wanted to be invisible as much as I do right now.

I'm determined to hold it together as we walk to our seats in the waiting room. Toby, less shaken now, finds a *Highlights* magazine, which strikes me as bizarre. How many children regularly visit the Branson police station? Enough to warrant a children's magazine subscription, evidently.

I pick up the *Branson Courier*, and my eye stops on a statistic that says southern Missouri is considered the meth capital of the entire country. Missouri had more meth-related arrests last year than any other state—by a three-to-one margin. Twenty percent of arrests occurred after an explosion that caused the house to burn. I swallow hard, as if there's a bitter pill that hasn't quite dissolved stuck in back of my throat.

Toby complains that he's hungry. I'm at the mercy of the good people of Branson. The nameplate on the receptionist's desk reads "Marjorie Miller." Summoning a smile, I smooth my hair, nod toward Toby, and ask Marjorie, a plainly dressed woman with an impressive salt-and-pepper bouffant, for some crackers.

"Sure, honey, let me reach into the snack basket here and see what we got."

She twists in her secretarial chair and rolls back to the black file cabinet behind her. Opening the bottom drawer and exposing her oversize pink underpants as she bends over, she comes up with a six-pack of bright orange crackers with peanut butter. "Here ya go, hon."

I accept them gratefully with no thought that even twenty-four hours ago, I would've cringed and rejected the preservative-laden snack.

"They're orange," Toby says, as he holds the package about one inch in front of my nose.

Marjorie chuckles.

I kiss his forehead and laugh for the first time since I was in a tube on the lake, behind a boat. Before I heard a clunk on the marina deck. It feels like that was a year ago.

"They're cheesy," I say, opening the package for him. "Some kinds of cheese are orange, right?"

"There idn't no other color of cheese in Branson," Marjorie says. "Where y'all from?"

"Arizona, right outside of Phoenix."

"Y'all come for the lake?"

I sighed and shifted Toby from one hip to the other. "Guess we should've stayed at the lake."

"I was wondering," Marjorie said.

Toby doesn't want to eat the crackers at first, so I take a bite. With a goofy expression, I make a circle motion in front of my midsection and say "yum."

Marjorie chuckles again, obviously enjoying having a three-year-old in her office. Toby eats his crackers and plays peek-a-boo with her between bites. When he's finished, she shows him the trash can and helps us find the water fountain.

"Do you have little ones?" I ask.

"Three grandbabies," she says, turning around a studio-posed picture for me to see. Her grandbabies are freckled, lanky adolescents. "They're getting so big. I miss them being little."

"Good-looking kids," I say. "They look happy."

"They're a handful." Marjorie glances at the clock. "Ernie should be here pretty soon. I think he's waiting to see if Kay has cooled off yet. She probably will."

"I hope so."

"She's been through so much. First her boy, then her husband." Marjorie shakes her head. "And the way John went—well, he loved that dog, didn't he?"

I nod, sick that my heart leaped at this tidbit of information.

"It's a shame," Marjorie said.

I nod again.

"So you gotta bear with Kay. She's not herself right now. It's not like her to make a fuss."

I force myself to leave it alone. "Could I borrow your phone? I need to call my husband."

Eric's phone goes straight to voice mail, so I leave a message that I don't have my phone but to call back on this number. I look for a clock and realize we've been here almost forty minutes. How long can it take to clear this up? Toby, thankfully, has settled in on my lap while I read, and he falls asleep in minutes. His body seems to keep me warm and grounded. I realize, too late, that I forgot to tell Eric we're okay.

Finally, Ernie shows up, but he speaks only to Marjorie. "Kay's not answering her phone," he says, "so you might as well add her to the system." Without even looking my way, he returns to his office.

Marjorie waves me over and asks to see my identification.

"I don't have it." Controlling my voice, but feeling that warrior drum in my chest again. "He wouldn't let me get it out of my car."

"That darn Ernie. You didn't argue with him, did you?" She gives a little grunt as she bends and digs in her desk for a preprinted form. "Arguing makes it worse. He's hardheaded. Everybody knows that." She squints at her monitor as she hits the same key over and over, until she finds her place. "Okay, hon, this won't take long. Name?"

I sit in a small kitchen chair at the end of a metal desk while she types the details of my existence. I hope Toby stays asleep until Eric gets here. When she is finished with me, she takes us back into an abandoned office. I guess I'm in the system now.

I am going to have a police record. Me. Toby's mom. A grown woman with a child in my care and I'm about to be arrested because . . . why? It all starts to collapse on me. What was I thinking? How could I drag Toby along, without any inkling of what we were walking into? We could've died. What kind of mother am I? I steer Toby away from processed food like it's poison, but I lead him into a situation where he's looking down the barrel of a shotgun? And I completely freaked out in front of him, which makes it a thousand times worse, and I was so stupid that I threw a loaded gun (!), and my son watched me shove a grandmother to the ground like she was the criminal. Who am I? I can't imagine what Toby must think.

I'm so relieved that he's still asleep and doesn't respond when I know my tears are soaking spots on his little T-shirt.

It's almost 10:00 a.m. before Marjorie tells me I have a call. She transfers it to a rotary phone on the abandoned desk in the office. It's Eric.

196

"I don't even know how to tell you this," I say in a low voice so Toby won't hear. "But I'm okay. We're both okay."

As soon as he realized I was gone, he called my cell phone. When I didn't answer, he looked for my backpack and didn't find it. He never found my note, the one designed to keep him from worrying. He called the police, who told him we had to be missing for twenty-four hours before they could do anything. He lied and told them there was a break-in at the condo so they would come. He stayed and paced, getting madder and madder as he waited for the police to show up and write a report. That's when he went to the parking lot and realized the car was gone. He called the hospital. Nothing. That's when he took his cell phone and started out on a run, looking for us. He'd been to the marina and ran all the way to the grocery store, looking over his shoulder as cars passed him on the highway.

It breaks my heart to picture him this way. I'm sick to my stomach as I try to explain. Detained, that's all. I can't even say the word *arrested*. It's not official yet. Not until they confirm whether she wants to press charges.

"Press charges? For what?"

I can barely choke it out. "Trespassing."

"What?" I can hear him absorbing this. "Where did you trespass? Where did you go?"

"Please. It's been a long, bad morning. Can we do this later? I'm not trying to be evasive. I'll tell you everything when I see you . . . but the short version is, I found Kay Robberson."

"Shit."

There's no way to explain myself. I can't even start.

"Tell me you're kidding."

With a big sigh and a completely flat tone, I realize I don't have a choice. It will only make it worse if I'm too much of a coward to own up to it. I don't deserve the luxury of choosing my time and place; I have to do this on the phone. Right now. "No, she's a real person. I found her house; Toby asked for her . . ."

"Dammit, Shelly." I have thrown one too many rocks against his calm exterior today, and I can hear it crack. He takes a big breath. "I thought you were done with this."

I break down sobbing. "I am now. I promise."

"Don't even start with that," he snaps. "I don't want to hear it."

"Please, Eric. I know you have a lot of questions—"

"No, I don't." He pauses. "Yes, I do. I have one question."

"Anything."

"Was it worth it, Shelly? Just answer that one. Was it worth it?"

I swallow thickly and whisper into the phone, "No."

No response.

Finally, he says, "Is Toby safe?"

"Yes." I clear my throat. "We're in an office. They won't release me until . . . They're waiting to see if she'll drop the charges."

No response, but I sense a faint, subtle shift. I push the receiver to my ear and can almost hear him make a decision. I know he can do this—put aside his reaction to something and focus on how to fix it.

In a lower, more deliberate tone, he says, "I'm coming to get my son."

"You're so mad at me." I try to keep my voice from trembling, but I can't. His fix doesn't include me.

"We can talk about that later." I can almost hear him raking his fingers through his hair. "Look. Can you hold it together? Just don't make things worse, all right?"

I get a visual image of myself windmilling a rifle into the air. Knocking an elderly woman on her ass. Shoving my son to the ground. A shiver of shame rolls over me, and Toby stirs in my lap. I know how I sound.

I whisper into the phone, "I think I'm losing it."

"I'm on my way."

I will make it right with him. I have to.

Toby and I sit in a boring tan-carpeted, beige-walled office full of nothing but a metal desk and a secretary's lopsided swivel chair with the tweed seat coming unraveled. Marjorie brings in another metal folding chair so there are two chairs for us. I'm tempted to try to get her talking again. Once she leaves, I poke around the desk, holding Toby with one arm while I explore with the other. The metal desk drawers are all empty, not even a stray paper clip. The air conditioning fan starts up. I'm freezing in this stupid tank top. I'm glad for the warmth of Toby's body on my chest.

I sit down in one of the chairs. Toby nestles in and falls asleep again. My eyes are scratchy and dry but I can't sleep. This thought won't leave me alone: Toby still didn't get to deliver whatever message John Robberson wanted him to.

Eric's question reverberates in my mind. Was it worth it?

No.

That's the bottom line. I will never know what any of it means— the plane crashes and fires and Thud and Kay—and I have to start making my peace with that. "I'm not going to find out," I say out loud.

I'll go back home and repair my relationship with Eric. Get my real life back.

Yes. That's what I need to do.

Having made a decision, I feel lighter. However, Toby doesn't. My leg is falling asleep from his weight, so I shift him from one leg to the other. In the process, I jostle him awake. I try to settle him back down, but he's up now. I can anticipate what's coming next. I get up and try the door and can't believe someone locked it from the outside. Toby is holding the front of his pants and giving me the face. I knock on the door.

A police officer, a young guy with a greasy complexion, follows me to the restroom and stands outside the door while I help Toby.

The officer waits on me, and I am acutely aware that he is probably listening to me pee and flush, whether he wants to or not.

I wash my hands and face. I run my fingers through my hair and wish I had a scarf or hat or something, but I manage to feel a little more civilized. We return to the office, and I'm still keeping my arms close to my chest to cover my bra-less shape. As we walk back, one of the officers sees Toby and offers him a stale jelly doughnut that was left over in the break room. He likes it. Of course he does; it's like crack. I think it's the first time he's had a jelly doughnut, or any kind of doughnut for that matter, and now I'm going to have to explain to him why we're not having another one.

I'm getting back to my sense of myself.

Not long after we return to the empty office, there's a knock on the door. "Someone here to see you, Mrs. Buckner."

Good. I don't have a watch and there's no clock on the wall, so I'm not sure how long we've been in the office. When the officer opens the door, I gasp when I see it isn't Eric but Kay Robberson who walks in.

"Oh. Oh," I say, eyes refilling, I hold out my hand to shake hers. It seems a completely inadequate gesture for the situation, but I can't think of anything better to do. All I can do is choke out, "I'm so sorry."

She shakes my hand but doesn't say anything. I fuss with Toby and make him stand up in front of me. I put my hands on his shoulders, facing her.

Kay says, "I'm not pressing charges. Ernie told me I didn't need to come in here, but I believe in doing the right thing. Everything happens for a reason."

I am speechless.

CHAPTER TWENTY-NINE

JUST PLAY ALONG

She waves off my pathetic, repeated apologies. Clearly, she's not here to forgive me. She's here for Toby. She leans down to his level and asks, "Now, is there something you want to say to me, young man?"

My heart does a backward somersault, and I hate myself for it.

He shakes his head and pulls on my pants leg.

I lean over and whisper in his ear, "It's okay, baby. This is Kay. Tell her what John Robberson told you."

Kay squats until she's looking Toby right in the eyes.

I'm proud of him as he maintains eye contact. His voice is clear and true. "Don't be mad about the dog."

The corners of Kay's mouth pull low. "John Robberson told you to tell me that?"

Toby nods.

"Okeydokey." She nods her head. "You tell him I'm not mad anymore." Her voice is thick, but only for a split second. She straightens up and says, "All right?"

Then, out of Toby's earshot, she says, "See, it's like when they find a monster under their bed. If you play along, talk to the monster, it goes away. I don't think John Robberson is going to bother your boy anymore."

Play along?

The flicker of hope inside me gets blown out like a birthday candle. If she's just playing along . . . it means nothing to her. Eric's words echo once more: "Was it worth it?"

A fresh wave of shame crashes over me, cutting off my air. "Thank you," I manage to say. I clear my throat. "And I'm sorry."

Hand on the doorknob, she turns and looks me in the eye. "We're all done here, right?"

"Right. I won't bother you again."

"See that you don't."

—

Eric shows up about ten minutes after Kay leaves.

"Am I glad to see you," I say, releasing Toby so he can run to his dad.

Eric scoops him up. In a low, careful voice, he says, "Everything okay here?"

"Can we go home now?" I start to cry. "Please. I'm exhausted."

Without taking a step toward me, he says, "I was thinking on the way here; you really need to talk to someone."

"Talk to someone?"

"Maybe someone here. I could take you to the hospital. Just to get you stabilized."

It takes every ounce of diplomacy I have to convince my husband to let me shower and sleep before I do anything else. Maybe because I look like I've had the flu for a week, he agrees. To assure him that I can think rationally about the fact that I acted so irrationally, I calmly agree to see my therapist, Anna, as soon as we get back. His jaw clenches and unclenches four times before I can tell he decides not to push it.

He's not furious. It's worse than that. He feels sorry for me. As if I could be any more ashamed, somehow that's the icing on the cake. He thinks I'm fragile, which is the condition of a thing before it breaks. It's too late for fragile.

We head back to Arizona, Eric driving the entire way without an overnight stop. I have no tears left as I sit in the passenger seat, embroiled in shame. We will not talk about this in front of Toby. That may be the only point of agreement between us right now.

CHAPTER THIRTY

UNFINISHED BUSINESS

When I return from my weekly session with Anna, Toby is waiting for me in the garage. He must've heard the electronic door opener engage; it's as loud as a chainsaw. He's jumping up and down, right in the middle of my space, waving to me. It's like coming home to a new puppy. I've spent the last hour crying, so it doesn't take much to trigger more tears. I blink them away and roll down my window.

"Toby, move back to the doorway so I can park. I don't want to run over you."

He comes up to my window instead. "Where were you?"

"Talking to my friend Anna. But I'm here now."

"Can I sit in the front seat?"

"Sure."

He rides shotgun as I pull into the garage. When the car stops, he leaps, unencumbered by a seat belt, into my arms for a hug. This makes me cry, too.

"Go get Daddy, now, okay?"

I turn off the ignition and wait behind the wheel. Eric clips Toby into his car seat and takes his place without a word to me. This does not make me cry. I'm used to this part. It's been like this ever since we got back from Branson.

Anna says the only way I can rebuild Eric's trust is to tell the truth. So, instead of Date Night like some couples have, we have a weekly Confession Session. Usually, he chews in silence while I tell him the truth about every lie I told, all the stuff I left out, and exactly how crazy my thinking had been. According to Anna, he's supposed to tell me how he feels (but he hasn't and I can't make him tell me or even bring it up). So far, he just keeps explaining how he tried his best to talk me out of each particular incident. He listens. He doesn't get mad. He's tolerant.

So, once a week, we drop Toby off with the babysitter and negotiate our way through a painful, unwieldy meal in an out-of-the-way restaurant. We don't want anyone to see us. It's like we're having an affair, only in reverse. We go out because we're trying to keep these conversations as compartmentalized as possible. I refuse to have this talk at home. I don't want to pollute our space. I don't want to glance over in the middle of an argument and see something like the placemats we brought back from Jamaica or anything that reminds me of the good times we've had. Because then they'll be tainted.

Today, Toby's at the movies with his sitter, and we're at a super-slick commercially successful coffee shop with no soul, in the middle of the afternoon, splitting a prepackaged fruit cup. He holds up a mushy square that used to have a color.

"What is that? Is it supposed to be pineapple?"

"No, I think it's honeydew melon." I smile. "Well, maybe its ancestors used to be in the honeydew family."

He pops it into his mouth. "I can't do this too many more times, Shel."

"Me neither." I sigh. "Let me just get through this last part, okay? The Branson part."

"Can we make this the last one? What does Anna say?"

"Eric. We've been over this before. She says it's important for me to say it, so there are no more lies between us."

"No, I mean today. What did she say to you today? Does she think it's working?"

I sigh. "She said if we keep pulling up the roots to see if the flower is growing, the flower doesn't have a chance to grow. She means . . ."

"I get it."

"It's been good for me, Eric."

"I know," he says. "That's why we're doing it."

"You don't get anything out of it?"

"If it works, I get my wife back, right?" The corners of his lips rise. His teeth show. He's not quite smiling, but I can tell he's trying.

"If it's any consolation, I should be able to get through the rest of it today. So this should be the last time."

The corners of my lips rise. My teeth show.

"I feel like we're accomplishing something, then." He pushes the fruit cup away. "All right. Let's hear it."

I start where I left off: my meeting with Kay. As I go through the details, Eric seems to be in a better mood. He asks a few logistics questions. He's not sulking this time. It almost feels like I'm telling a story instead of confessing my crazy. I take it step by step. Finding the mailbox. Standing on her porch in the dark. Holding Toby up for her to see. Stupidly, not saying a word to her.

Eric said, "The whole thing would've gone differently if you'd waited until a normal hour and talked to her."

I stared at him. Told him the rest of it, the gun, knocking her down . . .

"Kay's a tough old bird. I'm surprised she didn't get up and finish you off."

"How would you know?"

"I'm just going by what you've told me about her. We've talked about her so much, I feel like I know her."

"It will be easier to get through this if you stop pointing out what I should've done differently."

"You're right. I'm sorry."

I keep going. I can't get through it without my voice cracking and my eyes continually stinging. The humiliating ride in the back of the police car. The annoying Ernie. The mercy of Marjorie and her orange crackers. The waiting. And finally, the shock of Kay showing up. The shame of that last hope in my heart as it withered with the phrase "playing along."

Neither of us speaks. He hands me a tissue.

"I'm so sorry, Eric."

"You can stop apologizing now." He hugs me. "We're done. You said it; I heard you. I forgive you. Now you forgive yourself."

"We have to be extra honest with each other," I say. "No more secrets between us."

"No more secrets."

—

Oasis Verde may be a planned community, but nothing stops the Arizona sun in August. Dry heat, okay, but it is a full 110 degrees in the afternoon. Lakshmi's been in India visiting Nikhil's family for a month, so she's been out of the loop. We have a lot of catching up to do, and it's way too hot for us to meet at the park.

We decide we'll take the boys to an indoor playground that resembles an overgrown bounce house. If we go early in the morning, the older kids won't be there yet and the boys can run around without fear of a twelve-year-old trampling them.

We get settled in one of the brightly colored plastic booths with a clear view of the boys. Sanjay and Toby are flinging themselves face first into a four-foot pylon that resembles a punching bag. After she tells me about her trip, Lakshmi says, "Okay, your turn. What did you do while I was gone? Did you go to Branson?"

"Boy, did I."

Lakshmi's eyes light up. "What happened?"

Telling the whole story sends me back to the mindset we'd shared, which feels like a guilty pleasure. She wants to know every detail. I indulge her with energy in my voice, until I get to the point where Kay pulled a gun on us. Lakshmi has a stricken look on her face.

About that time, the boys start yelling, "Look at me! Momma, look at me!" and we turn to watch them swing from a rope into a pit of foam blocks.

"Okay, go on. She obviously didn't shoot you. What happened next?" Lakshmi asks. "Did you ever find out why Toby was supposed to meet Kay?"

The guilty pleasure is now all guilt and no pleasure. I trudge through the rest of it, all the way up to Eric's insistence that I return to therapy and our marathon of coming-clean sessions that followed.

"Wow," she says, sitting back in the booth. "That's a lot to take in. How are you doing?"

"I'm okay. We're in a good place now."

"Can you do it? Just let it go like that?"

"I have to, Lakshmi. It's not that I don't believe there was something . . . spiritual, or mystical, or whatever . . . It's more like I'm just really, really clear on the cost. At the end of the day, it's not worth it. I was risking my marriage; my family; my sanity, even . . . for what? I still can't answer that question. So it's not worth it, whatever it was."

"I understand."

"So, for a while at least, it would help me if we didn't discuss it."

"Sure. That makes sense," she says.

The air between us has changed. I can't put my finger on it, but I appreciate that she's trying to meet me where I am. It's almost like we've been working on a project together, and now it's over. I excuse myself and find the restroom. When I return, Lakshmi is deep in thought, watching the boys play.

"Everything okay?" I ask.

"Look at them. They're not playing the airplane game. Or the fireman game. Is Toby still talking about John Robberson?"

"Yes, but not as much. Something changed when we were there. I haven't brought it up."

"Probably best," Lakshmi agrees. "At least you've got some peace now."

"Well . . ."

"No?"

"You know how sometimes you lie in bed when you can't sleep? And you replay every humiliating thing you've ever done? Do you do that?"

She says, "I try not to, but I know what you mean."

"Well, the one I can't shake is that I *tackled* the poor woman. Knocked her flat on her back. Someone's grandmother. I could've broken her hip!"

"She was fine when she came to see you and Toby, wasn't she?"

"I got the impression that if she was hurt, we would be the last ones to know it."

"Stubborn?"

"Proud. I think she was determined to do the right thing, as far as she understood it."

"Well, that's admirable, isn't it?"

"For her. It makes me feel worse! I'm always going to be That Crazy Lady who came to her house and threw a fit. I wish I could talk to her now. Apologize. Tell her I'm normal again."

Lakshmi says, "Sounds like you have a little unfinished business."

"I'm going to finish it, then. I'll write her a letter," I say, feeling more certain than I have in weeks. "It worked with Eric. I need closure on this."

CHAPTER THIRTY-ONE

HITCHHIKERS

I'm putting the nozzle into my gas tank at the Mini-Mart when I see Wendy. I haven't been back to our playgroup since that embarrassing encounter in the grocery-store juice bar, and I haven't seen Wendy since the night we sat on the curb waiting for the fire truck. I wave and she walks over from her gas pump to mine.

"I was just talking about you!" She gives me a quick hug and tells me about her friend who owns a coffee shop downtown. Trying to build business, her friend added a hypnotherapist who does sessions on weekends. "You should go see her. My friend says she specializes in getting rid of soul hitchhikers."

"Hitchhikers?"

"People who die suddenly and don't know they're dead. They latch on to other souls, and the only way to get rid of them is to go see her. Isn't that brilliant? I thought of Toby immediately and told her all about him."

"You told her about Toby?"

"Think about it! It fits the profile. She says she'd have to see him to know for sure, but maybe he picked up a hitchhiker. See? That could be what his imaginary friend is—a soul hitchhiker. It's like a cross between a ghost and a reincarnation! It explains everything!"

"Well, that's a new one." I manage a teeth-only smile. My gas pump cuts off with a loud clunk. "Excuse me," I say, as I reach for the handle.

"Here—let me get you her card!" She runs back to her car, fishes through her purse, and comes back with a thick mocha-toned business card with a stenciled logo. It's clearly a labor of love. I hate to drop something that well crafted into the trash at the Mini-Mart, but I hear the crazy in Wendy's voice. I wonder if I used to sound like that. I'm pretty sure I did.

That's what Carla told me, when we finally got a chance to have one of those late-night marathon calls and I told her the Branson story. What a contrast to the painful confessions I had to make to Eric. When I told her what I did, she could not stop laughing.

"You did what?" she hooted, after I described each of my flagrant errors in judgment. It's not that she missed how serious it was or how desperate I'd been; this was her gift to me. She helped me separate from it just enough to look at it from the outside in, like I was a lunatic in a slapstick comedy trying to solve a mystery that existed only between my ears. It's a relief not to constantly look for hidden interpretations.

Like when Toby talks about John Robberson now. He doesn't play the game every day anymore, but he did try to wink at me this morning. I just winked back.

The entire conversation strengthens my resolve to write Kay a letter. I don't have to overinterpret anything; I just need to finish my business with her so I can move on.

"I don't think I'll be needing this," I say out loud inside my car as I slip the hand-crafted card into the no-man's-land side pocket of my driver door. I wave goodbye to Wendy, hoping she didn't see me talking to myself.

CHAPTER THIRTY-TWO

QUIT WITH THAT

*D*ear Mrs. Robberson,

  Hello. I'm Shelly Buckner. Maybe you've forgotten my name, but I'm sure you remember meeting me over the Fourth of July weekend. I know I promised you wouldn't hear from me again. I have to trust in the decency you showed me when I was at my worst, even as I ask you to indulge me once again.

  I returned to my home in Arizona, deeply ashamed of my behavior toward you. I won't drag you through the convoluted thinking that led me to your doorstep, but let me assure you, I understand now that I was very confused at that time. I won't bog you down with all the possible explanations, because none of them can justify my actions.

  I need for you to know I've come to my senses. I'd like to express my regret at dragging you into the drama I concocted. I'm so sorry to speak such nonsense about John. It was ridiculous to conclude there was any connection between my son's imaginary friend and your deceased husband. I can only imagine how hurtful it must have been, how insulting to John's memory, for me to say the crazy things I said. It was presumptuous of me to speak with any authority about something I couldn't possibly know.

In short, I know how inappropriate it was for me to even approach you, much less the way I did it. You were right to order me off your property, and I am deeply ashamed that even then, I couldn't stop myself from continuing to harass you.

I'm ashamed my son saw me in such a state, and I'm sorry to have created a threat. Of course, you felt the need to defend yourself. As you probably suspect, guns frighten me. I overreacted (to say the least!), and I understand I made the situation even more dangerous. I am absolutely mortified that I attacked you. It was a fear reaction on my part, but I know that doesn't excuse it. I can't stop thinking about it. I'll never forgive myself if you're experiencing any continued symptoms as a result of my impulsive behavior.

I would like to offer to pay for any damages I caused on your property or for any injury I caused. Please send me any medical bills or receipts and I will take care of them right away.

I am so deeply sorry. You showed your true character by coming to the police station. I couldn't appreciate it then, but now I see the wisdom in your actions. You showed great kindness to me—and to my son. Thank you for providing a wonderful example of compassion and old-fashioned decency. You gave me a good lesson in mothering that day.

I lost my own mother before Toby was born, so I always search for wise women to inspire and instruct me as I try to find my way. You've been one of those for me. I hope you can find it in your heart to forgive me. I take full responsibility for my behavior.
Thank you,
Shelly Buckner

I needed to write it. I picked at it and pulled it apart about fifty times, sleeping on that version twice before I could mail it, trying to demonstrate both humility and some level of mental clarity.

I chat up my mailman, mentally flowcharting his explanation of the stops my letter will make between Oasis Verde and a black mailbox on the side of a rural highway in Branson. For three days, my conscience crosses its fingers that the letter will go undetected and make it up the long driveway, all the way to Kay's kitchen table, before she notices my return address. I'm hoping she won't tear it up or mark it "return to sender" without opening the envelope. She doesn't have to answer, but it will eat at me if I think she hasn't even read it.

Almost two weeks later, I'm still chatting up the mailman, still pretending I'm not flipping past the dry cleaning coupons and bills with a hidden purpose. I find a greeting-card-sized envelope with cutesy puppies printed on the back lapel. I flip it over, read the return address, and let out a squeal right there on the sidewalk. I jump up and down, wagging the letter in the air like it's a winning lotto ticket. Inside: a single sheet from an old-school steno pad, the kind that has the spiral at the top. Kay's handwriting looks like she's in junior high, with lots of loops and kind of a backward slant.

I can't stop smiling as I begin to read.

Dear Shelly,

You don't have to worry about me. Don't be so hard on yourself. And I don't need your money. I got a pension. It's clean between us now, so quit with that.
All right then.
Kay
PS: Your boy was real sweet and I liked meeting him. Ask him what kind of dog.

I stop smiling.

CHAPTER THIRTY-THREE

COMING SOON

Should I be worried?"

Eric shakes his head, but I can't tell if it means "No, don't be worried," or "Holy shit, this is weird and totally inappropriate and why the hell is she asking Toby anything if she thinks it's all a big game and we just need to play along?"

"Do you think this is just her way to play along?"

"Yeah," he says, "I bet that's it. Maybe she's just showing you that she's still playing along."

"Should I answer it?"

Opinion is divided on that question. Pa has been out of the loop on many of the details of the Branson trip, so he was surprised to hear that Kay even existed. He didn't see what all the fuss was about.

"She's an old lady. When you get old, you don't get to see many little kids. You look at them and it makes you remember when your kids were that little and it makes you happy. That's all. I bet she doesn't have any other little kids to dote on, so she's borrowing yours. Will it kill you to throw her a bone? Send her a picture of Toby and ole Thud; she'll get a kick outta that."

I catch Carla on the phone, between airports, to get her perspective on it. She gives me the down and dirty. "Let's break it down. Two choices. You're either going to answer her letter or you're not. If you don't, what happens?"

"She either stops writing or she keeps trying to contact me."

"If you do answer it, what happens?"

I hesitate. "Same. She either stops writing or she keeps trying."

"So it doesn't matter what you do, does it? She's throwing it out to see if you take the bait. If you don't, see what happens. She may go away on her own."

"What if she doesn't go away?"

"Then you have to decide whether or not you want to hear what she has to say." Carla laughs. "And whether you can keep from going postal on her. She's like your mental-health litmus test. If you can be around her and not freak out, then you know you're over it."

Lakshmi wants me to respond, out of sheer curiosity. She thinks Pa's idea about sending a picture of Toby and Thud is a great compromise.

I don't trust my gut reaction anymore, so I keep weighing the pros and cons. To clear my mind, Eric and I take Toby on a walk around the neighborhood after dinner. As we pass Mrs. Gilliam's house, Toby stops to call her cat, Pickles. He raises his voice to exaggerate the emphasis on the second syllable. Mrs. Gilliam hears Toby's signature call and opens her screen door. Eric and I wave from the sidewalk and let her have her time with Toby, both of them giggling as he strokes Pickles right under the chin, like she taught him.

"Old people love Toby, don't they?"

Eric looks at me. "I know what you're thinking."

"It feels mean not to answer at all. After all I put her through, if I can do something small like send a picture, maybe it will make her happy, and we can end it on a positive note."

Eric sighs. "Is there any logical reason to tell this woman what kind of dog was in Toby's imagination?"

"You're right, there's no logical reason. It's an emotional reason. I will feel better if I can do something for her, even if it's just a picture. I feel I owe her that much."

"Okay. Fair enough. Next question: Is there any actual risk?" He answers his own question. "No, unless it acts as a trigger for you."

"I can't think of anything she could do or say that would trigger any further action on my part."

Dear Kay,

I'm glad to hear you're doing well. I asked Toby what kind of dog, and he told me the same kind as our dog Thud, a Dalmatian. I'm sending a picture of Toby and Thud from last year. Unfortunately, I don't have a current picture because poor Thud died a few months ago, quite unexpectedly. My husband Eric used to run with him every morning. When they stopped for water, Thud swallowed a bee, which caused his throat to close up. It broke our hearts to lose him like that. I think Eric misses him the most.
Thanks again for responding.
Shelly

By the end of the week, I get this letter—same loopy handwriting, same cutesy stationery, but a completely different tone:

Dear Shelly,

I knew it was a Dalmatian! See, John had a thing for Dalmatians. He was a fire chief (did you know that?) and he got it in his head that every fireman needed a Dalmatian. Well, he got Duke first, but it didn't take long for him to get sick of the dog going to town on his leg, if you know what I mean, so we got Daisy. Next thing I know, we got puppies all over the place. I threw a fit and he talked his fireman buddies into taking a few. They paid good money for 'em, too. So now John's got it in his head we're gonna get rich on this, and he goes out and buys himself another female and next thing I know, we're breeding them at home. Duke was always his favorite, though. Went to work with him every day. The kids in town looked for him, riding up front, even with the sirens blaring, on the way to a fire.

We had a boy, too, and he loved them dogs. If the puppies wanted to come in the middle of the night, I'd let him stay up and wait. He was sweet about it, always wanting to pet Daisy or Delta—that was the mommas' names. He learned though—you let 'em alone and let God get the job done. If there was a runt in the litter, he'd love on that one more than any of the rest.

Not John. He didn't love them puppies. He loved old Duke. So when it was time to sell the puppies, we'd let John take them to town. We'd stay back and give Daisy and Delta some extra TLC on those days.

Now with John and Duke both gone, I know what it is to miss your dog, and I wanted to tell you, I'm friends with Duke's breeder and he's got a boy puppy ready to wean, so I went ahead and put down a deposit on him for you. Don't fuss about it—just let an old woman do some good in the world, all right?

There's a little hitch, but I got it all worked out. I was gonna just see if I could put the little pup on the airplane, but my breeder buddy says no way, no how. Says there's a kennel virus they get on planes and it kills puppies all the time. Says the only way to get this puppy from me to you is for me to take it to you. So that's what I'm gonna do.

I don't want to put you out or anything. You don't have to do anything, just don't be a pill and ruin my fun. It'll do my heart good to see that little squirt meet his new puppy for the first time. I'm *leaving today and I expect I'll be at your house sometime Tuesday afternoon. I take a lot of stops when I drive, so don't worry about me.*

I ain't asking. I'm just telling you I'm coming. It'd be real good if you were home to meet the puppy so I can be sure he's all set.

All righty then.

Kay

CHAPTER THIRTY-FOUR

NO BIG DEAL

W hat do we do?"

My hands are shaking as I hand the letter to Eric. "She says she's going to be here Tuesday. Tomorrow."

He snickers. "Well, we sure didn't see that coming, did we?"

"We have to stop her."

I run inside, find the number, call her home phone. Eric follows me and stands by my side as I squeeze my eyes and will her to be in Branson, at home, with nothing to do except answer her telephone. I try to visualize this scenario, but all I can conjure is the predawn light on her porch, the weight of Toby on my hip, and the smell of manure in her flower beds. And a now-familiar shiver of shame.

"She must've already left. She's driving here. Right now." I pace in a circle. "What are we going to do?"

Eric says, "Looks like we're going to get a puppy."

"What about Toby?"

"We just tell him she's coming to visit and bringing us a puppy. We make him think we bought it from her. She's just doing us a favor," Eric says. "That's what we tell everybody. We don't have to make a big deal out of this."

"It *is* a big deal."

"It's weird as shit, I'll give you that. But it doesn't have to be a big deal. She wants to come, fine, we let her come. We treat her like we'd treat anybody else. We normalize it."

"Really?"

"Yes. We'll play with the puppy, hang out with her, have dinner together, and let her say what's on her mind. Obviously. That's what's going on. She's got something to say to us, and she wants to do it in person." He hugs me. "It'll be okay. There's nothing she can say that's going to change one thing about our family. Except we'll have a puppy when she's gone."

"Toby will love that."

"And the rest, as long as you can stay grounded, is just an old woman who needs to talk about her husband. It won't kill us to hear her out."

I wait until bedtime, when I know I've got Toby's attention. I teach him Pa's "zipper on the lip" gesture—not so he'll keep a secret, but just so he won't interrupt me before I can explain the situation. I tell him the good news first: a puppy. He starts jumping up and down, but he zips his lip and turns the key, as instructed. Once he's got his imaginary key tucked into the waistband of his pajamas, I tell him the other part: Kay is coming.

"How do you feel about that, Toby?"

He points to his lips, pressed tight in a line.

"Use your key."

He lifts his pajama top high over his belly and holds it up by hooking his chin to his chest. I smile at his earnest effort and near-sacred handling of the tiny invisible key. When he inserts it into the corner of his smile, I wish it could somehow unlock the depth of his toddler insight about Kay's visit.

I ask again. "Are you excited about her coming here? Will you be happy to see her again?"

He shakes his head and bounces in his bed. "Puppy!"

"What if she wasn't bringing a puppy? If she just came to visit by herself, would you be happy to see her?"

He shrugs.

"Let me ask another way. Is there anything else? Before, you would always tell me she was mad. Are you still worried about that?"

He shakes his head. "She's not mad. She said so."

"I see." I rub his back in a circle. "You can put the key back now."

I call Lakshmi and ask her to meet me at the coffee shop. After she's finished reading the letters, her eyes are bright. She carpet-bombs me with questions, none of which have a clear answer.

"Maybe she's still mad about the dog," she concludes.

"Toby says no."

"Does John Robberson know that? Because he's still here, right?"

"Toby still talks about him," I admit.

"See, I don't get that part." Her voice is bouncing like an animated dot over song lyrics. I'm supposed to sing along. "If all he wanted was for her to forgive him about the dog, and she has . . . See what I mean?"

"Kay told me she was just playing along."

"But Toby didn't hear that, did he? So does John Robberson know she was playing along? That she didn't really forgive him?" Lakshmi asks. "Maybe Kay somehow knows *that*, and that's why she's coming."

I look at her a long time before answering. "Lakshmi. You know I can't speculate with you."

"I'm sorry, but how can you not?" she asks. "How is it for you now? John Robberson doesn't exist, no matter what Toby says?"

"I don't know what John Robberson is to Toby. I don't know what Kay's going to say when she gets here, but as long as it doesn't hurt Toby, what does it matter? Nothing about him hurt Toby—I did. Every problem I ever had with John Robberson, I brought on myself. I'm just choosing not to do that this time. Eric's right. If we don't make it a big deal, it's no big deal."

"I consider it a big deal if this woman is in your house and you don't even ask the most obvious question of all. If you can't even bring yourself to ask—"

She sees the look on my face and gives me a hug. "You're killing me. You know that, right?"

I return the hug. Before we part, she whispers, "At least find out why she's mad at the dog. For me. I'm begging you."

CHAPTER THIRTY-FIVE

WHAT ABOUT THE DOG?

When Kay rings the doorbell, I'm pulling gingerbread cookies from the oven. The house smells cozy and inviting, and Kay comments on it as soon as she steps inside the door. I reintroduce Toby. He holds out his hand and says "How do you do?" like we practiced.

Kay shakes his hand with mock formality. "How old are you again, little squirt?"

"Almost four."

"Well, I swear you've grown so much, I thought you must be five by now. You look like you're fixin' to start kindergarten."

Toby beams.

"Come on, I have a surprise for you."

She takes Toby by the hand and leads him to her car. From the backseat, she pulls out the crate that holds our new puppy.

Kay looks different than I remember. Of course, the first time we met, she was in her nightgown. Even after her long drive, she looks more pulled together than I expected. She has a wide, square face, with a Dutch jawline and fair, freckled skin. She's short and heavyset, but her legs are muscular and don't have an ounce of fat on them. The backs of her hands are covered in age spots. Her gray fuzzy hair is shorter now, and I notice she's tucked the ends behind her ears. She's wearing shiny pink lip gloss. She must've stopped and freshened up before she got here.

Toby lies on the ground and squeals as the puppy licks his face. He runs in circles on the tile kitchen floor and the dog slips and slides, yapping the whole time, while Kay and I watch.

"What's his name?" Toby asks.

"Let's wait until Daddy gets home to decide. We can just call him Puppy for now." I turn to Kay. "You can stay for dinner, right? Eric will want to meet you."

We take Puppy on a walk, and I show Kay around Oasis Verde. We make small talk about her drive and her antics with the puppy. I tell her I've invited Pa for dinner, which leads to a long conversation about my mom. I take Kay to the urban farm, and on the way back, I introduce her to Mrs. Gilliam and we pet Pickles. Toby shows Kay how to stroke him under the chin.

Kay hasn't said one word about John Robberson, which is a relief in one way and a disappointment in another. It makes it easier for me to insist that she stay with us overnight. I've decided to hold back until she brings it up. When we return to the house, she says she's tired and goes to rest in the guest bedroom. I call Eric and ask him to come home early.

Right before four o'clock, Toby hears the garage-door opener engage and makes a run for it. He flings open Eric's car door, and the puppy leaps right into Eric's lap before he can get out of his car.

"What's his name, Daddy?"

"I don't know yet, Tobe. You'll have to help me think of a name, okay?"

Kay must hear Eric and Toby playing with the puppy in the living room a few minutes later, trying out new names for him.

Eric still has a mustache, trimmed short these days. It's not much more than an extra line of reddish stubble on his top lip. That puppy looks like he's trying to lick it right off Eric's face.

Kay says, "Looks like you two are long-lost pals."

He stands to greet her, pulling the puppy away from his face long enough to say, "He knows he's home. We're trying on some names for him." The puppy licks his open mouth. "What's your name, big guy?"

She says, "His grandpa's name was Duke. But you name him whatever you want."

John's dog, I observe but don't say.

Eric gives Kay a welcome hug. "Thank you for bringing him. I'm glad to finally meet you. I feel like I know you already."

I don't know anyone who would describe my husband as a hugger.

Kay says, "Oh, you're a charmer! I knew I'd like you the minute I saw that mustache. All John's pilot buddies wore mustaches. They thought they were hot stuff." She laughs. "You don't fly planes, do you?"

"No, ma'am, but I wouldn't mind trying my hand at it," he says with a twinkle in his eye.

"Don't put ideas in his head!" I warn, taking her question as a second cue that she's ready to talk about John now after going radio silent with me this afternoon.

Toby takes the puppy into the backyard, jumping and yipping as they go. My hand shakes a little as I pour three glasses of fresh-squeezed lemonade, so I distract Kay by handing her the tray of cookies I baked earlier.

She chuckles at Toby playing with the puppy. "Boys and their dogs."

Okay, that's three. I'm going in.

"Kay. Forgive my curiosity, but I would love to hear what you make of the message Toby gave to you."

"You mean what he said about being mad about the dog?"

"Yes."

"Well, I know what the little squirt was talking about."

"Really?"

Kay looks at me. "Not at first. But I been thinking about it, and I think I figured it out."

I realize I'm holding my breath, so I make a conscious effort to inhale. Exhale. Inhale. Eric reaches for another cookie but doesn't say anything.

Kay brushes her hand through her hair and takes a deep breath. "Well, for it to make sense, I have to start a ways back."

Twenty years back, when John decided to be a firefighter. He'd come back from Vietnam injured, and his recovery had been long and tedious for both of them.

I add, "It's hard. I don't know if I told you, but Eric had a serious accident, and we all suffered together for months."

"She doesn't want to hear about that," Eric says.

"John came home on an honorable discharge, but that didn't mean he could find a job. Not one he wanted, anyway. Some of his buddies signed up to go fly again, but he didn't want anything to do with that. He was lost for a while there. He took odd jobs, worked construction awhile, fiddled with cars, but everything bored him. Then he took to listening to the police scanner late at night. I guess he was trying to find something exciting. Sometimes he'd go out of his way to drive by the spot on the highway where an accident had been. He had bad dreams and woke up mean. He was flat-out restless."

Her words ring true with me. That's what Eric was right after the accident: flat-out restless. It must be a common reaction to a life-changing injury. I never thought about how Eric might share characteristics with soldiers. I always thought his was an easier injury. It's not like someone shot him down out of midair and tried to kill him. It seems that would be different, if you were hurt defending yourself. Getting hurt in an accident, well, that didn't seem as . . . noble. I wonder if John Robberson felt lucky. I wonder if Eric feels lucky—or dumb.

Kay's still talking.

"Next thing I know, he's chasing fires. The local guys—they had his number. Didn't take much to talk him into doing the training and joining the club. So I'm thinking that's good, right, because now he's coming home all tuckered out every day. And finally, he's sleeping. And once he starts sleeping again, he's back to his old self."

Yes. That's right. When Eric started running, he started to sleep differently. As still as a corpse. I remember it. He didn't even move in his sleep. If he fell asleep on his back, he'd wake up on his back. Well, except the nights when he'd sleepwalk.

Kay says, "Our whole life got better after that. Next thing we know, I'm pregnant and now nobody's sleeping again, but we're happy this time. We both got something to do. I got the baby and John's got his fires. Over time, he worked his way up and became the fire chief, about the time JJ was in high school."

"JJ?"

"John Jr. We called him JJ."

Vaughn Redford. What did he say again? I close my eyes until it comes to me.

Let go.

Eric stands up and shoves his hands in his pockets, looking out the window at Toby playing in the backyard. "Just stretching my legs. Don't mind me."

"Anyway," Kay continues, "JJ thought his daddy hung the moon, even though he was gone a lot, putting out fires and saving people. By the time JJ finished high school, John was the fire chief.

JJ took classes at the community college, but it didn't suit him, so after he came back from his stint overseas, he did the training and became a paramedic."

"Saving lives runs in your family," I say, hoping she doesn't elaborate on the "stint overseas." I don't think I could take it.

"I wish staying alive ran in my family."

Nobody knows what to say to that. We all take sips of our lemonade.

Kay says, "See, JJ died on the job. His heart was in the right place; you see a body lying in a house fire, you try to save 'em. They didn't know back then what they was up against. 'Course, that's when John got so interested in catching crank dealers."

"Excuse me?"

"Crank. It's all over the Ozarks." Kay looks at us. "You know. Meth. They hide out there in the hills and cook it themselves. Half the time, they don't know what they're doing and blow their houses up right under their own noses."

"Guess they're not all chemistry teachers first."

"No. It idn't like on TV," she says. "Nowadays, we know all about it, but I'm talking the early days, back when the drugstore wouldn't think twice about selling a hundred packages of cold medicine to any old scroungy rat with rotten teeth. Before the fire crews started telling each other to wear a gas mask if they smell rotten eggs at the scene."

My head jerks toward Eric, but his back is turned.

Kay goes on. "They started seeing bad dogs on chains, guarding empty shacks. The law was catching on, but the tweakers were meaner and stayed one step ahead. Back then, it was a police matter, and John liked it that way."

She takes a quick sip of her lemonade. "All that changed in one day. JJ was out doing his job. He answered a call, saw somebody inside a burning house, and went in to help. When he ran through that door, I guess he didn't think to look for fishing wire stretched across about knee level . . ."

Tears burn down the side of her nose as her gaze intensifies on my patio door. Her finger jerks three times, tracing an invisible set of connections: one, from the bottom third of the door, straight up the door frame, pointing, two, at the ceiling, in the corner, wordless as her finger jolts diagonally, three, accusing a spot on the nearest side wall.

There.

In the silence, I cannot bear to look at the same wall Kay sees right now. Mine is painted a creamy bisque I'd worried looked too dingy.

Eric turns to face us and says, "You don't have to—" but before he can finish, his knee knocks Kay's lemonade off the coffee table. The glass breaks on the hardwood floor just as she swipes her finger in the air.

"Pipe bomb full of nails."

"Oh my God," I gasp, not sure whether to look at her or the broken glass.

Eric doesn't say anything. He's picking up the broken pieces. I hand him a stack of napkins and try to focus on Kay. She turns to me as if Eric has disappeared under an invisibility cloak.

"Caught him full in the face." Kay clears her throat. "He didn't suffer. We couldn't even have an open casket. John never let me see him. You know how hard it is to believe your boy is gone when you can't see it with your own eyes?"

Eric slinks toward the kitchen trash can, never making eye contact. I'm too horrified to move, much less say anything.

"I got to sit with him one last time. John went with me to the funeral home and made sure they kept his body all covered up, but he pulled JJ's hand out from under the sheet. I must've sat there crying and staring at his left hand for an hour before John made me leave."

I have to close my eyes against the image.

When I open them, Eric must've slipped back into the room with a fresh glass of lemonade, because it has magically reappeared on the coffee table and he's standing in the same place, his back turned to us, looking out the patio door.

Kay says, "He was right to do it that way. I needed to know, but some things you can't unsee. I got my pictures and my memories. I can hold my head high. JJ died a man of honor."

I manage to choke out, "Kay. I'm so sorry."

"Me, too, hon. Me, too." She wipes her tears with the back of her hand and says, "Everything happens for a reason, don't it? It was a hard lesson we got handed, but God made sure something good came out of it. That's when John got that training going for all of 'em—police, fire, medical—so they could do their jobs without dying of good intentions."

I say, "John was a man of honor as well. To be able to take his grief and channel it into something that helped others."

"At first, that's what it was—helping other people. But after a while, it was like his new job was running drug dealers out. He was happy to hold his crews back while their houses burned to the ground. Sometimes I wondered if he was a little too happy."

My head is about to burst. Eric still hasn't said a word. His back is still turned to us, his hands jammed deep in his pockets.

"Kay. Thank you for sharing that with us," I say. "You've been through so much, and your family is extraordinary."

"But?" she says, with a weak smile.

"But I have to admit, I'm trying to put this together with Toby's comment. Where does the dog come in?"

"I'm getting to that part," Kay says. "I think I told you John had a thing for Dalmatians. Old Duke rode to work with him every day."

"Yes," I say.

"On the day John died, his crew saw his pickup truck when they pulled up to the fire. They didn't see Duke, so they assumed John was around back. The crew was putting on the hazmat suits when the fire let out a big roar and the back part of the roof collapsed. They went around back and, sure enough, John was lying there on the floor with flames all around him and Duke half burned up at his feet."

Kay hates it when you go back for the dog. Toby's words echo in my head.

"Were you there?" Eric asks, turning around, with almost an accusatory tone to his voice. "Did you see it happen?"

"No, but I can put two and two together," she practically barks at him. "The dog was inside the house. Did you miss that part?"

"You got it all figured out then, don't ya?" Eric turns his back on us. "Excuse me. Nature calls." He strides toward the hallway bathroom.

"Eric!"

He doesn't answer.

"I'm sorry," I whisper to Kay, nodding to Eric's back. "He's not usually like that."

"Men," she says with a roll of her eyes, as he closes the bathroom door. "They're all like that."

"I know, right?" We snicker together, and I feel a little twinge of guilt, like I'm making another one of those doofus husband jokes. I'm glad Eric's gone for a few minutes.

I lean in. "Toby's message missed the point, didn't it? You were mad, just not at the dog."

"Bingo. You know that. I know that. But my bonehead husband don't know that." She laughs. "Funny, idn't it? I didn't put it all together until the little squirt showed up. See, I used to think once you went to heaven, all of a sudden you understand things that never made sense to you on earth. But after what Toby said, now I think that idn't true."

I say, "I'm sorry, I'm not following you."

"Look, you didn't know him, but John was a man's man. Which means he was dense as a fence post.

"Dense as a fence post?" Eric says, returning to the conversation. "I can't leave you girls alone for two minutes."

She snorts. "Did I say *was*? Scratch that—he *is* dense as a fence post. Evidently heaven doesn't fix that."

"What do you mean?"

"After Toby came to see me, I ran into this trainee guy at the grocery store. And I don't know him from Job, but maybe he's trying to make me feel better; he stands there in the potato-chip aisle and tells me how I can't blame John for going in after ole Duke. It just showed how much he loved that dog."

Kay snorts in disgust. "A lot of people said that to me, right after the funeral. They meant well, but it don't change anything. Widow of a dog lover is still a widow. But I can't say that to this dumb kid, so I just stand there and sure enough, he's not done bringing me comfort, so he has to go on about how much he learned from John. Let them tweakers burn, he says to me. They got it coming to 'em for what they did to JJ."

Her whole face twists like she's wringing out a dirty mop. "That's when I dug up the report. There were three bodies in that fire. Two burned up. And John. I cornered his old buddies, but they kept telling me there was nothing he could do about those bodies. He couldn't go in without backup."

She continues, "So I asked them why he didn't have backup. Even I know that idn't procedure. Why's he the only one on the scene?"

"You said he got there early," Eric says.

"Right. Think about it. He got there early enough to know there were people inside." Kay's voice is steely, indignant. "And will somebody please tell me why he idn't in a hazmat suit? If he got there early, he had plenty of time to suit up."

"So?" Eric asks.

"So if he had any intention of going in after them, he'd have suited up." She raises her voice. "But he didn't suit up, did he? No, He didn't even try. He stood there and let them burn."

I'm taken aback by the bitterness in her tone, but I know in my gut she's got it right.

"He wanted revenge," I whisper.

"And revenge turned his heart black," Kay snaps. "Killing them idn't gonna bring JJ back, now, is it?"

"He's not supposed to go in without backup," Eric says, with an edge of irritation in his voice.

"Then why's he going in for his dog? With no backup? Tell me how that makes him a hero. Tell me how a hero cares more about a dog than a human!"

There's no good answer to that question. I scramble around for something, anything to say. "He was grieving. He got confused, right? It's . . . understandable, isn't it?"

"It's hateful," Kay spits. "He's supposed to save people, not let them burn. It doesn't make it better to know the only thing he's sorry about is that his dog got caught in it."

"Oh, Kay."

"I can't unknow what I know. Ever since Toby said that to me, it put me on a path to finding the truth. Worst of all, now I know John still don't think he did anything wrong."

I don't know what to say.

She looks up at the ceiling of the living room and shouts, "Mad at the dog? You know who I'm mad at, you old coot!" Kay keeps looking up, long after she's stopped talking.

The silence is taut, keen, otherworldly. I half expect the TV will turn itself on all of a sudden. Instead, Eric jerks the patio door open with a grunt.

His motion seems to jolt Kay back to reality. She looks around, almost as if she's forgotten I'm in the room with her.

"I'm sorry. I don't know what got into me." She picks up her lemonade glass and takes a big gulp. "I said too much. I don't tell that story back home. The ones who know what John did, they don't see nothing wrong with it. He tried to be good, he really did. Anybody back home will tell you we had a good life together."

"Of course you did."

She looks past me, her eyes focusing on Eric playing with Toby and the puppy in the backyard. "I haven't said enough about that. I don't want you to think poorly of him."

I say, "I think John doesn't want you to think poorly of him."

CHAPTER THIRTY-SIX

BE CRAZY WITH HER

When Eric gets back from his run, he hops in the shower. I hold the shower door open so I can keep my voice down and Kay won't overhear. "Don't you think it's awful that Toby's message made things worse for her? It feels like we've been a party to spoiling her memories. It would be easier for her to grieve, wouldn't it, if she could just remember the good parts?"

So many people do that; it seems like they forget their loved ones had any flaws at all. That's how Pa seems to me. Kay's the opposite.

"Toby didn't make it worse," he assures me as he steps out of the shower.

"She's so bitter. It breaks my heart," I say. "Thirty years together and then she finds out she's been married to a self-appointed vigilante. It's like she didn't know him at all."

"You don't know if he really was a vigilante. Or if she's telling the truth." He towels off. "Maybe she just needs to talk. So we let her talk. As long as you're okay."

"I'm okay. And you're right; she said there's nobody in Branson she can talk to."

I wonder if she feels everyone thinks she's crazy when all she's trying to do is speak the truth. Well, I know how that feels. That must be why she's here. She's counting on us being crazy with her.

Pa's arrival cues Kay to reemerge, all freshened up, like nothing happened. She's wearing soft khakis, a simple mint green T-shirt, and a cross necklace made of turquoise and silver. She's reapplied lip gloss, and her newly fluffed hair is neatly tucked behind her ears.

Pa hasn't gone to quite that much effort, I'm afraid. At least his retirement suit is clean. All he wants to know is what I cooked for dinner. "Pot roast," I tell him. "Now go out there and be nice to my guest."

Toby brings his toy F-105 to the dinner table and shows it to Kay before we even get napkins in our laps. "See? Thud."

"John flew a Thud," Kay says, surprised.

"I know," Toby says, unsurprised.

"Her husband was a fighter pilot in 'Nam," Eric explains to Pa, as if this is news.

Pa whistled. "Fighter pilot, huh? So what's his story?" He looks at me. "All them pilots have one story they tell over and over."

"You know it. Crashed his plane," Kay says. "Some kind of dive-bomb. And he'd go on and on about the bomb not dropping and how smart he was to roll the plane the opposite way."

My leg starts shaking under the table.

"Does that make any sense to you?" she asks. "It never made any sense to me."

Eric practically jumps out of his chair. "Yes! Yes! Because that's the only way it would work."

"You act like somebody's about to drop a bomb on you," Pa chuckles.

Eric sits back down. "It's simple physics, really." And then he goes off on a long, complicated explanation. For a while, Pa tries to keep up with him, but Eric is clearly talking only to Kay. Judging by the look on her face, Eric could burp right now and she'd swear it turned into cotton candy.

"But it didn't work, did it?" Pa asks. "You said he crashed, right?"

"Something went haywire and the cockpit filled up with smoke. He had to eject. Slammed into a tree on the way down and broke his leg."

"Which leg?" Eric asks.

"That's it." I push back my chair, scraping it on the floor. "Everyone ready for coffee?"

As they head to the living room, Eric drops back. He looks at me and winks. "Left leg." He turns with two cups in his hand. "Like in Toby's game."

"What are you doing?" I whisper to his back.

"Playing along, that's all," he says and hands Kay her decaf. "No big deal."

"Really? Because it's starting to sound like a big deal, Eric." He doesn't hear me. I head upstairs to put Toby to bed.

He's still asking questions of Kay, the two of them ignoring Pa altogether. Eric's not playing along. He's mesmerized. After two solid hours of John the Hero Pilot, the fascination factor is way down for me. It's almost as if the Kay who yelled at her dead husband this afternoon bears no relationship to the Kay entertaining my husband tonight.

And worse, the late-night Eric, who's now absorbing John Robberson stories like a kid trying to put his mouth over the end of a fire hose, bears little resemblance to this afternoon's Eric, who seemed on the verge of fact-checking her account of the deaths of her son and husband.

When I return, Kay says, "There she is. Now, let's talk about something else."

"We don't have to," Eric says.

"No, no. I got carried away, remembering the good times. It's nice to talk about something other than fires and choirs."

"Fires and choirs?" I ask.

"That's what John used to say all the time. He put out fires all day and I sang in the choir at our church, so if we talked about our day, that's what it would be. Fires and choirs."

Eric explains to Pa, "He was a fire chief, too."

Pa says to me, "How 'bout that."

I pat him on the knee and snuggle up to him on the sofa.

Eric quizzes Kay about John's training program. They are facing each other in armchairs across the room. Pa begins to slip sideways against my shoulder, so I jostle him and tell him to drive back to his hotel while he's still awake. I wish he were staying here instead of Kay.

Once he's gone, Kay says, "Your daddy's a nice man," as she settles back into her armchair. Eric turns down the TV volume on a late-night talk show and asks about John's crew. She tucks her hair behind her ear as she considers where to start. He leans in, unaware that I've taken my place on the sofa. I stare at the muted celebrity interview on the screen, observing how the deferential gestures of the host seem to trigger a corresponding laugh track that plays live in my living room.

When the band comes on, I yawn conspicuously and wonder aloud about where the puppy should sleep.

"Let's take him to our room," Eric says to me. Turning to Kay, he adds, "Guess we gotta call it a night."

"John used to turn in first, too. 'You coming or what?'" She giggles. "That's what he'd say if I was too slow to follow him. 'You coming or what?' Used to drive me nuts."

Eric helps me move the puppy's crate into our room and heads straight to the bathroom to brush his teeth.

"Are we going to talk about what happened today?"

"It's late, Shel. We've got time." He spits into the sink. "She's staying an extra day."

"What?"

"We decided while you were upstairs with Toby." He leans down to pacify the puppy whining in his crate. "You were right. The best thing we can do is listen, help her remember the good times."

"Is that why you kept encouraging her?"

"Of course."

I take my time brushing my teeth and cleaning my face. The light's off when I crawl into bed. "Are you asleep? Because I really think we need to talk—"

"Hush, woman." He binds his arm around my waist and heaves me underneath him. He buries his face in my neck, resolute. He doesn't even take time to undress. He yanks his boxers halfway down and presses himself on me, insistent and sudden. It's over within two minutes. He doesn't say a word or make eye contact with me. He rolls over and is asleep before I can ask what just happened.

My head is spinning.

CHAPTER THIRTY-SEVEN

CHARMING KAY

Pa heads back to Tucson, Eric goes to work, and I've got to entertain Kay for another day. I call Lakshmi and give her the five-minute recap. It's all I can manage for now.

"I'll tell you every single word she said, I promise. But today, swear to me—no direct questions. Not one."

"Everything okay?"

"Just bring Ms. Pushpa, okay? Meet us in the park. Ten minutes?"

Not only will Ms. Pushpa be a good distraction, I'm curious about how these two will get along.

They're polite, of course. Just like moms of any age, they find the common ground: their kids. I fall under the familiar spell of Ms. Pushpa's voice and can't help smiling at the melodic emphasis on the second syllable of her words, the run-on quality of her sentences.

In her atonal Ozark accent, Kay begins to describe John and JJ's military service. I brace myself the minute she opens her mouth. I just can't run two marathons in a row.

I don't know if Kay has picked up on my story fatigue, but she spares us the details and tells Ms. Pushpa that both men made it through the war but are deceased now.

"Your son, as well?" Ms. Pushpa, a devout pacifist, reaches over and squeezes Kay's hand. "Such a terrible tragedy. You have sacrificed greatly."

The two older women sit together in silence, nodding and holding hands. Even Lakshmi seems to take this at face value.

I'm a horrible person sometimes. Why can't I cut this woman some slack? I have to keep reminding myself of this: Kay is grieving. Somehow, we're a part of her process.

Eric comes home from work early and plays with the puppy on the front porch with Kay while I make a quick run to the Oasis Verde farmers' market. When I return, nobody offers to help unload groceries. I hear snorts and snickers coming from the porch. I haven't seen Eric this animated since Thud died.

When I glance out the window, Kay leans forward and slaps him on the leg. He holds his hand up to the side of his mouth, whispers to her, and sits back with his eyebrow cocked, checking her reaction. I turn back to the groceries and hear another whoop of laughter.

It's good they're getting along so well, I tell myself. I look again, in time to see Kay's awkward attempt to hike up the back of her powder-blue stretch pants, harrumph, and resettle into the patio chair. I have to smile. She's seventy-something. Let her get comfortable.

I know, without voicing it, that there's no way I'd leave my husband out on the porch, laughing with another woman while I'm inside cooking their dinner, if she were young and cute. I clang a couple of pans when I don't really need to and interrupt them a few times, asking Eric to do simple things like put ice in the water glasses and make sure Toby's washed his hands. I know, even as I'm doing it, that I'm being silly.

Eric helps out, laughing and joking all through dinner. Kay is livelier than she was the night before. While the two of them carry on, oblivious to the rest of us, I spend most of dinner either explaining their comments to Toby or encouraging him to eat instead of play with his food. It seems like all I contribute to the conversation are anecdotes about Toby.

I feel completely boring. There's that toxic word again.

When Kay asks how we got to Arizona, Eric tells his go-to story. He was twenty-two years old, still a senior in college, with an offer to come to Phoenix for a job interview. He was so nervous, he gulped down three glasses of water and ended up next to this executive at the urinal. Eric is milking the story for all it's worth, even standing up to demonstrate, as if Kay's never seen a man pee. Only in the story, Eric's too paralyzed to pee and lets out a loud fart instead.

Kay hoots as Eric sits down, hanging his head in mock shame. They are laughing so hard they both have tears sliding down their faces.

It's funny. The first nine hundred times you hear it. I contribute a little *huh-huh* noise to the mix. Kay nods, wiping her eyes, and gives a winding-down laugh, *hoo-hoo*. She takes a big swig of the overly sweetened iced tea I made for her, emptying the glass.

"Let me get you a refill." I leave the table, return with a full glass of tea, pick up Toby, and carry him upstairs for his bath, all without a word or even a glance from either of them.

When we come back down the stairs, I think we surprise Kay and Eric, who are still sitting at the kitchen table, amid the dirty dishes and empty glasses, engrossed in conversation.

"Well, look at you two! Let me get these nasty leftovers out from under your noses." I begin clearing the table, and Kay quickly jumps up and helps. Eric keeps Toby occupied in the living room until we start the dishwasher. I bring in a tray with three cups of decaf and four dark chocolate squares.

Toby, all squeaky clean and in his pajamas, jumps up and down for his chocolate, a treat for him. At first, he wants to share it with the puppy, but Kay invites him to climb up in her lap instead. She points to an airplane on his pj's, and he tells her the right name for it. After he goes through them all twice, she begins to give the airplanes increasingly silly names, like Herbie or Jed or Putter-Poot. He giggles with each one.

She's charmed every man in my family.

CHAPTER THIRTY-EIGHT

I'M RIGHT HERE

I excuse myself to tuck Toby into bed. Kay and Eric's voices fade as I settle in to read Toby's favorite book a second time before he starts to get drowsy. I rub his back and roll the moment around between my thumb and finger, savoring every touch and snuggle. When I hear his breath deepen, I press my lips to his head, inhaling the little-boy scent. My heart is as full as the moon outside Toby's window.

I gently pull his door closed and dawdle in the hallway, preparing for reentry from the lovely quiet cocoon of his bedroom. I hear their voices, low and serious, as I reach the nook at the end of the staircase. I hesitate before I enter the living room when I hear him say, "It's the deepest regret of my life."

I turn my back to the built-in bookshelves near the bottom of the stairs and stand flat against the wall, bare feet on the hardwood floor.

She says, "It's so nice to hear you young fellows talk like that. When JJ was born, John was out in the waiting room, smoking and pacing. Babies were women's work. So if he showed up late, I don't even think I would've noticed."

"Oh, she noticed all right."

"It's different these days. Men and women expect different things than they used to." Kay sighs loudly enough that I can hear it. "But you were late, huh?"

Eric laughs at that and explains that he wasn't simply late; he missed it altogether. He tells her he didn't remember anything about the day and had to piece it together from what others told him later. "The guys I work with told me that all of a sudden, toward the end of the afternoon, I jumped up from my cube, yelled something about having a baby, and all they saw was me running down the stairwell. Then, less than three minutes later, they see me burst back into the work area, rip open my top drawer, throw Post-it notes and a stapler into the air, grab my keys, and sprint to the garage."

Kay giggles.

"And I found out from the doctors, about two days later, that an eighteen-wheeler hit me head-on, and I broke my leg and had some internal bleeding."

I can't make myself walk into the room. I find it interesting what he doesn't say. He never describes the accident as his fault. And that's always how he talks about his injuries: a broken leg and some internal bleeding. That's the dinner-party anecdote version. Not a clue as to the real extent of what happened.

She says, "That sounds pretty bad."

"Well, it was kind of touch-and-go there for a while. I actually died on the gurney in the X-ray room. No pulse, no breath, nothing."

He never talks about that. To anyone. He's got a touch of bravado in his voice, but I hear the confessional tone underneath. He obviously wants her to know this. With difficulty, I swallow the lump in the back of my throat.

"Yep, they split me wide open. You know how on TV, they always use that thing that looks like a reverse bear trap, stick it in the sternum and crack it open?"

"That's not always what they do," Kay says.

"Right." He sounds impressed. "That's what I was going to say. They only do that in surgery. So I don't have one of those scars. Mine is under here," and he picks up his shirt and shows her the scar from the gash under his ribcage.

Long pause. The air goes stale.

"Oh." Her voice is thick and syrupy.

I poke my head around the corner. I see her fuzzy gray hair but not her face. Eric's back is to me. He doesn't speak, but he's still holding his shirt up, high, so his elbows are pointing to the sky.

She clears her throat and asks, "Does it hurt?"

"Not anymore."

"You know, my friend Barbara, she's a nurse, and she told me there weren't too many young men walking around with this kind of scar."

Her words don't match the tightness in her voice. It sounds like she's trying hard to make her vocal chords do something they can't. "Most people with this scar don't live to show it to anyone."

"You okay?" he asks, relaxing his arms a bit.

She closes her eyes. "John had this scar."

No response.

"The EMT did that to him, even before they got to the hospital. He had smoke in his lungs, but one of the boys told me his heart stopped as they were loading him into the ambulance. The EMT was JJ's best friend. Couldn't stand to lose John, too. Cut him open right there, before they pulled away from the scene."

The longer she talks, the lower her voice. "They cut him," she repeats.

"Did you see it?"

"At the hospital. They cleaned him up and had him all tucked in like a baby, but I pulled back the sheets. I had to look at all of him. I don't think it sunk in until I saw that horrible cut, right there, just, just . . ."

In a heavy voice, he says, "Just like this?" and raises his arms again.

She nods slowly but doesn't say anything.

My lurching stomach crashes like the wave of a hurricane, trying to erode the seawall of my stance. I'm afraid to move. I can barely breathe. I can't take my eyes off them. I hear a low noise, almost like a sob.

When Kay asks, "Is it okay?" she's not asking whether the injury has healed yet.

"Sure. Go ahead."

Kay Robberson is feeling Eric's scar, running both her hands from one side of his chest to the other, and swaying her head with the movement. She's almost in a spell, with her hands together and her eyes closed and tears escaping down the lines in her face. She's murmuring something, but I can't make out the words. My eyes lock on them, as if I'm in a trance.

This continues for a full minute, maybe two, with him holding up his shirt and her swaying like that. She ducks her head lower, and I have to stand on my tiptoes to see. The color drains out of the room as her face moves near his scar, with her hands still on his flesh, and she holds her cheek against his chest. I can't see the expression on his face. He bends his head forward, like he's watching, with care, the same way I used to watch Toby while he slept in my arms. He's still holding his shirt up above his nipples, frozen in the pose, elbows still crooked high.

A shudder starts in the back of my neck and snakes its way down my spine. I retreat into the safety of the nook and shake my head until I can see color in the world again—the amber tones of the hardwood floor under my feet, the cinnamon in my toenail polish. Gradually, I regain the sensation of the cool floor on my feet; the reality of my physical position in the world occurs to me like a seeping stain.

There has to be a logical explanation for this. Something I haven't considered. Something I don't know about her. I nod my head slowly, starting to understand. Poor Kay. She's got dementia. Like that rant the other day. I wonder if she even remembers it now. Clearly, she's delusional. Completely disoriented.

Poor Eric. I wonder if he even realizes what's going on. How awkward for him. I don't want to make it worse, but I wish I could give him a heads-up. I hope he tries to bring her out of it without embarrassing her. I'll wait until the moment passes.

I can't stand it. I poke my head around the corner again.

Eric finally lets go of his shirt and takes her head between his big hands, his long fingers in her gray hair, his face close to hers. She's crying now and won't look at him.

It's awful. He's always so uncomfortable when women cry.

"Hey." He says it so intimately that I do a double take. He doesn't sound *uncomfortable*. He doesn't sound one little bit *uncomfortable*.

"Look at me," he tells her, and she moves her head a smidgen. "In the eye."

She balls her hands into fists and starts pounding on his chest. "Why?"

"You know why."

I want to scream, *No she doesn't, Eric. What are you doing to this poor woman?* I lean in to get a better view.

She moves her hands up to her cheeks, on top of his hands, gripping them hard. She slowly shakes her head from side to side, and she's moaning something, but I can't make it out. No? Is she saying no?

He starts nodding, in the same rhythm as her head shaking. "Kay. I'm here. I'm right here."

It's like watching a snake charmer. Bizarre. I've never seen him like this. He's holding her head and won't let her go. They stay like this for a long time. A really long time. He nods, yes, yes, and she's crying and shaking her head, no, no, and he keeps nodding.

I feel as if a sticky spider web has fallen on me, gluing me to my spot, and all I can do is stand there, mesmerized, agreeing with Kay, shaking my head right along with her. No. No. No. Whatever it is, no.

Finally, her head stops shaking. She looks at him, straight on. Her expression is still. Her hands are still gripped tight, on top of his. They're locked together.

I hold my breath. My pulse pounds audibly against my temple, *lub-dub . . . lub-dub . . .*

She blinks her swollen lids. When she speaks, her voice reminds me of an eel emerging from a dark, dim cave.

"Are you . . . ?"

He nods.

". . . John?"

His entire face cracks into a grin. "I'm right here, sugar."

She clasps her hands tighter, still on top of his, on the sides of her face.

"I'm right here." He says it again, with no hesitation. "I'm right here."

She swipes his hands off her face, and for a split second, it almost looks like she's about to kiss him full on the lips, and I can't tell whether I see my husband pull away from her or if I simply absolutely need to see that.

I take a rapid and deliberate step into the living room.

"Eric?"

Before he can answer me, Kay reels and slaps him, open handed, right across the cheek.

CHAPTER THIRTY-NINE

WHAAAAT?

O w!" He's holding the side of his face, turning toward her. "What was that?"

I stride into the middle of the living room, holding my arms out like a traffic cop. "What's going on here?"

"Git!" Kay jumps off the sofa. "You get away from me!" She backs up into the hallway, looking over her shoulder, toward the guest-room door.

He's struggling to stand, but his foot gets caught between the cushions. He finds his footing and takes a step toward her, away from me. "Talk to me!"

She bucks backward and shrieks, "No!" as she runs into the bedroom and slams the door.

I follow her before Eric can go much farther. He obeys my arm signal to halt.

"Kay?" I say into the closed door.

"I shouldn't be here," comes the muffled response. "I shouldn't have come."

I can't tell if she's afraid or pissed or what. Hell, I don't even know what to think or how I feel. I stepped into the living room on sheer instinct—some inexplicable urge to interrupt whatever was passing between them, an unconscious reaction to protect what's mine. Now I'm having the adrenaline shakes. I can't tell if I'm afraid or pissed or what.

I don't know if I should try to talk to her or Eric first. I look over at him. He's not afraid or pissed; he looks like he's just woken up.

I lead him back over to the sofa. "Eric? What happened?"

Suddenly, Kay's door explodes with energy, the doorknob slamming into the wall. "Stay back," she hisses at Eric through clenched teeth. Her suitcase, only half-zipped, knocks over a porcelain lamp that shatters as it hits the hardwood. I hear Toby call out, and I step toward the stairs in case I need to go to him, which means I also step directly in Kay's warpath.

She bumps me, hard, as she jerks past. My head bangs into the corner of the stairway.

"Ow!"

She grunts, throws her arm out like a left hook to reposition the purse sliding off her shoulder, and doesn't slow down.

"Hey!" Eric calls out, reaching for her arm and missing her by a centimeter. "Don't you run out on me!"

She whips open the front door, turns, and spits, "How dare you!"

I reach for the puppy as he bolts past me. Before Eric or I can get to the open front door, we hear the ignition. He calls after her several times before he decides to chase the puppy. I stand in the driveway, watching Kay's escape from Oasis Verde.

I don't know why she came, and I sure as hell don't understand why she's running away now.

Eric returns with the puppy. I have to touch the little guy just to make sure I didn't make it all up. That fifteen pounds of squirmy white fur is the only concrete evidence of Kay's visit. The night air is still, the park empty. It feels like I've just lived an episode of *The Twilight Zone*. Neither of us says anything for a long moment.

"Umm . . ."

"Yeah." He turns and dumps the puppy in my arms. "You stay with Toby."

"What about you?"

Without a word, he makes a beeline for the house, leaving me on the sidewalk. I wait, expecting him to return. Instead, our Prius squeals past me, Eric hunched over the steering wheel, apparently in hot pursuit of Kay. The puppy whimpers and strains to join the chase, his toenails scraping against my belly.

"No!" I clamp him tight against me as I pivot a hard turn toward the still-open front door, determined not to let a puppy get the best of me.

CHAPTER FORTY

WHO ARE YOU RIGHT NOW?

The house looks like thieves have ransacked it. I put the puppy in his crate and start to sweep up the remains of the broken lamp. My heart is pounding in my ears as I bend over to replace the broom and dustpan in the pantry closet. I stare at my sofa, half expecting to find a bloodstain, but all I detect are telltale indentations on the pillows. I place my hand on one, but there's no trace of body heat. Eric's phone is on the coffee table. I have no idea where he is or how long he's been gone or how long he'll be gone. I have no idea what to say to him when he returns.

I turn toward the guest room as if I'm in a trance. I strip the bed and cringe as I collect the bath towel, still damp from Kay's shower. An unfamiliar toothbrush lies askew in my sink. I swipe it into the trash, pick up the linens, and start the washing machine. A shiver runs down my spine, and I stand in the laundry room until I hear the water reach the fill line and the agitator begin to churn. I go to the kitchen and wipe down the countertops until my fingers are sore and the smell of bleach makes me dizzy.

As much as I'm supposed to want Eric to show up and explain it all away, in my gut, I don't want to be here when he comes back.

I'm not sure who's going to show up. I put down my sponge and take the stairs, two at a time, on the way to Toby's room. Just as I'm about to wake him up, I realize Eric has the car. Unless I'm willing to take Toby and carry him—where?—in the middle of the night? No.

I'm stuck here.

That's when I finally start to cry. I back out of Toby's room but stop short of my own bedroom. I end up a crumpled mess in the hallway, trying not to allow full sentences to form in my head. Trying not to admit how scared I am.

I hear the garage door open. I jump to my feet, my back pressed against the wall, my eyes wild. Footsteps in the hallway. On the stairs. He knows exactly where I am.

I dart as far as I can from Toby's room before he sees me. I fumble to find a pose that won't give me away. He's standing right in front of me, still not saying a word.

I choke out, "Did you catch her?"

"No."

"What happened?"

"I don't need you jumping my shit about it. She got away, all right?" He goes into the bedroom—my bedroom—and mutters, "You coming or what?"

My stomach plunges. On sheer instinct, I turn and sprint to Toby's room, my footsteps slapping against the hardwood floor. Before I can get there, my bedroom door seems to explode as the doorknob bangs a hole in the wall.

"Dammit," he bellows, yanking the door free. "Where do you think you're going?"

I whirl toward him and hiss, "Lower your voice."

"Damn, woman. After all I been through today."

I do a double take.

He mocks me with his own double take, complete with a sneer.

I shake my head.

"Quit looking at me like I got two heads. It's just me."

"Is it?"

"What's that supposed to mean?"

"Who are you right now?"

His eyes narrow. He strides toward me. I wish I could suck those words right back down my throat, but there they are, hanging in the air between us like a toxic gas. I step forward so he won't come closer.

"See for yourself. Look at me," he says, his voice eerie and insistent. "Right in the eye."

I can't do it.

A jet stream of fright hits me full-on, square in the sternum, knocking me down, backing me up to Toby's door. One knee slams on the hardwood floor as I twist and bolt upright again. I can't breathe. I pluck Toby out of his bed and hide his face in my shoulder.

I lurch toward my backpack, jam my feet into flip-flops on my way to the garage, and whip open the driver's door to squeeze behind the wheel with Toby writhing in my lap. I start the car over Toby's cries, my headlights glaring at the stranger's shadow haunting the doorway. I push the button to the garage-door opener, and the chainsaw buzzing noise seems an appropriate soundtrack that both echoes and amplifies my fear. The three seconds it takes for the door to open feel like three hours.

Almost as if John Robberson is acknowledging that I finally realize the extent of his invisible influence on my life, he decides to let me go. If he wanted to trap me inside the garage, he could do it with one push of that square white button only inches from his shoulder. If he wanted to burn the house down with me in it, he could've done it. John Robberson has been calling the shots for a long time.

CHAPTER FORTY-ONE

WHAT HAS CHANGED?

I 'm worn out by the time I reach Pa's house. I see the lights flip on. I tell him we need a place to stay tonight, and that's enough for him. He pulls out the sofa bed for Toby. I have nothing with me, no clothes, not even a toothbrush, so he digs around until he finds a new one in a drawer, still in the plastic wrapper from the dentist's office.

He asks if I want him to throw my clothes in the wash while I sleep. I bury my face in his shoulder like I did when I was a little girl. My nose is runny, and he rocks me back and forth while we're still standing.

"All right, baby girl. All right. We'll talk about it in the morning."

On the way to his second bedroom, I ask if he has any sleeping pills. He retrieves a prescription bottle, which alarms me a bit since I was expecting an over-the-counter option. I'm too tired to question it. I take one and lie down to wait for the chemical blanket of drowsiness to envelop my head.

Pa starts the washer. I hear the water rush in, then an electronic chunking sound as the water stops and the agitator begins its work. It makes me think of my mom, who often put in a load of laundry before bed. As I succumb to sleep, I feel a nudge from her, almost a tuck-in.

I sleep late. I hear Toby and Pa making breakfast noises, so I reach for my phone and send Eric a text.

We're at Pa's. Don't call me. I need some time.

My phone rings immediately. I mute the ringer, stare at his picture on my screen. If I don't answer, he's going to ride his bike all the way to Tucson.

"Eric?"

"Shel." He sounds like himself again. Relieved. Worried. Like he misses me. "Are you okay? Toby?"

"We're fine." I pause. "Did you sleep?"

"I must've. When I woke up, it took me awhile to figure out that you were gone. Thought you went out to get breakfast or something."

"Eric. Do you even remember what happened?"

"That's why I wanted to talk to you. When are you coming home? We need to do a serious recap."

"How about you give me what you've got?" I say, still needing to hear him sound like himself again. "You start."

"Sure. Okay." He pauses. "How far back? The first day Toby talked about John Robberson?"

I can't keep from recoiling when he says the name. I get out of bed, trying to find enough space in my head to actually have this conversation. I pace a few steps, then sit on the bench at the end of the bed and close my eyes against the waves of emotion, willing myself to float instead of drown.

"No, Eric, let's jump right to the part where Kay said, 'Are you John?' and you said, 'I'm right here.'" With the phone tucked against my shoulder, I open my palms, holding the question between us, even though he's not in front of me. I'm begging him to attach a rational explanation. "What was *that*? For you, I mean?"

"Can we start at the beginning?" he asks. "It will make more sense, I think."

"Does any of this make sense to you?"

"Let's just try, okay?" He pauses, taking my silence as his answer. "Remember that day? At the Boneyard?"

"Yes." I pull a pillow to my chest. "Well, no, actually, I wasn't there. Remember?"

"Right," Eric says, "Toby was with me. But I didn't know anything had happened. But you picked up on it, Shel. Right away. I tried to tell you it was nothing, but you wouldn't let it go. You knew."

I can hear the smile through the phone lines, like he thinks this is some kind of victory he's conceding.

"You didn't listen."

He lowers his voice. "I know. I'm sorry. I didn't piece it together until Kay got here. Really, not until yesterday."

"Come on. We both know this didn't start yesterday."

"Right," he says, excited. "When did it start?"

I roll my eyes. "You tell me. When did it start? For you?"

"Does March 16, 2010, ring a bell?"

"The day Toby was born? Yeah, Eric, it rings a bell. I was there, remember?"

"I know." There's a long silence before he speaks again. "I wasn't. Remember?"

I swallow my indignation.

"I was gone for eight minutes. I came back," he says, "but I don't think I came back alone."

My chest feels hollow.

He says, quickly, "I didn't realize it at the time. Toby was the first one to know. I think he can see me, or maybe just hear me . . . both ways."

"What are you saying?"

"Shel. You were right all along. Only it's not Toby. It's me. I'm John Robberson."

Certain words, when combined and spoken at a certain time in a certain way, seem to reverberate on a frequency below cognition. That's how this feels. Like someone has hit a gong, and the lowest possible vibration echoes in the chambers of my soul.

"How long have you known?"

"One day." I hear him shuffle the phone from one ear to the other. "All the data was in one place, and just now, boom . . ."

I'm sure he's making a hand motion of some kind.

He continues, "The barrier collapsed. And all this data is falling into place, like the blocks in Tetris, and as soon as it lines up, I get it, and I can make room for the next bit of data coming."

It makes sense. That's exactly how Eric would process it. John Robberson bubbled up on him from a sinkhole he's been vigorously denying. A little too vigorously.

"You should've told me."

"I couldn't tell you something I didn't know," he finally says.

He couldn't know until Kay showed it to him. Kay. Not me. It's stupid, but I feel a pang of jealousy. I swallow the tears and choke back the truth that refuses to be swallowed.

"So which is it? Are you my husband? Or Kay's? You can't be both. That's the rule, right? One soul at a time. So which one am I talking to right now?"

"I'm still me. I didn't go away. The night of the accident . . . I just . . . I don't know—picked him up, like a hitchhiker. Without knowing it. It's more like he jumped into the backseat without my permission."

"And Toby?" I'm sick to my stomach. "What have you been saying to Toby?"

"Nothing."

"Bullshit. He's not making it up. He hears someone talking to him. Whispering."

Eric's voice is deliberate. "If you're going to make me guess—and believe me, it's sheer speculation on my part—I'd say he hears with his heart, not his ears. We'll have to ask him. I would never hurt him. I would never set out to deceive you. I wouldn't do that. You know me."

"But I don't know John!" My heart is thrashing in my chest. "That's my whole point. You've been whispering—or letting him whisper—all along, and you don't even know."

"But I'm not dissociating. I would have gaps. I don't have gaps."

"So you do remember the eight minutes?"

"Okay, I had one gap. But not after that." His voice is deliberate. "Shel, you have to believe me. I did not consciously allow him to communicate with Toby. I never sent Toby any messages—not in my thoughts, not by taking him aside and whispering to him in secret, nothing like that."

"Oh, God. The sleepwalking." I gulp though my sobs. "You do it in your sleep."

We both recognize it, but our reactions are polar opposites. I'm sick to my stomach with shame for not protecting Toby, and he's acting like he won a round of *Jeopardy!*.

"Of course! That's helpful. It makes sense, doesn't it? Think about it as a struggle going on internally, kind of a fight for my consciousness."

"It doesn't make sense. At all."

"Ian's party. I was drunk. My consciousness was altered and all that stuff about the plane came out. That's when he shows up. When I'm sleepwalking. When my guard is down."

"The game," I say, my voice cardboard flat. "You wouldn't stop with the game."

"Now that was weird," he says. "Every time, the details were clearer."

"So you knew *something*." My vision contracts, my line of sight a laser beam of indignation. "You should've said it then."

"I wasn't sure what it meant. If anything. And you were acting so . . . well, I couldn't predict what you'd do. I wanted to figure it out first."

"And you couldn't." My knuckles are white on the edge of the pillow, and my voice crackles with anger. "So you made it about me."

My mind's eye is full of images: the pathetic look on his face as he picked me up at the police station. The sickening tension in his jaw on the ride home, the hardening of his gaze born of a certainty that he'd married an emotional invalid. I remember the genuine shame I felt. The hours of therapy. Those conversations—the painful confessions of all I'd done behind his back, the apologizing.

"What about after Branson? I poured my soul out to you. For weeks. You could've told me then."

"I didn't know what it was! Think about it. Why would I interrupt you, as you're telling me all these things, to tell you about stupid shit that didn't make any sense to me? And okay, I was pissed off. It didn't make any sense. I thought it didn't matter. I thought it was over."

"It matters."

"I'm sorry."

"It's not over."

"I know."

"Aaaargh! I hate this." I drag my hand through my hair. "I don't know what to say. I'm going to need some time, Eric. I'll call you back."

Pa apologizes for his refrigerator contents. He offers to drive me to the grocery store, unaware that it's the very place I first heard John Robberson's name. We push Toby in the cart.

It's the oatmeal cream pies that get to me. I face the packages of baked goods and cry.

As we return, I get stuck behind a hybrid minivan crawling down Pa's street at a snail's pace. As we pass, I see the shadow of a driver peering at mailboxes. The van stops in front of Pa's driveway, and I know who it is even before Lakshmi hops out of the driver's seat and runs to hug me.

"What are you doing here?"

"Would you believe I was in the neighborhood?"

"No. Definitely not."

She hugs Toby, who is disappointed that Sanjay isn't with her. He runs inside.

"Eric called me. He thought maybe you'd want someone to talk to." She looks back at her van. "I brought my mother with me. I hope it's okay."

We open the passenger door. Ms. Pushpa throws her arms in the air in delight, still in her seat belt. She reminds me of Toby in his car seat.

Pa and Toby are putting the groceries away when I bring my guests inside and introduce them. I make coffee for Pa and chai tea (with the tea bags from Lakshmi's purse) for everyone else.

At first, Pa joins us at his kitchen table. The conversation is awkward. Pa and Ms. Pushpa are comically polarized, him in his industrial-gray coveralls and her in a deep burgundy sari with gold threads in the ornate trim. Pa doesn't seem to know where to look. Ms. Pushpa's exposed aging midriff, between the draping folds of her sari, forces his eyes above her waist, but the dark red dot between her eyebrows prevents him from eye contact. I continue to put my father in these painfully unfamiliar situations, and I love him for making the best of it.

He takes a big sip of coffee and says, "First time you've ever been to Tucson?"

"Yes. Yes, it is." Ms. Pushpa smiles at him with passive peacefulness.

She is obviously and patiently waiting for him to go away so the women can talk. Ms. Pushpa isn't rude, but she does nothing to encourage a conversation with him. I've not seen her like this before. Then I realize she's here at Lakshmi's bidding for a specific purpose, and it has nothing to do with Pa. I ask about the banking errand he said he needed to do.

As soon as he and Toby leave the house, I wonder which of us will start. I have a tiny déjà vu moment going back to all those project update meetings I used to facilitate. I glance at Lakshmi, half expecting her to provide handouts.

She says, as if on cue, "Let's get started, shall we?"

Reliving last night's experience isn't difficult until I realize how much I can't really explain. My eyes prickle with involuntary tears.

"Last night, it felt like Eric was gone completely and all that was left was John Robberson. You should've heard the way he talked."

Lakshmi hugs me tighter than we've ever hugged. Ms. Pushpa's tiny hand strokes the back of my head, which is buried in Lakshmi's shoulder. When I pull back, Ms. Pushpa hands me a tissue.

Lakshmi says, "So, what does he have to say for himself?"

I blow my nose. "Today, he sounded like Eric again. He says it was like flipping a switch."

"Flipping a switch?" Lakshmi snorts. "John Robberson's been here a long time."

"But now Eric knows." I sigh. "I thought we were done with John Robberson. But not after Kay. I should've never allowed her to come."

"Ah. Kay." Ms. Pushpa nods. "What do you make of her? Do you think she was aware her husband's spirit was in Arizona before she made the trip from Branson?"

"No way." I shake my head. "She'd never even met Eric."

"What do you make of her reaction?"

"I don't know if she was mad or scared. Or both. The second she found out, she didn't want to have anything to do with Eric. Or John."

"It's too bad." Ms. Pushpa says. "In her spirit, she was compelled to come, but ultimately she could not receive the very thing she sought."

"Closure?"

Ms. Pushpa nods.

"Well, John didn't get his closure, either." I sigh. "You know what I keep turning over and over in my mind? If Eric has been carrying the soul of John Robberson all this time, then which one have I been married to for the past three years?"

Ms. Pushpa speaks up, without hesitation. "Your husband."

"So you think I should turn around, go back home, kiss whoever is inside my husband's body, and pretend nothing happened to his soul?"

She says, "No, no, not at all. What you call a soul, I would call the atman. The spiritual essence of a person, yes? I believe the universe is vast and the atman lives on. It is not for us to attempt to interrupt the karma of another. We must honor the progression of the atman. The soul's journey."

"Eric's journey is getting highjacked. By someone who doesn't want to finish his own journey, evidently."

"The only thing that has changed is that you understand a bit more. So John Robberson has attached himself to Eric—what is the true significance of this? The universe accommodates all. The atman, with all its influences, existed before and will exist again. As will yours. And mine. For this life, in this flesh, he is your husband."

"It feels like I'm married to Kay's husband. Eric has changed. He's a completely different person, not the man I married."

"He was your husband then. He is your husband now." Ms. Pushpa squeezes my hand. "You speak as if he is the only one who has changed. Surely you are not the same. Even a stationary stone over which a river flows changes its shape and texture over time. The river flows differently because the stone is there. Transformation is a part of life. We mature, moving from our childish concerns to our adult responsibilities. We change when we become parents. It's expected that someone might change, like your husband did, after recovering from a near-death experience. I have been fortunate enough to benefit from life experiences, and these have changed me."

I shake my head. "This is different."

"How?"

"There's a difference between normal human development and a third party swooping in and taking over your husband's body."

"Again with the talk of 'taking over the body.' You must open your mind. The soul is not a 'thing' that can be pushed to the side and bullied away."

I don't know what to say.

Lakshmi shakes her head at her mother. "Don't lecture her now. We're not here to make it worse."

"Perhaps there is more to your husband than you can visualize. This is not necessarily a bad thing." Ms. Pushpa intertwines her fingers and gently shakes her clasped hands, as if she were trying her best to sprinkle drops of comprehension in my path.

"Allow it to be a good thing," she whispers.

I bite my tongue. For the first time, I think Ms. Pushpa doesn't know what the hell she's talking about.

CHAPTER FORTY-TWO

LEARNING TO LIVE WITH IT—OR NOT

Not long after Lakshmi and Ms. Pushpa leave, Pa settles into his recliner. He makes sure I see the deliberate flexing of his toes before he says, "Let's hear it, baby girl."

I kiss him right above his crazy eyebrows. He holds my face close to his, and neither of us moves. We are forehead to forehead. I close my eyes and hold the moment. He nods his ancient head, and it feels to me like he understands everything in the world.

I tell him I believe John Robberson is a soul hitchhiker. That he wasn't ready to go. That he somehow latched on to Eric in order to get to Kay so she could forgive him. That Kay resents what she found out after his death.

Pa shakes his head. "Nah. I don't buy it. I met the woman. All she did was brag about her hotshot husband."

"I think she was overcompensating. She told us all this horrible stuff about the way he died, and she was so mad at him. She must've realized she said too much. It's called denial, Pa. I saw both sides of her. She's bitter, trust me. She needs to forgive him." I shake my head. "She can't grieve properly until she does. She's stuck."

"Well, following that line of thinking, I figure you're all stuck." He bobs his head, as if to absorb the weight of his opinion, which has seemingly plunked itself into place. "She's stuck with the truth and she don't like it. John Robberson's stuck to Eric, whether he likes it or not; it's too late to second-guess that one. Eric just figured out he's stuck with this John Robberson fella. So the downside of believing all this, as far as I can tell, is that you're stuck with both of 'em, aren't ya?"

"Unless Kay forgives him. Then she can go on, and it releases him to be in peace."

"You sure about that?"

I sigh. "Not really."

"Well, I'm no expert, but I'd be mighty surprised if it's that easy. The way I figure it, there's only a couple of ways this is gonna go." He counts them off on his fingers. "One, she forgives him. Or not. Two, he goes away. Or not. Which, in my book, baby girl, is none of your business."

"How can you say that? John Robberson made it my business."

"Sorry, baby girl, but you're the one making it your business— which brings me to number three," he says, pulling on his third extended finger. "Once you get one of those 'or nots,' there's only one thing to do. You learn to live with it."

"How can I learn to live with it?"

"*That's* your business. That's what life is all about. Playing the hand you're dealt."

I have to let that one sink in awhile. I bite my tongue for the second time that day.

"You sound like Ms. Pushpa."

"I seriously doubt that."

"It's true. You're saying it in different ways, but ultimately she said I should accept it. And you think I should forget this nonsense.

That it's none of my business. I need to learn to live with it. That's what you said, right?"

He sighs. "I can see that you're gonna do what you're gonna do. Maybe you're right and I'm an old fart. If she forgives him and he goes away, you're done with it."

"And if not?"

"I just hate to see you decide you can't have a happy marriage unless you can fix somebody else's unhappy marriage. Especially since one of 'em is dead and the other one doesn't want anything to do with you. Seems to me it would be easier to figure out how to live with what you've got." He pushes the footrest of his recliner into the upright position. "Now if you'll excuse me, I have to get my beauty sleep."

I grab a light cotton sweater, wander out onto Pa's front porch, and settle into a lawn chair in the night air. I reach for my cell phone. When he answers, I can't tell who it is. It's Eric's voice, but I can't tell which one of them is talking. So I hate it, but I have to ask.

"Eric? Is that you?"

He hesitates. "Yeah. Come on, Shel. I mean, what am I supposed to say? Yeah, it's me."

"This is going to be weird."

"Not unless we make it weird. It is what it is."

"Can we talk?"

We're on the phone for hours. Listening. Explaining. Recapping. Apologizing. Negotiating. No more secrets. Again. By the time we hang up, we have a plan. Core competency of the Buckners? Making a plan and making it work. No matter how ridiculous the problem we're trying to solve. Step one is agreeing on the problem. Step two is agreeing on the goal.

No matter what Ms. Pushpa and Pa say, learning to live with it is not the goal.

CHAPTER FORTY-THREE

PHASE ONE—KAY

E ric and I get right to work. Phase one, step one: contact Kay. In a world where we're all so overconnected, it's amazing how hard it is to reach someone who doesn't want to be reached. Kay's not exactly on Facebook. I leave a message on her home phone, which she doesn't answer. We give it a week before we decide it might work best if I write her a letter.

Dear Kay,
I'm not quite sure what to say about the way our visit ended.

"Don't say that," Eric advises, looking over my shoulder. "I don't think we should mention it. Just write to her like nothing happened."

I reach for another sheet of stationery.

Dear Kay,
Toby loves the puppy. We named him Buster. He's growing like a weed! Already, his legs seem like they're two inches longer than when you were here. His spots are starting to show, too. He's got a

*big one right at the base of his tail. The ones around his face look
like freckles. Here's a picture.*

"That's good," Eric says. "Should I put Toby in the picture? Or
just Buster?"

"Just the dog, I think. I don't know if Toby is a trigger for her.
We don't want to make it worse."

The process of getting a decent picture of a rambunctious puppy
distracts Eric long enough for me to write the rest of the letter in
peace. I won't try to name it, whatever transpired between her and
Eric. I refrain from speculating about John's unfinished business. If
there's one thing I've learned about Kay—and I'm sure she would
deny this—the direct approach absolutely does not work with her.
If we're going to talk again, it's going to be on her terms. All we can
do is extend ourselves. I'm not sure I could hit the right note if I
had to say it, especially not to her face, so I'm grateful for the smoke
screen the letter allows me. No matter how I feel, we have to leave
the door open.

> *I wanted to say I'm sorry for the awkward way our visit ended.
> I understand if you need some space, and I want to make sure you
> know we hold no ill will toward you. I hope you feel the same. Your
> visit affected me (and my family) very deeply. We will never regret
> meeting you or forget your connection to us. We mean no harm.
> Please write to me and at least let me know that you received this
> letter.*
>
> *We consider you a part of our family.*

Maybe I went too far with that one. Even as I write it, I'm convinced she's going to call bullshit on me. But I don't erase it, and I
tell myself it wasn't too much.

Two weeks later, I'm keeping watch on our mailbox as if it's going to vaporize when I'm not looking. Lakshmi catches me checking it one more time on my way to the park. Toby runs ahead of me with Buster on the leash. I wave and join her on the patterned blanket that has absorbed all our park conversations. We sit side by side in the shade.

"Nothing yet?" she asks, watching me cram the junk mail into my tote bag.

I shake my head and watch Buster drag the two boys on laps around the park. "It would be a lot easier if she'd just answer one way or the other. If I knew for sure that she absolutely refuses to allow any contact . . ."

"Um . . ."

"I know, I know. Fourteen empty mailboxes in a row. That's an answer, isn't it?" I bark out a noise that's supposed to sound like a laugh.

"You knew it was a long shot, right? Given what you know about her. She was furious when she left."

"At John?" I ask. "Or Eric?"

"Does it matter?"

"Probably not," I admit. "All that matters is whether or not she can get over it. And it doesn't seem like that's her strong suit." I flop onto my back and pull at my hair, making a face. "Aaack!"

"Momma?" Toby flies his airplane nearer to us.

"I'm okay, baby. Momma's just ripping her hair out, that's all. Go crash your plane."

Lakshmi gives my arm a squeeze.

I sit up and turn toward her, sitting cross-legged. "You're right. I need to face reality. She's not going to write back. Even if I call her every day, she won't answer, and even if she did, she wouldn't let me or Eric anywhere near her."

"I'm sorry," she says. "Are you giving up on phase one?"

"Not unless I have to. There has to be another way to reach her."

"You could go back to Branson."

"Yes. We know how well that worked out last time."

"What are you going to do?"

"I'm not sure. We can't force it. She needs to be receptive in order for this to work."

———

As we return home from the park, we wave as Eric turns off the mower to greet us. Toby wedges himself between us, holding our hands, begging us to swing him. One, two, three, whee!

Eric beelines for the refrigerator and tosses me a bottle of water while Toby goes upstairs to play. Eric glugs his entire bottle without taking a breath. When he's finished, he gives me a big "aaah!" like Toby.

"You know, we could call her church. Maybe tell her pastor that we need to talk to her."

Eric's face contorts, like he just licked a lemon.

"Think about it," I say. "We could tell him we're trying to make amends. Convince him that she needs to hear us out. To give us peace in our souls."

He says, "You're working on the assumption that he knows. What if she hasn't told him anything about us? Then we've created a problem for her, and she'll have to explain it. Or lie. Either way, it's not going to make her want to talk to us."

"Do you think she's told anyone?"

"I don't know," he says, on his way to take a shower. "I'm not clairvoyant. Your guess is as good as mine."

"Well, not really," I mutter under my breath. John Robberson knows whether or not Kay would tell her pastor. He probably knows the best way to get her to talk to us. But the more we bring John to the surface, the higher the risk that Eric fades away. That's a risk I'm not willing to take if there's any other way.

One of my conditions, as we'd determined our strategy, was that we'd set limits. No matter how much mental shuffling I manage, I still don't want to be married to John Robberson. I want to be married to Eric.

After much discussion, and after Eric spent two days poring over all those lists I'd made back when I was observing Toby, he saw the pattern: John Robberson was only strong enough to appear when Eric was in a reduced state of consciousness. So we agreed that the best way to control John's appearances was to shut off those avenues.

So Eric doesn't drink anymore. I joined him out of the same compassion he showed me when I was pregnant. We don't really miss it. Sure, it might be nice to have a cold beer on a hot day, but it's easier to not have it in the house. We weren't everyday wine-with-dinner kind of people anyway. Binge drinking just doesn't hold the appeal it did in college.

We lock the bedroom door, and I keep the key. No more sleep-walking chats with Toby. We both agree Toby has to be protected. We're not taking any chances.

The first rule about John Robberson is that we don't talk about John Robberson. Eric doesn't want this to become a dinner-party anecdote, the interesting thing about us that others discuss among themselves. He believes it would damage his reputation at work and make him the object of ridicule. He thinks it makes him sound stupid.

The fact that it's true doesn't make it easier. For Eric, it actually makes it harder.

I think he doesn't want to talk about it because it makes him vulnerable. The unimaginable has happened. We don't have a way to talk about that in our culture.

So we set limits. He's been even more diligent than I expected. After he read about the effect of music on brain waves, he made one more change. When he runs, now he listens to a book or podcast instead of music. He doesn't like it as much, but we agreed it's best to keep his cognitive functions alert. When he finishes his run, he calls me and I try to talk him out of his jelly doughnut cravings, like an AA sponsor.

That's right. Jelly doughnuts.

We've been piecing it all together—all the unconscious influences. Naming the dog Thud, getting a Dalmatian in the first place, the mustache, all that flight jargon, the bomb story, even the CPR on Toby—we think all these came from John Robberson. But when Eric told me about jelly doughnuts, it knocked the wind out of me.

We've always been in complete agreement about food—organic, whole grains, nonprocessed, no chemicals. Nothing fried. Ever. I've never nagged him like I do Pa; I don't have to. If anything, he's more adamant about it than I am.

Every day since he started walking again, he's made his way to Sunshine Doughnuts to purchase and consume not one but two jelly doughnuts. He's been covering it up the whole time.

He says, "I finally understand food addiction. I'm powerless. One is not enough; it has to be two. And not the regular glazed kind; they have to be the kind with gooey stuff in the middle."

"Yuck!"

"I know! I feel like shit and keep going back for more. I crash, like, within twenty minutes." He laughs. "The guys in my group tell me they think I'm sneaking a smoke because I go outside and walk around the building every day now at the same time. Why do you think I'm running so much?"

"I had no idea."

"Hey," he says, "do you think it's like the people who get transplants and start craving the food their heart donor wanted? Maybe this is my version of the oatmeal cream pie."

CHAPTER FORTY-FOUR

HONEY SWEET

Since I've had eggplant coming out my ears, I'm baking a gigantic vegetarian casserole. We've invited Ian and Mamie, Lakshmi and Nikhil, and Carla and her (surprise!) fiancé, Steve. It's the first time we've met him. This is the same guy she was moaning about at Ian's party. He used to be her client. He also used to be married. As of last month, he's neither. They've known each other for two years, but they've only officially dated for thirty days. Thirty. Three-zero.

"I'm happy," she tells me. "So be happy with me."

Maybe there was a time when I'd try to tell her what to do with her life, but I'm waaay past that now.

It's the first time we've tried to integrate our Oasis Verde friends with our old crowd. I know Lakshmi and Nik don't seem to go out much, so I want to make sure she's comfortable. I'm not sure anything is going to make Nik comfortable, so I can't worry about that. At least I know he likes eggplant.

It's also the first time we've entertained since we found out the truth about John Robberson.

"Want me to set out a wine glass for you?"

"Sure," Eric says. "I'll fill it with water; nobody will notice. But you go ahead and have a glass so it's not so conspicuous."

"I think Steve is the only one who doesn't know. I'm not sure how much Carla's told him."

"Ian and Mamie don't know," he says. "Unless you've spoken to them."

"Not about this."

"About any of it? Shel, I can't have him even joking about it. Ian knows some of the guys at work."

"I know. I haven't said anything," I say. "Lakshmi and Nik won't say anything."

"Think it will be okay to put some music on?" he asks.

"Eric. Of course." I turn to fold napkins. "You're doing fine. I don't think a little background music is going to be enough to give him the upper hand."

Carla's early and doesn't ring the doorbell; she just "yoo-hoo"s to get the party started. Right behind her, Steve shows up with two bottles of wine—in each hand. He's gracious and almost embarrassingly glad to meet us, but I get the impression he's a little . . . disappointed, maybe, that we don't have two wine glasses at each place setting and two more available for backup tastings. I've got four red glasses and four whites, total, and every one of them is on the table.

"No way I'm getting away with water tonight," Eric whispers.

"It'll be fine," I assure him.

The sauvignon blanc is divine. Carla and I take ours into the kitchen and finish the salads. She's planning her wedding even though they're eloping. They're getting married on a beach in Cabo San Lucas next weekend.

"You mean eight days from now?"

Eric comes in with one arm around Steve and raises his glass. "Here's to beach weddings!"

Ian and Mamie show up next, straight from a friend's gallery showing. When Lakshmi and Nik arrive, Carla and Steve share their news, which kicks off a long discussion about weddings that lasts until well after we're at the dinner table. Lakshmi's wedding ceremony lasted three days. I would've loved to see it: the henna hands, the opulent saris, the rituals, especially when they put rice on each other's heads.

"What were your vows?" Carla asks. "We're debating between writing our own and saying the traditional 'to have and to hold' thing to each other."

Eric and I opted for the traditional vows, mostly because I didn't have much confidence that I could come up with something more meaningful. I didn't want to look back and realize my most sacred pact on earth was based on some lame, sappy song lyric.

"They're based on the Seven Steps," Lakshmi explains. "Not everyone has the same vows. We stayed pretty close to the Hindu ritual. The steps are: healthy living, spirituality, wealth, trust, fertility, longevity, and lifelong partnership." She counts them off on her fingers and looks over at Nik. "Am I missing one?"

Nik's expression breaks into a true, clear smile that I haven't seen before on his face. He picks up his glass and lifts it to Lakshmi. His voice has just the right measure of Ms. Pushpa's sing-song accent.

"May the night be honey-sweet for us. May the morning be honey-sweet for us. May the earth be honey-sweet for us and the heavens be honey-sweet for us. May the plants be honey-sweet for us; may the sun be all honey for us; may the cows yield us honey-sweet milk. As the heavens are stable, as the earth is stable, as the mountains are stable, as the whole universe is stable, so may our unions be permanently settled."

His words hang over the table like fireflies. Mamie grasps Ian's forearm and squeezes it. The music from the stereo picks up where our voices left off. Bluesy tones from a saxophone fill the air, making

Nik's glass, which remains in the air, seem like an invitation for his wife to join him in his memory. She lowers her eyes and nods before her glass meets his, with a faint clink that feels like a kiss. The rest of us are holding our breath.

"Honey-sweet," Steve whispers, raising his glass.

"I feel sorry for you, buddy," Ian says, "because that, my friend, is a freaking hard act to follow."

"It is," Lakshmi agrees, when the laughter dies down. "But did you notice what is not included in those vows?"

We shake our heads.

"Love. We never look each other in the eye and promise to love each other unconditionally forever."

"You're kidding," Carla says. "What about the 'I cannot live without you' part?"

"Even better, the 'you will not live without me' part," Ian laughs. "Is that the most elegant veiled threat you've ever heard?"

"Are you the most cynical person I've ever met?" Carla asks, before turning back to Lakshmi. "Why is there no promise to love? Does that bother you?"

"Not really. Don't you think everyone's marriage would be a little better if they simply agreed to live cooperatively with each other?" Lakshmi says.

"Of course, but isn't that implied when you love someone?" Mamie asks. "Isn't it just a different way to say the same thing?"

"Let me put it this way: if you couldn't have both, which would you want? Living peacefully together, or being 'in love'?" She uses air quotes.

"What's the matter? Don't you believe in being 'in love'?" Steve asks, mimicking her air quotes.

"It's just not enough."

"Well, I'll give you that one," Steve says, "but it's also not enough to just peacefully coexist. I had that—for eighteen years.

But I don't think we were ever in love with each other. Whatever we had, it fizzled, even before I walked down that aisle. She's a decent person, a good mom. She had her interests and I had mine. We pulled our weight. But at the end of the day, we built two parallel lives. It was fine. Just fine." Steve pauses and takes a sip of his wine. "I got so fucking sick of being fine. I was like a hollowed-out tree in the middle of the forest. The only reason I was still vertical was that the branches of the other trees kept me from falling over."

"Hollow is the right word. You should've seen him," Carla says. "Poor guy. The first time I took him to lunch, he told me he'd rather eat than have sex."

"Now that's just sad," Ian says.

"That's also no longer true," Steve answers with one eyebrow raised. "No offense to your eggplant, Shelly."

Eric hasn't said a word during this whole conversation. He's a checked-out, edited-down version of himself. He's one step away from hollow. Honey-sweet isn't really an option for us, as long as John Robberson's hanging on.

"It's time for phase two," I tell him as I wipe down the kitchen sink after everyone is gone.

"You make the arrangements. I'll show up," he says, tucking me under his arm as he flips off the kitchen light.

CHAPTER FORTY-FIVE

PHASE TWO—JOHN

I recognize the sign from that handcrafted business card as we enter the coffee shop Wendy recommended. We enjoy our coffee, read the paper, and refuse to speculate about what the next hour holds. It's going to mean everything—or nothing.

Right on time, a fit middle-aged woman in loose clothing comes to our table, discreetly introduces herself, and invites us to her office. We take our places on a burgundy tweed loveseat across from her floral armchair. She's got nurse's hands—short nails, thick palms—hands that look like they could hold you if you fell. She offers me an herbal tea but recommends that Eric refrain until the session is over. Between sips, she begins talking about releasing spirit attachments and allowing them to continue their journey to the light. After all we've been through, it shouldn't seem this silly, but I can't help smiling. Look at us. We're in Woo-Woo Central, and Eric doesn't even wince—maybe because it looks more like a therapist's office than a séance den. It gets serious when we actually write her a check. She gives us a receipt, takes out a legal pad, and asks us to start at the beginning.

It would take too long to tell her everything we know about John Robberson, so we focus on the unfinished business he has with Kay. She doesn't interrupt or ask questions. She doesn't even raise an eyebrow at anything we say, which is oddly validating. When our words stop falling into her lap in a jumble, she says, "I think I have enough to begin."

I don't see how she can have enough information, but I've never done this before. I can't shake the impression that her certainty is a cover for her flakiness. I'm going to be really sad if I smell Thud at any point in this process.

We follow her to a second room, which is noticeably warmer. "Hypnosis and shivers don't go together," she jokes. Eric and I emit an identical nervous twittery chirpy noise, which makes us laugh—which works out because she thinks we're laughing at her little joke. He gives me a hug and tucks my shoulder into that space under his arm where we fit together.

There's a large mocha-colored recliner in the center of the room. He settles in as she dims the lamp nearest him and takes her place in a gray swivel chair, the kind I had in my cubicle at work. She has the legal pad in her lap. I stand on the other side of the chair, holding his hand as long as she'll allow it. I have a tiny flashback to when Eric's hip pins were taken out. I stood by his side and felt exactly like this as I watched the anesthesiologist start the IV and ask Eric to count backward from a hundred. Helpless and hopeful at the same time.

Only this time she's the one counting. Eric's eyes are closed. I take a seat and place the noise-canceling headset over my ears; it's a precaution necessary to keep me from being hypnotized as well. As a result, I can't make out the words, only a monotone hum. Several minutes pass. My dulled auditory function sends my eyes scanning for clues. She's facing Eric, so I see the back of her head, the curve of her shoulders, the texture of her ribbed cotton knit jacket. I'm directly across the room, so I have an unobstructed view of his lanky body stretched out on the recliner, footrest up, arms extended, head tilted back slightly. He looks a little . . . deliberate, maybe, in his relaxation.

The hum continues at a plodding pace. What's designed to help him relax seems to have the opposite effect on me. I fidget in my chair as discreetly as possible, watching Eric the whole time. His expression is softer now. Slow. Hum. Breathe. Deep.

His left leg twitches and his chin jerks in response, which reminds me of little Buster, letting out puppy yips while chasing squirrels in his sleep. I nod approvingly. It can't be much longer until she gives me the signal.

Eric's eyes flash open and he says . . . something. I rip off the headphones.

"It's not working," he says, sitting up. "I'm just pretending to be asleep. I'm fully aware of my surroundings."

In a soothing monotone that's not much different from the headphone hum, she reminds him that the hypnotic induction phase is gradual. His awareness of surroundings does not negate the effect. She suggests that he interpret any ambient noises as confirmation that he is safe. She asks him to close his eyes and starts over. At the beginning. I replace my headphones and try to find a comfortable position in the musty upholstered armchair in the corner, a little more helpless and a little less hopeful now.

Finally, his head lags, ever so slightly, and the hypnotist holds a Ping-Pong paddle up past her shoulder, our agreed-upon signal that I can remove my headphones.

She requests permission from Eric's higher self to scan his body for additional spirits. I suppose he's hypnotized at this point, but when he agrees, the "yes" sounds like it comes from his regular voice, so I'm not sure. He opens his eyes, then closes them without her direction. I suppose that's how a person starts scanning for extra spirits. It seems like he knew exactly what to do. We sit in silence and wait. I hold my breath, counting, *one Mississippi, two Mississippi.* I have to breathe before I see any movement or change in his expression. At *thirty-four Mississippi,* he scratches his nose.

I'm not so sure about this.

Finally the hypnotist asks what he finds. He doesn't open his eyes, but he reports, in his regular voice, a darkness in his solar plexus. She calls forth the spirit and asks it to speak through Eric without harming him, to identify itself.

I'm not supposed to be surprised when John Robberson begins to speak, but I get chills when I hear the familiar change in Eric's tone. Not that he has some crazy demon voice, but the effect is just as scary—and strangely incongruent with what I see. Eric looks like he's asleep in the recliner, but the longer he talks, the more I think he should be pacing the room and waving his arms around for emphasis.

That part doesn't seem to surprise the hypnotist. I wonder if anything surprises her.

She asks in that low monotone, "What happened to your body?"

"Well, I sure as hell didn't run into a burning meth lab with no backup."

I jolt upright and stare at him. Eric's face looks like a cross between a swagger smirk and a chin jut, but his body is still stretched out on the recliner as if he's lying on a beach.

"What happened to your body?"

"They threw us both in and left us for dead. I didn't go *in* for the dog. I was trying to get *out* with the damn dog."

Wait. What?

If I had an air horn, I would honk it right now, just to stop everything. Punctuate the moment. I want time to freeze everybody in the room except me, so I can get up out of this stupid chair in the corner and pace in a circle until I know what the next question should be. I've got a whole list: Who is "they?" What about the other bodies? Were they already dead when you got there? Or did you stand by and let them burn? When did "they" show up? Before or after the fire started? Does Kay need to forgive you, or do you just need a chance to set the record straight? Are you even telling the truth right now?

None of these questions are asked. She doesn't understand enough to know what she should ask. I'm annoyed that I didn't insist on giving her more details while I had the chance. I hope she doesn't blow it.

The hypnotist doesn't miss a beat. She doesn't even act like she heard him.

"What happened to your body?"

"I woulda been fine if the roof had held."

"What happened to your body?" she intones once again, annoying me further. I'm not supposed to say anything, so I bite my lip.

"I'm telling you! The roof gave way. The smoke got me. What else do you need to know?"

I want to raise my hand like an overeager kindergartner, but I'm stuck with this woman who clearly wasn't even listening in our prep session or she'd know what to ask. It matters whether or not John Robberson was an arsonist, like Kay thinks. Or the victim of a crime, the way he's making it sound now.

"What was the last thing you saw while still in your body?" she asks.

"I don't know. Everything went dark."

"What did you do then? Where did you go?"

He's slower to respond this time. The swagger smirk fades. "I woke up and bumped into this guy who looked like he was going somewhere. I grabbed a hold and followed him."

No. It can't be that random. It just can't. I can barely stay in my chair.

The hypnotist clarifies the point. "That guy was Eric."

He shrugs.

The energy in the air changes, almost as if we just walked into a different room. I'm still trying to catch my breath. I want her to slow down. It feels like it took us a long time to get here and she's just racing around, like a grocery shopper cramming things into her cart so she can run to the checkout counter. *Ask him*, I want to say. *Ask him why. Why Eric?* But no, she's on to the next thing.

"Are you aware you are attached to Eric now?"

"Sure."

"Are you aware that you are causing a detriment to Eric and his family?"

"No. I ain't hurting nobody."

My eyebrows rise into my hairline, but before I can even formulate the words, she's on to the next question.

"Are you aware you are holding back your own spiritual development?"

"I don't know about that." He's still sprawled out on the recliner, and his arms haven't even left the armrest.

"Let me put it another way. If you knew you were causing a detriment to Eric and blocking your own path, how would you feel about that?"

"I don't see how it matters."

"What if I told you there is a better place to attach, a place for us to go when our body dies? It is preferable to staying attached to Eric, in every way. In this place you grow and learn and eventually come back in a new body of your own."

"It idn't up to me, as far as I can tell." He snorts. "I tried. She don't wanna hear it."

"Who?"

"Kay. She got it wrong but she idn't gonna listen now."

"We're all listening," the hypnotist volunteers, a bit too eagerly.

Silence. Almost as if the line dropped, she can't get another word out of Eric. Or John Robberson.

No, no, no . . . this can't be the end of it. Her back is toward me, so I can't tell if she's as concerned as she needs to be. She certainly doesn't give herself time to contemplate. She asks the wrong questions again and again, with the now-grating monotone, seemingly undeterred by the excruciating silence each time.

"What does she have wrong?"

Silence.

"This is your opportunity to set the record straight. What do you want to express?"

Silence.

"What is the message that's blocking your path?"

Silence.

I feel a nudge and it's just enough. I can't sit here in my corner any longer. I know what to do. I slide off my chair and creep up behind her, until I'm close enough to whisper. "Ask him if he'll talk to me."

She ducks her chin and whispers, "That's not how it's done."

I say, loud enough for him to hear, "Tell him I have a message from JJ."

His eyes flip open and he bolts upright in the recliner, body cocked like a pistol. His gaze, flat and vacant, bores past the hypnotist like she's a glass windowpane.

"JJ?"

"Yes!"

The hypnotist holds her arm, outstretched, in front of my face, her hand obscuring my view, breaking my eye contact with him.

"What about JJ?" he asks.

I push her arm away and take a wide step in front of her, using my butt to block her access. My sudden movement causes him to flinch backward in his chair. He looks down at his chest and starts to shake his head.

"You don't know what you're doing," she says, her voice trembling but, amazingly, still maintaining a semblance of that soothing monotone. "You're going to lose him."

"Help me, then," I whisper, under my armpit.

She stands up between us, then reaches out to Eric and places her hands on his eyes to close them, the way people do with a corpse. He lies back against the recliner and she murmurs to him until he's relaxed again.

She says, "There is a message from JJ. Do you want to hear this message?"

"What do you think?" His eyes are closed, but that energy is back in his voice.

She opens her thick palm and steps back to allow me to speak. She whispers, "Get down to eye level."

I squat next to the recliner.

"Here." She gives me the chair and pulls up a footstool for herself. She murmurs in my ear, "Slow voice. Low. Nothing sudden. No sharps. Don't touch him."

She says, "I'm inviting Shelly to interact with you now."

"Yeah, yeah."

My heart is in my throat, but I've never been so certain about what is expected of me. What he needs from me. What could happen now.

"I'll tell you what JJ said. It's important. But first, you have to listen to what I have to say."

That snarky smirk is back on his face. "Fine," he says, and turns his gaze toward me, opening Eric's eyes, not seeing me at all.

It's so clear to me. I can tell the difference. I feel like I just swallowed a superhero pill. I can do this. I set my lips in a tight line.

"Fine? That's how you're going to play this?" I swivel in the chair, away from him, and say to the hypnotist, "I think we can stop the session now."

She startles. "Are you sure?"

I keep my back turned to him but speak loudly. "He needs to hear this more than I need to say it."

"Dammit."

I swivel until I'm facing him again. He closes his eyes and leans back in the recliner. "You win," he says.

I can hardly believe this is happening. My mouth is dry and I have a million questions, but I'm laser-clear in my heart. "John Robberson, you're in the wrong place and we both know it. You need to explain yourself to Kay, and you can't get to her because you're attached to Eric. Am I right?"

"Except she won't listen so it don't matter."

"It matters. You know it matters." I lean in, soften my tone. "Or you wouldn't try so hard to communicate with her. Am I right?"

"Suppose so."

"So there's a part of me that can understand how much you need to be heard. I want you to know that." I pause. "Toby tried. He really did."

"He messed it all up. That's why she's got it wrong now."

"See, when you say things like that, then there's this other part of me . . ." and I have to swallow to keep from screaming, ". . . that thinks you should know better." I pause, breathe through my nose, rise from the swivel chair, and put my mouth one inch from his ear, careful not to touch him. "Toby is an innocent little boy." The rest of it comes out low, through my clenched teeth. "How dare you ask this of him? Listen to me, John Robberson. You. Leave. My. Kid. Alone. Got it?"

"Got it," he whispers.

"If you do that," I say, my heart still banging in my ears, "if I ever get the chance, I will try to get you in front of Kay. But I am not spending my life chasing down your shit, so you have to come to terms with that. And when it comes to my family, you have to Back. The. Fuck. Off."

"Got it."

"Say it."

"Okay."

"Okay." My heart is pumping like a piston in my chest. "Give me a minute." I have to shake the adrenaline out of my system, so I walk to the other side of the room, jump in place, flick my hands, exhale hard a few times, and nod to the hypnotist, who watches the entire episode without comment.

"Thank you," I whisper to her as I return to the chair. "Is he still there?"

She nods.

"Now, if you're ready to hear it, I'll tell you about JJ."

"I'm ready," he says.

"I'm not going to get into how it happened, and I didn't even know who JJ was, or what it meant when I heard it, but here it is." I pause. "JJ says let go."

No response.

"Let go. That's what he said. Just like that: let go."

In a low voice, as low as the murmur that brought him forth, he says, "Let go of what?"

Of all the things he could've said, that was the worst option. *Eric*, I want to say. *Let go of my husband. Let go of my son.*

My eyes fill with tears, and my throat feels like I've swallowed a bee. Every thought stings deeper than the last. There's so much letting go that needs to happen.

Let go of your pride. Let go of trying to clear your name. Let go of your pain. Let go of your need for revenge. Let go of your fear. Let go of your refusal to let the truth be the truth. Let go of everything you think you can control and see what happens.

Finally, I find my voice. "He just said let go. That's all I know." I step back, find my chair in the corner, and let the hypnotist finish the session.

CHAPTER FORTY-SIX

ALL TOGETHER NOW

Eric doesn't remember anything, so I'm glad the hypnotist gave us the audio file. Sharing a set of headphones plugged into his laptop, we listen to the entire session that night, legs under the covers, leaning against propped pillows. When it's finished, Eric closes the lid and folds the headphones in a neat symmetrical coil before he says anything.

"He wasn't a vigilante."

"He's telling the truth?"

"I think so," Eric says. "It feels like the truth."

"Since when do you rely on your feelings?" We both snicker at that one.

"Since when did you become such a freaking ballbuster?" He imitates my voice on the tape. "Back. The. Fuck. Off."

We dissolve in laughter. When we catch our breath, he says, "We really need to contact Kay. Tell her the truth."

"Oh, Eric." The minute he says her name, it feels like a boulder rolled onto my chest. "And then what?"

"Then he goes away."

"We don't know that." I try to sigh, but I still have that boulder on my chest. "We don't know how this works. Nobody does. We're right back where we started."

"We're not," he says, taking my hand in his. "We're together now."

CHAPTER FORTY-SEVEN

COSMIC RESPONSIBILITY

I t's been three months since that session. The John Robberson phase of Toby's life has passed, just like all those books said it would. He put his airplanes away. We don't talk about broken legs and dogs in fires. He and Sanjay play soccer now on a little pee-wee team. Several times a week, Eric comes home from work and plays slow-motion goalie with them.

We haven't heard a word from Kay. Not that I expected we would, but a lack of closure is a bit like a loose string on your sweater. You know you're not supposed to pull it, but it's right there.

Lakshmi is still convinced that if Kay heard the whole story, the stars would align, some cosmic shift would occur, and John Robberson's spirit would be magically released. And furthermore, if that happened, Eric would undergo a personality change, and any complaints I've ever had about our marriage would disappear.

"Do you hear me complaining?" I ask.

Eric and I made a new rule when it comes to our friends. We talk to each other first. So if we have a disagreement, I can't go running to my girlfriends to vent. Anna calls it triangulating, when you invite a third party into your relationship.

So maybe we're overreacting, but given what we've been through, Eric and I decide to implement this rule. Neither of us confides in anyone else until we've talked it out and come to some resolution. We have to agree on our story before we tell it to anyone else. It sounds like a little thing, but it took a lot of conscious effort on my part. Especially at first. I didn't realize how much I'd relied on Lakshmi and Carla to help me make up my mind about how I felt about Eric. But now, I have to work it out with him.

When the conflict is over, we can tell our friends about it. But nobody gets the chance to come between us anymore.

Well. We're not counting John Robberson. We're learning to live with him. With all the unknowns. Eric practices mindfulness. I don't know if he's so present there's no room for John Robberson to show up or if after that session the old guy listened to me and backed off. Or maybe he listened to JJ and finally let go.

I've made my peace. After the session with the hypnotist, I thought a lot about why John Robberson latched on to Eric. Maybe it was nothing more than random timing: the eight minutes Eric's soul was vulnerable coincided with the time John Robberson's soul left his body.

I have no idea how a soul gets from Branson, Missouri, to our little Oasis Verde. Surely there were lots of other souls departing during those same eight minutes. Other near-death experiences. Coma patients. Babies being born. I can almost picture this autobahn of souls, running right over our heads, jammed with traffic, zipping around with no speed limit.

Why Eric?

I have no idea. I don't know why he came, and I wouldn't presume to know when he should leave. If it's part of Eric's soul's journey to pick up a hitchhiker, then we'll just have to make room for him.

When I look into my husband's eyes, I don't see John Robberson. I see Eric in a different way. It feels like I'm looking back seventy-five years, maybe longer. I wonder if he sees years and years past in my eyes.

If it could be true for Eric, it could be true for me. Who knows who we were, or who we'll become? All we can do is take what we know and make the most of it. Now that we know that Eric is/was John Robberson, what difference does it make, really? Do we have a different cosmic responsibility than anyone else on the planet?

Well, in one way, I think we do.

CHAPTER FORTY-EIGHT

NEXT OF KIN

Right after Thanksgiving, my phone rings in my purse, which is on the other side of the room where I've been painting leaves with Toby. I have red and purple water-soluble paint on my fingers and, knowing I can get the resulting stain out, I wipe them on my jeans before digging into the small side compartment that holds my phone.

I don't check the caller number. I'm too busy giving Toby instructions to finish the leaf he's on and assuring him I'll be right back. I lurch a hello at whoever is calling.

"Mrs. Buckner? Shelly Buckner?"

"Yes, this is she."

"This is Patricia Fenton. I'm a social worker at Skaggs Regional Medical Center in Branson, Missouri, and I'm calling at the request of Kay Robberson."

Kay's name is like an electric shock to my system.

"Yes!" Walking out onto the patio with my phone, I ask, "Is she okay?" I wave Toby to the backyard. He scampers out, wiping his painted fingers on his shirt.

Ms. Fenton explains that Kay has had an accident. While she was attempting to hang her Christmas lights, her ladder tipped and she went down hard, and she was admitted at the hospital last night with a broken hip. One detail makes me sit down on my patio and swallow hard: Kay had to crawl inside to reach her telephone to call nine-one-one. Ms. Fenton estimates that, judging by the near-frostbite on her toes and fingers, Kay may have been lying in the snow on her own front porch for several hours, until well after sundown. "She must've hit her head, or the pain caused her to black out. We're not exactly sure. She doesn't remember."

I picture Kay's porch, imagining it covered in ice and snow.

"She had surgery first thing this morning. The doctors say she's strong and tolerated the procedure well. But as you may know, recovery is difficult for this kind of thing."

"Of course."

"Mrs. Buckner, that's why Mrs. Robberson asked me to call. She has no family here. She's got a good support group in her church, but she needs . . . well, she's going to need some consistent help."

"Uh-huh."

"Starting today. Maybe tomorrow."

"And . . ."

"And she listed you and your husband as her next of kin."

—

The very next day, Eric and I are sitting at her bedside, and not one of us is acting like this situation is as weird as it actually is. I guess that's our coping mechanism. The only thing Eric and I agreed on during the plane ride was that we would under no circumstance bring up the subject of John.

"When people ask, Kay, what do you tell them? How are we related?"

"I tell them the little squirt is my godson."

Sure. How else can we explain how our families are spiritually related, except through Toby?

Eric tackles the insurance, and I make arrangements for a nurse's aide. We coordinate with her church and its impressive prayer chain as well as casserole-toting friends who will make sure she has a hot meal and some company every day.

While Eric's away working on insurance details, Kay says, "Sit down. I've got some things to say. And then I have a favor to ask."

"Sure."

She swallows, clears her throat. "They told you what happened?"

"Yes."

"Well, I bet they didn't tell you everything. You're the only one who will know what I'm talking about."

"Okay."

"You know I fell. I laid there on my porch a long time. I didn't know if I was ever gonna get up. You know what I did as I laid there?"

"What?"

She shakes her head slowly. "Well, I'm supposed to pray, right? I even said the words, but they weren't going nowhere. You know how that is? Like you're talking to the inside of your own thick skull."

"That's pretty common, I think."

"No. You're not getting it. I could not pray because I was so busy cussing John." She gives a little snort-laugh. "I'm still so mad at that man."

I nod, hoping she can't hear my pulse from there.

"It doesn't matter now. It doesn't bring JJ back, and it doesn't bring John back. It doesn't do me one bit of good to stay mad."

"No, it doesn't," I say.

"Once I got that out of the way, laying there flat on my back like that, something new burned a hole in me."

"What?"

"What if it was my time? What if I died right there? I have to tell you, there's a big part of me that wanted to. I thought about seeing JJ, and then it hit me."

I waited.

"He's not there."

"John?"

She leans in and whispers, "How can he be there waiting for me, when I seen him here, with my own eyes?"

"You mean, in Eric."

She nods slowly, her arms crossed.

"It's time for him to go. I've been thinking about it. If he ain't gone by now, he idn't gonna go unless he knows I need for him to be there when I show up. So I have a favor to ask."

She fidgets in her hospital bed, straightens the sheets, and glances at the door. "I wasn't ready before, but I am now. Will you let me talk to John again?"

"Oh, Kay." Now it's my turn to fidget. I fight back the temptation to flood her with details of all we've been through. I struggle with whether to tell her about JJ's message. For the first time, I wonder if it was meant for her instead of John. Or for me.

Let go.

"I'm not sure it will work," I finally say.

"Me, neither."

———

Eric walks into her hospital room, rolling a thick stack of papers into a cylinder. "All done." He smacks Kay on the toes with the papers and gives her a wink. "How's it going there, Sugar?"

I squeeze Kay's hand. "Let me think about it."

Eric flips through channels and stops on *Let's Make a Deal*. I can feel Kay's gaze, but I don't make eye contact with her. Eric and Kay play along with the game show, but the commotion of it irritates me. The nurse comes in to check Kay's vitals, and Eric starts fussing around with the dinner menu even though we don't need to order for another couple of hours.

I don't know why I'm procrastinating. There's only one thing to do.

When the show is finally over, I stand up to give Eric a hug. "I think I'm going to step out now. Kay has something to say to you." I smile at her as I leave and whisper, "Good luck."

I step into the hallway, waiting until I'm well out of earshot before I allow myself to collapse into a waiting-room chair. I'm not sure how long I sit there before a familiar realization emerges from my core: the unimaginable could be happening right now. Anything is possible.

I shift in my chair and feel a slight nudge in the small of my back. *That's right, Mom. I can deal with it either way. I know that now.*

I probably should check on them. I look at my watch. I'll give it about eight minutes.

ACKNOWLEDGMENTS

I owe many thanks to the people in my life who have supported this work. Thank you to my agent, Emmanuelle Morgen, for seeing the potential and making it happen; Christine Pride for her smart insights and feedback; and Danielle Marshall, Jenna Free, and the team at Amazon Publishing for helping make one of my dreams come true.

Writing is a solitary pursuit, but it is made easier within a community. Thank you to my writing group in Dallas—Shilpi Gowda, Dr. Cindy Corpier, Erin Burdette, and Cindy Jones—for getting to know Shelly and Eric and Toby before everyone else and for advising me on what they would and would not do. Thank you, my fellow word warriors in The Big Three—Lia Eastep, Julie Stewart, Bridgett Jensen, Jackie Gorman, and Katy Yocom—who know exactly what it takes to wake up every morning with the audacity to believe that we have something to say. Thank you to the talented writers I met in the Spalding MFA program, including my thoughtful mentors: Robin Lippincott, Kirby Gann, Mary Yukari Waters, Ellie Bryant, Rachel Harper, Julie Brickman, and the indomitable Sena Jeter-Naslund. And my fellow students who read an early draft and gave feedback that made a difference: Elaine Little, Graham Shelby, Mary Lou Northern, Tay Berryman, George Schricker, and Karen Mann.

Thank you to my friends who support the creative process in their own ways: specifically, Jackie Sherman for walking every week with me and my imaginary friends as I was writing the first draft; Dr. Jim Schroeder for helping me imagine exactly how the worst-case scenario might go; Dr. Vinita Schroeder for her vacation super-powers; Nancy and Rick Rome for encouraging words and a glass of good wine at the right times. Thank you to my first and best mom-friends: Shannon Hollingsworth for letting me read out loud to her; Quitze Nelson for letting me be nosy about things I haven't had to live through; Lorie Leigh Lawrence for her talent in making everything look better.

Thank you to my family—Tom, Hugo, Morgan, Michael, and Matt—who all contributed to this work in their own ways, which perhaps they didn't realize as it was happening. Thanks for sharing in the unspoken assumption in our family that creative work is worth doing. And finally, thank you to my Jenkins family roots: my mom, who took me to the public library every time I asked; my dad, who taught me to work hard; and my sisters, Peg and Pam, and my brother, Gary, for putting up with my storytelling back when it was just lying and maybe not so entertaining.

ABOUT THE AUTHOR

Lori Reisenbichler has told stories her whole life, most recently onstage at the Moth and Oral Fixations. She holds an MFA from Spalding University and has served as an editor for the *Best New Writing* journal. *Eight Minutes* is her debut novel. She lives in Dallas, Texas, with a charming devil of an architect. They have three grown children. When she's not writing, she throws dinner parties and cheers way too loudly at sporting events.